*A More
Innocent Time*

A More Innocent Time

a novel by

Eugenie Hill

TAPLINGER PUBLISHING COMPANY
New York

Published in 1979 by
TAPLINGER PUBLISHING CO., INC.
New York, New York

For my mother

Part I

⋴§ ONE §⋗

A bell clanged somewhere in the dusty distance. Eleven small boys in the traditional prep school garb of gray shorts and gray pullovers scuffled and stirred.

"Time for your Latin now, boys," the new mistress said brightly. "And I'm off to teach English with some older boys, the Fifth form. After that it will be break. We're all looking forward to that, aren't we?"

"Yes, Miss Vale," the children chorused in dutiful sibilance.

As the new mistress got to her feet they formed a ragged line at the door. She experienced an odd reluctance at leaving the drafty, high-ceilinged room where she had been at work for the past three days. The business of teaching was very strange to her still, although it couldn't be called difficult.

The day of a St. Fenrins boy was ritualistic and straightforward. She had little more to do than follow closely the timetable in meticulous copperplate inherited from an elderly predecessor. With the little boys there were no discipline problems. Now, for the first time, she was about to encounter a form from the Upper School.

"No running!" she admonished automatically as she prepared to follow the children through the door. Their receding footsteps were measured at first but soon speeded into a scamper as they rounded the corner and disappeared from her sight.

Conscious that she was late, Agnes Vale hurried across a quadrangle at the back of the main building. Outside what was known as New Block she collided with a portly, youngish man in a tweed suit.

"Whoops!" He steadied her. "Fifth are assembled in anticipation of your coming," he said. "All breaths are bated. You realize you're about to make history? Never before has an upper form at St. Fenrins been taught by a member of the fair sex!"

"It's a daunting prospect for me," she said. "They're not going to like it, are they?"

The portly young man smiled. His name was Justin Lord. He taught History as well as being responsible for the Choir and was one of the few on the staff who had treated Agnes in an easy manner from the start.

"It's precisely what they need, my dear," he said airily. "I won't say a woman's touch—influence is perhaps more le mot juste. Simply make a firm start, and you can't go wrong. See you afterwards in the Masters' Common Room."

As he moved off, fluttering his fingers, Agnes Vale envied him his good luck in not being an innovation. Stiffening her shoulders, she entered the form room.

Ten pairs of eyes swiveled to the doorway. Sputtering giggles broke out and were suppressed as with quick steps she sought refuge behind the master's desk.

None of those who faced her could have been more than eleven years old. Yet in this context, and in comparison with the seven-year-olds she had just left, they seemed quite disproportionately and disconcertingly mature.

"My name is Vale," she announced, to break a silence that was in danger of becoming protracted. "You'll have heard that I'm to take you for six periods a week."

She repressed a temptation to throw herself on their mercy by telling them that she was entirely new to teaching, and hurried on, speaking so rapidly of syllabuses and the complaints of the language masters about their inadequacies in grammar that it was doubtful whether they caught all she said.

"I thought we'd make a beginning by taking a look at clauses," she finished, twisting the modest engagement ring on her finger compulsively. "If you will turn to page sixty-four in Blackman. . . ."

The boys looked disappointed. Already their initial alertness was slackening off into a scraping of shoes and a sliding about in seats. When, after a few moments of desultory discussion, they settled without animation to a written exercise, the new mistress stared about her with a sense of relief. I'm the outsider here, she thought. Everyone else—these boys, the masters—is so entrenched.

"Please, shall I go on to the next exercise, sir?"

The voice interrupting the muted activity seemed preternaturally loud. There was a faint titter, and everyone stopped working.

"You are . . . ?" Agnes said to the stocky boy who had spoken.

"Blount s— I mean ma'am." His already ruddy cheeks turned a deeper hue.

"We haven't settled what to call you," a dainty blond boy with what she considered to be a pert expression called out. "Ought we to say 'ma'am'?"

"That's rather Victorian," Agnes said. "Miss Vale, I think."

"Surely 'ma'am' would be logical as we call the masters 'sir,'" suggested someone else.

"I prefer Miss Vale," she said, to settle the matter. "Yes, do start a new exercise, Blount."

Reluctantly the class settled again. They'll take advantage if I'm not firm, Agnes thought gloomily. All this giggling and whispering. And so sure of themselves! They're a patrician-looking lot, too, on the whole. Ruling class and all that. What am I doing here? Harold and I could be married already. I could be in Chicago with him now. Why on earth did I insist we should wait until he comes back?

She glanced down a list with which she had been furnished, trying halfheartedly to put names to faces. A couple had "Hon." in front of them. That was unnecessary and archaic, surely. Joe Stratton, her prospective father-in-law, had told her that St. Fenrins had once even boasted a prince as a pupil. That was long ago, in the heyday of private schools, before things started to slide.

O'Higgins . . . Fildman . . . Karistides . . . A veritable United Nations here.

"What's your name?" Agnes suddenly addressed a good-looking, dark-haired boy who was staring at her with what she considered a supercilious expression.

"Me? Willoughby, Miss Vale."

He colored slightly at thus being singled out.

"Yes. And next to you?"

"I'm Karistides."

No blush this time. Agnes nodded. He would be the Greek, of course, a sturdy, dark-skinned boy with a sullen face.

"And you, who find everything so amusing?"

"Moss-Hemlock, Miss Vale."

The pert blond seemed blissfully unaware of the absurdity of it. Lucky for you, Agnes thought grimly, that you don't have to live in one of the developments in the New Town.

She went on around the room eliciting names that at once swam together meaninglessly in her head.

"Is it true you're a writer, Miss Vale?"

Moss-Hemlock again. It was Agnes's turn to flush as the eyes of the form turned collectively in her direction.

"What makes you think that?" she asked, frowning.

"Mr. Sergeant told us," the boy named Willoughby volunteered. "He said the person coming to take Junior Form was a writer and that was why he was arranging for you to take us for English."

"To give us the benefit of your expert guidance," the Greek boy beside him drawled.

"Hardly expert," Agnes said. "It's true I'm working on something, but—"

"Jolly interesting!" the boy named Blount said encouragingly.

"What sort of writing?" Moss-Hemlock persisted.

"A children's book, as a matter of fact."

This exhumation of something so personal threw her into confusion.

"What's it about . . . Is it a boys' book . . . Can we read it . . . What else have you written?" The questions rustled up and down the room.

"I can't go into details now," Agnes said hurriedly. "You really must get on with your work."

It was a relief that the bell saved her then.

"I must warn you that I shall expect more from you perhaps than even the masters do." She addressed the fidgeting form in what she hoped was a positive tone as Blount collected the exercise books. "English is very important to me. Not so much a subject, more a way of life."

There was a silence. The good Blount nodded. The Greek boy smiled without warmth.

"You'd better go now," Agnes finished abruptly.

They scrambled out, not looking at her, save for Moss-Hemlock who thanked her hypocritically for "an interesting lesson."

God, they think me a fool, she thought as the door closed on the last of them. We're opposites in everything, in outlook, in social class—and worst of all, I'm a woman. How on earth did I get myself into this?

A discreet cough caused her to glance up, and she saw the stocky Blount in the doorway.

"I'm Form Monitor," he said. "I'm supposed to see the lights are off."

"That's all right," Agnes nodded. "I'm finished here."

As she was about to leave the room, he called to her.

"I wondered, Miss Vale—" He approached, shuffled his large feet, stared down at them. "Whether you're planning to do literature with us. You know, poetry and stuff?"

"Why, yes." She was surprised. "I certainly hope so, once the grammar is sorted out."

"Good. I'm rather keen on poetry. We never do any, though. No time."

"I'm rather keen on poetry myself," Agnes said, amused.

"Interesting, your being a writer." He started to put his hands in his pockets, then withdrew them abruptly. "I rather think I might have a go at something similar myself one of these days."

Agnes smiled at him. As his eyes met hers for the first time, she felt as if some fragile bridge had been constructed between them.

"I'm to go to the Masters' Common Room now," she confided. "I'm afraid I'll never find my way."

"I'll take you," Blount volunteered at once. "I remember how many twists and turns there seemed to be when I first came here. You'll soon get used to it, though."

To the place perhaps, to the people never, Agnes thought, bracing herself as she followed him toward the main building for another assault on what hitherto had been an enclave of exclusive masculinity.

"Write for children? But I know nothing whatever about them!" Agnes had protested to Levy, her agent, when he first put it to her.

"You could always find out," he said easily. "It's a market that's wide open at the moment. I've a feeling you could break in. You've a straightforward, readable style, and you're sympathetic. Kids respond to that. Seriously, why not give it a whirl?"

Agnes hesitated. She had been a bright child and a promising student, and her ambitions had always been both literary and lofty. Yet here she was in her late twenties and had sold nothing more than a few magazine stories and articles, all lightweight. It was humiliating to her that her three novels with what she saw as serious themes had failed to find a publisher.

It was at about this time that Harold Stratton asked her to marry him. He was a solid, unfrivolous man, securely established in a career as an industrial chemist, not at all the sort of husband the romantically susceptible Agnes would earlier have envisaged for herself, any more than she would have imagined herself as a children's writer.

All the same, Harold's unequivocal admiration did not leave her unmoved. And life for her had always been what she designated as a series of Fresh Starts. Even if each was in some way a compromise and a diminution of the one preceding it, that, she told herself stoutly, was all part of the process of maturing, and she ought to make the best of it.

With this in mind she accepted both Harold's marriage proposal and her agent's advice. Her fiancé was to be abroad for six months at the laboratories of his firm's parent company, so she went to stay with his widowed father and schoolteacher sister at their house on the edge of a new town in Hampshire.

It was Harold's father who heard of the temporary vacancy at a nearby prep school and suggested that there she might gain experience in the teaching of boys. Agnes, who had hitherto worked at the BBC, had no teaching qualifications. She would, her future sister-in-law assured her with relish, have been unacceptable within the state system. But Tim Sergeant, the St. Fenrins headmaster, himself comparatively new to the job, had been prepared to take her on.

While walking about the grounds one afternoon a couple of weeks after her arrival, Agnes reflected that this was the most desultory part of her day. With the boys at Games, there was an uncanny silence about the place. The only sign of life was an old gardener who hobbled and toiled in a green baize apron while his assistant, a shambling simpleton, scrabbled in a flower bed muddy from recent rain and stared up at Agnes with a vacant grin as she went by.

Aimlessly she wandered toward the river, which constituted one of the boundaries of the school estate. At this point it was no more than a stream of brackish water moving sluggishly beneath a low sky. On the bank ahead of her stood a creeper-covered tower that had early captured her imagination. Someone had said it was occupied by the school's former headmaster, but she had never seen him.

As she stood staring into the water, reflecting that after her earlier heady expectations her recent way of life was as faded and low-key as the landscape around her, Agnes became aware of a low, insistent humming coming from the direction of the tower.

She followed the sound to a cluster of old-fashioned beehives set beside a crumbling wall at the rear of the building. A masked figure in a broad-brimmed hat was stooping over one of them. To Agnes the scene was reminiscent of a Dürer etching; the suggestion of something allegorical charmed her. She stepped toward the figure as it turned from the hives and removed the hat and mask.

Erskine Fawcett, she thought at once, facing an old man with papery skin and a shock of silver hair, the fabled former headmaster! She introduced herself. The old man smiled at her absently, murmuring something about having heard of her arrival "from Timothy."

"I suppose you find bees very restful after so many years of boys!" Agnes said brightly. "There's something so benign about them, don't you think?"

"Indeed." Erskine Fawcett nodded. "One associates them with much that is pleasant. Fragrance, sustenance, summer warmth—'*Sic vos non mellificates apes!*' " He murmured the tag without self-consciousness.

"I really must look at Virgil again one of these days." Agnes was always gratified when she recognized a quotation. "He's so absolutely right on country matters."

"You know Latin?" the old man said with approbation. "Few women do nowadays. You are most welcome at St. Fenrins." He stared at her almost beatifically. "Would you perhaps care for some honeycomb? Rather good, yes?"

Such a small thing, she thought, taking it, to please him so much.

"And here's young Lord," Erskine Fawcett said, staring beyond her, smiling still. "I have been making the acquaintance of Miss Vale, Justin. We have an acquisition, have we not?"

"Undoubtedly, Headmaster." The plump historian bowed. "We have been blessed."

"The choir . . . in slightly better voice last evening," the old man went on. "But you need to work on them, dear boy. They cannot all be natural singers like young Willoughby. Odd, when his father couldn't sing a note . . . The mother, of course—Sandy Holder—is greatly gifted . . . Well, keep at it, Justin!"

He nodded to Agnes, sawed with his hands in the air as if in benediction, and turned toward the hives again.

"The old boy's been a bit ga-ga for years," Lord muttered to Agnes as they moved off. "What have you there? Honeycomb? Sweets to the sweet! Obviously you scored a hit there, Miss Vale."

"Won't you call me Agnes? Things must have been rather different here in Mr. Erskine Fawcett's day."

"In his *hey*day, very different. He completely withdrew into himself after his wife died. That was when the big slide began."

"My fiancé's father was telling me that some of the best families in the country sent boys here once," Agnes said. "But there was some kind of scandal."

To her surprise, Lord blushed.

"Certain boys, certain masters . . . Need I say more?" he mumbled, looking discomfited. "I see not. You're percipient, Agnes. Agnes? Charming!"

"The place certainly looks as if it's seen better days."

"Quite. Numbers fell off, you know, when word got about. In desperation the Governors pensioned off old E.F. and appointed Sergeant. Can't say I covet his job. Uphill all the way."

"Who *was* St. Fenrin, by the way? I've never heard of him."

"Who has? Apparently he was some obscure Saxon martyr. Went in the last Vatican purge, I believe. I feel that's rather symbolic of the old school. We've pretty well lost our raison d'être . . . Excuse me just a moment. I spy Willoughby. Must have a word . . ."

He halted the track-suited Fifth-former skimming past them and briefly reproached him for a missed organ practice, before walking on with Agnes.

"Any game there is, and he's sure to be in it," he observed. "But he's not to be allowed to neglect his music. And he will argue! You heard him just now."

"What was it you called him? Goff?" Agnes said. "Is that really his name?"

"A diminutive. He was christened Godolphin, though he wouldn't thank me for informing you of the fact."

"How odd!"

"An old family name, I believe. Now, let me take you in to tea, Agnes. What is more, let me be *seen* taking you in to tea. It will be such a feather in my cap!"

Agnes doubted this, since the rest of the masters still seemed to find her presence an embarrassment and largely ignored her. All the same, Lord's banter made her feel less of an outsider.

Her class after tea was with Fifth. She found them sprawled across their desks talking loudly of their own concerns, but as soon as she appeared and called them to order they took their places in watchful silence.

Agnes set an exercise to which they settled without animation, and there was silence save for the rain, which now dripped beyond the windows.

I must try to stir them out of this apathy, she thought, marooned behind the master's desk. I ought to be teaching them to write. O'Higgins has the makings of a style, and Blount's vocabulary is remarkably mature, though the spelling's appalling. I'll try them with "The Neglected Grave" as an essay title. It might inspire them. They shall do it tomorrow.

"Finished!"

It was Willoughby, who in the first class had struck Agnes by the arrogance of his expression. In her mind he was bracketed with his friend and desk partner Karistides, the sullen Greek boy with uniformly brown hair and eyes and skin who executed all his work for her with a kind of competent negligence.

She got up and crossed the room. Willoughby rose to his feet and remained standing as she glanced over his book and told him to go on to the second part of the exercise.

As he reached out to take his book from her, their eyes met. Willoughby's were of an unusual color, a light brown, almost golden, with a hint of red in it. Now as they held hers unwaveringly she had the odd sensation that they were meeting on the same level rather than as a woman and a boy. His scrutiny of her face had about it a challenge that was wholly masculine. In the force of it she was more conscious of her femininity than she would have believed possible.

They stared at each other for several long seconds, their eyes seemingly disassociated from their bodies. At last Agnes smiled faintly. At once she saw in the boy's face a reflection of her own relaxation of tension. Beside them Karistides yawned audibly.

"Blount, you've misspelled four words in this line alone!" Agnes exclaimed, moving quickly on. "You must *think*."

That evening, as Agnes waited in the clearing air for her bus, her thoughts returned of their own volition to the wordless encounter with Willoughby. The long glance had had so much of a challenge in it. Was it, could it have been, sexual? Agnes shied away from the absurdity. He was no more than a child. Yet there had been nothing childlike in the look he gave her. He was a handsome boy. When he was grown, women were going to take notice of him, no doubt.

Of course there had been nothing sexual about it, she thought as she lay that night in her fiancé's bedroom. Even for her to conceive of such a thing was monstrous!

St. Fenrins was an odd place, monastic, enclosed, seemingly unrelated to the world outside. Already her imagination was becoming overheated by the atmosphere of it. It was fortunate that she was to be there for a short time only. Goff Willoughby. A look. Such nonsense!

Determinedly she filled her mind with wholesome thoughts of wholesome Harold Stratton until she fell asleep.

Throughout the rest of that autumn, life for Agnes was singularly uneventful. At the Strattons' she spent many hours working on her children's book and writing copious airmail letters to Harold. At the school, once the novelty had worn off, it began to seem as if she had always been there and that nothing could ever change.

The nature of the boys intrigued her. She had a strong sense of life teeming and rippling, but the exterior they presented to adults was blandly uninformative, and she could see no terms on which she might be admitted to their world.

When the last afternoon of the term arrived, the school chapel was packed with parents for the carol service. Agnes, who had always been fascinated by church music, felt a childlike sense of wonder as the choir approached, singing of Alpha and Omega, the faces of the surpliced boys transfigured by flickering candlelight, the unearthly purity of their voices borne to every corner of the old building.

When the service was under way, Willoughby had a solo, "I Sing of a Maiden that is Makerless." The unaccompanied notes soared with such unfaltering clarity that she felt ravished by them and was left shivering.

At the end of the service a Nativity play was performed on the altar steps. The star performer turned out to be Karistides as Herod. With no trace of his customary sullenness, he blazed his way through the role of the strutting tyrant, conveying with uncanny maturity all the bully's doubts beneath the bravado. Alone amid the solid schoolboy competence of the other actors, he revealed himself a natural.

As she walked away afterwards into the darkening afternoon, Agnes found her thoughts full of these two; of Willoughby, so fair of face, singing of the matchless maiden, and of Karistides, in his dark vitality bringing to life the cowardly and temporal king. Obviously here were two boys possessed of equally powerful but contrasting personalities. It was strange, she thought, that they also appeared to be close friends.

It was during Lent, that most interminable and uneventful of school terms, that Agnes entered Fifth form one dull morning in time to overhear a scrap of conversation.

". . . and much better anyway if he would let us dissect it while it's still alive," Karistides was saying.

"That would be perfectly disgusting, Andy," Willoughby said with a wrinkling of his aristocratic nose.

"But more *interesting*," Karistides persisted. "After it's dead, it's only a thing."

"Nevertheless, we can learn all we need to know from it in that state," Blount, a keen biologist, said earnestly. "As you're aware, I'm absolutely anti experiments on living animals."

"The same goes for me, every time," Willoughby confirmed.

"Well, if you're going to be sentimental," Karistides shrugged.

"Save the scientific discussions for Mr. Cooke's class and settle down now," Agnes called them to order in what she had come to recognize with distaste as her "school ma'am" voice. "Clauses yet again, I'm afraid. Oh, my heart sinks along with yours, Blount, but we really have to get on top of this."

During the oral part of the lesson she noticed that Karistides was casting covert glances out the window. His face showed something approaching animation, a spirit he never displayed for his work.

He was a child with whom Agnes could never feel entirely at ease. She found herself able to say little about his work. Grammatically it was correct, almost pedantically so, but there was no spark of vitality there.

When the boys finally settled down to write, she noticed that he was slow to begin. He now sat alone by the east window, since some of the masters had complained that he and Willoughby wasted time when they shared a desk.

After a few minutes Agnes left her desk and wandered about, glancing over the boys' exercises. By the time she reached Karistides, his head was bent and he was writing fast.

The eastern side of the classroom overlooked the vegetable garden, a flat and dreary spectacle at this time of year. Glancing out, Agnes saw that Karistides's attention had been focused upon the half-witted gardener's boy who was supposed to be digging in the potato beds. In fact he had laid aside his hoe and was engaged in a vigorous act of masturbation.

Hastily she averted her eyes and turned her attention to O'Higgins, while managing to look sideways at Karistides.

The expression on his heavy face was unusually pleasant. A smile played on his parted lips. Agnes was struck by his joyfully innocent air. When his eyes strayed to the window again, she maneuvered herself so that she, too, could look out.

He was still at it! Surely the wretched creature must reach a climax soon. Agnes was aware that her own indignation and repulsion were not untinged with fascination, which caused her to grow hot. It seemed as though the convulsive jerkings of the shambling puppet were for the benefit of the swarthy Greek boy.

As she found her way back to the sanctuary of the desk, she marveled that the rest of the form labored as phlegmatically as toiling peasants in a Brueghel painting over their adjectival clauses. She was afraid that one of them, glancing up, might notice what was going on. Mercifully, Karistides seemed content to keep the spectacle to himself. Agnes was alone with her knowledge and had no idea what to do with it. How would a man have dealt with the situation, she wondered.

Suddenly she longed for everything to be simple and two-dimensional again, the way it was in the children's book she was writing. As her glance moved over the bent heads to rest on those of the handsome Willoughby and the stolid Blount, she felt an absurd pang, as if their innocence were threatened.

Karistides was wriggling a bit now. Had he a sympathetic erection? It was not for the English mistress to go peering into the trousers of young boys. The situation was ludicrous and offensive to her.

The class ended at last. The boys departed in chattering ebullience. For once Karistides had a contented, satisfied look, too. Relieved to be alone, Agnes looked out the window again. Only the dreary beds were in view, a hoe stuck in a clump of soil, the tops of the potato plants faintly quivering. Of the gardener's boy there was no sign.

"Isn't that gardener's boy a bit unwholesome to have about?" she remarked casually at tea a couple of days later.

"You mean the loony one, Len?" asked Angus Ross, the Math master. "He's quite harmless."

"He doesn't have anything to do with the boys, does he?"

"I shouldn't think so. He wouldn't, would he?"

"I suppose not."

Agnes sipped her tea. Mr. Godball, the aged Classics master, chomped solidly through a substantial chunk of bread and butter.

"I feel I shall never get through to the Karistides boy." Again Agnes broke the silence. "I don't believe he likes women."

"Don't worry," Ross said easily. "The masters don't have much success there either. Sullen little devil! Still, it's understandable in a way. The boy and his sister were brought up entirely by English nannies. The family's filthy rich. They have their own island, but the parents are never there and the kids are left pretty much to their own devices. The Willoughbys are awfully good about having Andrew at their place during the holidays. It gives him some chance to be with a nice, normal English family, poor little sod!"

Angus reached across the table and helped himself to strawberry jam, and no one referred to the matter again.

In early March, Agnes, crossing one morning from the old school to New Block, was struck by a sudden mildness of the atmosphere. All at once she was conscious of the unbecoming cocoon of shapeless woolen clothing in which she had for long been sheltering from the chill and drafts of the school. It would be good, she felt, to have this soft air against her starved skin.

As soon as she was seated in Fifth form, she unbuttoned the immensely thick and shabby cardigan that she habitually wore. Sunlight shone through the big eastern windows and slanted full onto the master's desk.

Agnes shifted her chair out of its range and crossed her legs. The class proceeded sluggishly. Fildman read droningly. Slowly she began to unbutton a second cardigan. After a few minutes she took that off also. Beneath it, she wore a faded, shrunken blue T-shirt with short sleeves.

The boys had watched the peeling operation with covert fascination. When it was complete, Moss-Hemlock leaned across to his neighbor and murmured:

"How about that for a pair of tits? Not bad, eh?"

The reader happened to have paused at the end of a paragraph, and the words were clearly audible. Agnes colored. Karistides grinned. One or two of the others looked sheepish. Only Blount remained happily oblivious that anything untoward had been said.

"Fildman," Agnes said, studiedly fixing her eyes on the middle distance, willing her color to subside, "what figure of speech is being used in line fourteen?"

"Line fourteen . . . metaphor, Miss Vale," the boy said alertly. "He compares the sun to a great emperor."

"Correct. What I want you to do now is to go through the passage carefully and write down any other metaphors and similes."

There was soon silence in the hot room save for the scratching of pens. Agnes glared at Moss-Hemlock and mentally threatened him with detention if his work was as careless as usual. He's only a child, she thought, when he looked woebegone. But a male child, that was the rub!

Not for the first time she felt that she had come up against an aspect of the boys' natures which, womanlike, she might have preferred to ignore. But this is only prepuberty, she thought. I'd never be able to cope with adolescence. Of course the T-shirt *is* very tight. In future I shall certainly take care what I wear.

Alone in Harold's bedroom that evening, she stood before the mirror. She lifted her nightgown and stared critically at her breasts. She tried to envisage them as they would appear to male eyes and decided that they had a fecund look, like fruit ready for plucking and sucking.

In that moment she made a decision. Harold was to return from the States for Easter, and their plan had been to marry in the summer. Why wait until then? Her book, a rather stolid story about some boys who discover an abandoned gypsy caravan, was already completed and in her agent's hands. And only today Angus Ross had been speaking of an artist friend of his who wished to sublet a flat in the Old Town from the end of the month.

Of course I've promised to see the summer out at the school, Agnes thought, but I can as easily do that married as single. I'll write to Harold at once and put it to him. He'd like to be settled as soon as possible, anyway. It will be nice to be settled and secure. I shall like it, too.

She took one last, ironic look at her breasts before she let the nightgown fall and turned from the mirror. There was no need for this fruit to wither on the stem!

Three weeks later, at the end of the slow Lent term, she walked through the gates of St. Fenrins for the last time as a spinster.

ᦰ TWO ᦱ

"We'll never ever manage to call her Stratton," said Ben Blount. "We may as well stick to Vale."

"It's only for this term, anyway," Karistides remarked indifferently. "She's leaving at the end of the summer. Got to concentrate on the husband now!" He laughed.

Goff Willoughby said nothing. When old Serg had made the announcement of Miss Vale's new status, he had experienced a sudden, unaccountable, almost proprietorial rush of feeling that had brought a flood of color to his face.

Nor were the rest of Fifth unaffected by the event. Marriage was to them an enigma. They vaguely understood it as having connections with both love and sex. Of love they knew little and thought less; of sex they knew more and thought continually. In Agnes Vale they sensed a fusion of the two, and it increased her appeal for them.

The summer term was the easiest, the most careless of times at St. Fenrins. The old school, scented by roses, mellowed by sunlight, haunted by bees, came at last into its own.

On sunny afternoons the Culture Club met outside under the trees. Culture Club was a group formed by Agnes for the reading of poetry with the older boys. In spite of her vehement protests, it had never been known by any other name, and, much to her astonishment, it had been a success from the start.

Agnes Stratton was very relaxed with the boys now. She wore a light dress that emphasized her suntan, and she had pinned her long hair on the top of her head in a little knot from which escaping tendrils corkscrewed onto the back of her neck. Goff Willoughby saw with a stab of jealousy how, when she asked Karistides to read from Tennyson's *Ulysses*, their knees were touching as he shared her book.

"You have to be our Ulysses, Andrew," she was saying enthusiastically. "He's such a fascinating character, and you're exactly right for him."

Goff, watching them with knees and heads so close, scowled at the way his fool friend smirked and took it as a compliment.

Up to the time of Fathers Match, there was considerable speculation among the boys about "Vale's husband." A hitherto shadowy figure, seeming at times no more than a figment of her imagination, he was to be presented for scrutiny then.

The Fathers Match immediately preceded the summer half-term. Since most of the parents attended and took their boys away afterwards, it was one of the chief social events of the school year.

"Vale's husband" turned out to be a pleasant-faced, soft-spoken, unemphatic individual. His ordinariness was at the same time a relief and a disappointment to the boys. Against it, his wife was shown to great advantage. By happy chance the Fathers Match fell on one of the finest days of the summer. The new Mrs. Stratton wore a flowing dress of apple green with a matching velvet ribbon in her hair, and her manner had a joyful zest. Goff Willoughby, approaching her at the beginning of the Tea Interval, felt a stab of pleasure simply in seeing her.

"Miss Vale—I mean Mrs. Stratton—will you come and meet my parents?" he asked.

Agnes smiled at him, left her husband talking to Justin Lord, and allowed herself to be escorted across the grass. In his cricket gear, for already he was in the First Eleven, Goff had a sense that he looked particularly well.

His mother was outside the tea marquee in conversation with Erskine Fawcett, who had known her since she was a girl. Goff cleared his throat and waited for a natural break in the conversation to say:

"Mother," (these things had to be done properly) "this is my English mistress."

Sandy Willoughby turned and extended her hand. Slender and dark, with that tremulous look found in thoroughbred horses of uncertain temper, she was a woman who, in the fixed intensity of her gaze when pensive, was reminiscent of Berthe Morisot in Monet's painting *The Balcony*.

"Your English mistress, darling?" she said, with a hint of amusement in her voice that Goff failed to understand.

"Miss Va—, Mrs. Stratton, this is my mother."

The two women shook hands, murmuring appreciative banalities.

"Mrs. Stratton has been a valuable asset to the English department, Sandy," Erskine Fawcett said positively. "She could undoubtedly also have assisted with Classics, had the need arisen." His face colored faintly with pleasure at the thought. "Her leaving will be a real loss."

"So nice for the boys, having a woman to teach them," Sandy said. "They adore it, of course. Such a novelty!"

Goff's gaze flickered between Agnes, fair in her apple green, and his mother, darker, more muted, in her cream dress with a matching parasol.

". . . and such a pity Fitz, our youngest, doesn't start at Fins for another two years." Sandy smiled as she looked toward her second son, very like Goff but softer somehow, who was gamboling on the grass with a pert-faced elder sister. "Little boys do so love to have a pretty young teacher."

Looking up, Goff saw his father approaching, big and burly in white flannels, calling out something about securing a table for tea.

"A magnificent innings, Hillary," Erskine Fawcett said. "The old-timers are giving the boys a run for their money, as usual."

"Mrs. Stratton? Delighted." Hillary Willoughby shook Agnes's hand firmly. "You know, it was some time before I even realized Goff's English teacher this year was a woman."

"A teacher is a teacher," Agnes said. "The sex is irrelevant."

"Oh, I think it's relevant, even at this age. We weren't half so lucky when I was at Fins, eh, sir?"

"Less emancipated times . . ." Erskine Fawcett murmured absently.

"What about Goff, Mrs. Stratton? Any good?"

The father fixed Agnes with a businesslike gaze. He was as dark as his wife, but where hers was a sallowness, his blackness had a golden tinge. The hair on his head, as well as that faintly visible beneath his shirt, fairly curled and crackled with vitality. He exuded an air of total confidence.

"Goff's an all-rounder," Agnes Stratton said. "He'll do very well. Music is one of his strengths. He gets that from you, of course, Mrs. Willoughby." She smiled at Sandy, who stood with her arms wrapped around her younger son. "He has no problems with English. His style is competent and workmanlike."

"Isn't going to set the Thames on fire, by the sound of it!"

The father tousled Goff's hair.

A small boy came up then to take Agnes away to meet his mother. The Willoughbys went noisily in to tea with Erskine Fawcett. Goff trailed behind with a vague sense of disappointment he could not have explained. But he soon forgot it in the excitement of the second innings. The fathers declared one wicket behind at close of play, the way they often did, but it was Goff's own sixty-four that was generally regarded as being directly responsible for First Team's victory. He was glad Agnes Vale was there to witness it.

In the fine summer days of the second half of the term, Mrs. Stratton came to school on an old bicycle. When first she wobbled along the drive it seemed inexpressibly comic to the boys, but they soon came to accept it as natural. Fifth, feeling themselves in some way a special case, used to sneak clandestine rides on it along a grassy path near the shrubbery in Free time. The element of the forbidden in this added greatly to the enjoyment. Then one afternoon, inevitably, they were caught. In his confusion O'Higgins swerved from the path and tumbled on the grass.

"Really, I don't think much of your equilibrium, Arthur," Agnes said severely. "Even *I* do better than that!"

The Irish boy sprang red-faced to his feet while Willoughby righted the bicycle.

"And now I suppose you'd better all have a go," Agnes said suddenly, challengingly. "But don't for goodness sake fall off and injure your tiny selves, or we shall all be *dans la soupe!*"

The boys stared at her. Such a suggestion coming from a teacher was audacious; it bordered on anarchy. In the prim depths of their boyishly conventional souls, the members of Fifth were almost relieved that she was leaving. A woman like her could be dangerous.

"Gosh, thanks," said Blount, breaking the silence and taking the initiative, since the others seemed dumbfounded.

While he was waiting for his turn, Goff amused himself with a mental picture. He saw himself swerving against a root, falling off rather gracefully, lying there still with his eyes shut. Blount would speed off to fetch help. An alarmed Miss Vale would lean over Goff just as his eyes flickered open, biting her soft lower lip, her blue eyes full of trouble as she reached out . . .

Suddenly Goff saw clearly that she was putting herself at risk in indulging them and herself in this fashion. She was being irresponsible. And that rendered her vulnerable. All at once he felt she was within his power.

"You next, Willoughby."

She held the bicycle by the saddle. As he took it from her, their eyes met with an electric shock that was more potent than a contact of flesh would have been. In this moment they were equals. He had her now in the palm of his hand.

Elated, he pushed the bicycle to the top of the slope, mounted, shut his eyes, and zoomed down with his breath leaving his body. At the foot he slithered unharmed to a stop, passed the bike to Moss-Hemlock, and nonchalantly dusted his hands against his shorts.

"Bravo, Goff!" Agnes said.

When all had taken their turn, the group walked away companionably together.

"I do hope your bike hasn't suffered, Miss Vale," Moss-Hemlock trilled, as they strolled in a bunch with Blount pushing it.

"I don't mind if it has," she said. "I shan't need it much longer."

"What will you do," O'Higgins wondered, "when you don't have us to teach?"

"I shall have more time for my own writing."

"Shall you miss us?"

"I'll miss having someone to grumble at," she grinned. "But I'm not really a teacher, you know."

"You'll never teach any other boys, will you?" Goff asked.

He found the notion strangely gratifying.

"It's highly unlikely. You lot have been enough for one lifetime!"

"Do you realize," Moss-Hemlock said, "that this year you've grumbled at me more than almost anyone?"

"I only do it because I care," Agnes said. "Those who care always make the hardest taskmasters."

"Will you come back to see us?" Blount asked.

Agnes considered.

"I don't think so," she said at last. "Going back is always rather unsatisfactory. But you can have my address and come and visit me. You'll all be welcome any time."

"Couldn't you come back just once a week for Culture Club?" Fildman asked.

"That's tempting, but no. Let Culture Club stop now, before

you're bored with it. Next term there'll be something else." They had reached the rear of the main buildings. "Off you go," she said. "And if you're late for whatever you're supposed to be doing, you can say I kept you. Better not say why, though!"

She laughed happily and walked away from them, leaving the bicycle propped against the wall.

"That was good fun," O'Higgins said.

"She's not a bad sort, for a teacher and a woman," Blount conceded.

"I used to think she was a dragon," Moss-Hemlock reminisced. "She always picked me up on little things."

"She said people are hardest when they care," Goff said.

"Surely if you care for someone you want them to be happy? But how can they be, if you're always grumbling at them?"

"When people care, they want what's best for you," Goff said patiently. "They don't worry about your being *happy*."

"Then surely they're really being selfish," Moss-Hemlock reasoned.

The argument was becoming too involved for Goff. He preferred to remember simply that Miss Vale, who was young and pretty, had been for one tender moment in his power.

". . . and you do see, Willoughby, how a few more adjectives and adverbs would improve it no end," Agnes was saying earnestly. "Take this paragraph here . . ."

"Yes, Miss Vale," Goff said.

He concentrated on inching his hand toward hers. In a moment they must touch. A bee, fugitive perhaps from the Fawcett hives, was buzzing lazily on the sunny glass of the form room window.

"I always finish up by trying to write all the essays myself," Agnes said in a surprised tone. "But really it has to come from you, Willoughby, hasn't it?"

"Yes, Miss Vale," he answered dutifully.

His hand had reached hers. It lay with a faint pressure against it. For fully half a minute of silence, save for the bee's buzzing, they remained in contact. Then, as the bell sounded, she closed the book with a sigh and handed it back to him.

"Try, Willoughby," she said, gathering up her books, smiling vaguely at the rest of the form and wandering from the room.

"Poor thing, she certainly works at it," remarked O'Higgins. "I vote we give her a leaving present. There'll be the statutory book token from old Serg, but her own kids are too young to organize a collection."

"We could give her a book ourselves," Moss-Hemlock said. "You can't go wrong with a book."

"A cookbook, so she can make tasty things for her husband," suggested Fildman.

To Goff that seemed all wrong somehow, but he didn't say so.

"It's our last English class on Monday. You could give it to her then, Ben," O'Higgins said to Blount.

"With a kiss, of course," Karistides said with a grin. "Very sexy!"

"Oh I say, that's a bit much." Blount colored.

"When you present something to a man you shake hands with him," Karistides said. "A woman you kiss."

"But I really don't think . . . She mightn't like it . . ." Blount stammered.

I wouldn't mind kissing her, Goff was thinking, but of course they'll never think of me. I'm not Monitor, and my English is nothing special.

"Of course she'd like it, she's a woman, isn't she?" Karistides said witheringly, turning away bored toward the window.

"I'd kiss her," volunteered the hapless Moss-Hemlock.

"Oh, you'd kiss anybody," Blount retorted with contempt. "But I'm not going to do it. It's just not on. I shall simply shake hands." He nodded firmly, the matter settled to his satisfaction. "If that bee's still trapped, Andy," he called, "I'd better come and put it out now."

"Too late. It's dead already," the Greek boy said, adding enigmatically, "Poor bee!"

He shrugged, and thumped Goff, and the boys raced out into the release of the blue air.

The following week Agnes Stratton received the cookbook they had chosen for her. She shook hands with Blount and thanked them all gracefully. Two days later she left them.

She was not to come back to St. Fenrins in their time.

✌ THREE ✌

Goff Willoughby was strolling in the square of Andham New Town, his lip curling in faint contempt for those who jostled him continually. In front of Boots he almost collided with a woman coming out. As she raised her hand to steady him, he found himself staring at Agnes Vale.

"It's Goff Willoughby!" Her face lit with recognition.

A deep blush suffused Goff's face as he raised his cap.

"Good afternoon, Mrs. Stratton," he said.

"Of all people to see! What are you doing here?"

She sounded so amazed and pleased that his embarrassment faded. He had not thought of her consciously in months, not since the presentation was made. All that seemed infinitely long ago.

"I had a lift in with my father," he said. "My sister and I have to meet him in the Cock at six."

"So you're prowling about on your own. A post-Christmas spree? Splendid!"

She wore a belted coat with a collar and matching hat of some dark fur that made her look something like the women he knew at home. She began to talk about Fins, shifting the parcels she carried. It gratified Goff immensely to be able to let her know, casually, that he had been made skipper of the First Fifteen. She understood, of course, that he was fully a year younger than a captain normally was.

"And how about work?"

"Oh, that's okay."

They were staring at each other, still not moving on. It was she who suggested, though it was only just three, that they might have a cup of tea together.

"We could get some in Ashtons, in the High Street," Goff said promptly.

"In the Old Town? Do let's. We can cut through the graveyard."

The big clock in the tower of the church that divided the Old High Street from the New Town was chiming with a melodious and melancholy sound as they hurried along an elm-flagged walk, murky already in the winter light.

"Don't you get the feel of the past here, Goff?" Agnes said. "It's so strong it makes me shiver. Why do I have such a yearning for things I've never experienced? It all seems so much more alluring than the present."

She did not seem to expect a reply, and Goff vouchsafed none but simply nodded understandingly.

The Old High Street tried to pretend ignorance of its brash new neighbor beyond the churchyard. The Cock was an original coaching inn, and the shops and cafe had a similar air of conservative antiquity.

"Shall we sit in the window?" Agnes asked as they stepped inside Ashtons. "I do love to look out on the world."

She stripped off her gloves and unbuttoned the fur at her throat. She was wearing a high-necked dress of red wool that clung closely to the lines of her body.

As they studied the menu, Goff was conscious of his present money in the new wallet tucked snugly in his jacket pocket. He very much hoped to be able to pay for the tea. He pictured his former English mistress waiting as he did it, humbled by her female role. But he was nagged by the fact that she had invited him and so probably intended to pay.

"Have whatever you want," she said, confirming the suspicion. "The cakes are delicious, or you could have ice cream, definitely one of their specialties."

For herself she ordered tea and a slice of coffeecake. Goff was tempted to have tea also, to show himself her equal. Alas, greed won and he ordered a pineapple and chocolate sundae.

"You must tell me all about Fifth," said Agnes, leaning forward when the waitress had gone. "Though they're not any more, are they? Sad! I wish it could have stayed summer forever with us all just as we were then. How's my friend Ben Blount?"

"Oh, just the same." Goff felt a prick of jealousy. "He made a wormery last term. Just for a laugh, Andrew Karistides left the lid off one morning. The worms got out during old Cooke's class. One was crawling right up Jonny Fildman's leg. Ben had an awful job getting them all back unsquashed."

"It sounds fairly typical of Karistides! Mr. Godball has you for English now, doesn't he? I'll bet he finds your grammar ragged!"

"He hasn't said so. It's all awfully dry now. When we have poetry, which isn't often, it's just—you know—learn-Horatius-by-heart kind of thing. We miss Culture Club."

Goff had not in fact missed the poetry readings at all. It was only now, talking to Miss Vale like this, that he was suddenly convinced he had.

They waited in ritual silence while food and tea were set before them.

"What an enormous piece of cake!" Agnes said. "I doubt if I'll be able to finish it." Daintily she broke off a small piece with the little fork provided. "How frightfully butch you're all becoming! What an irrelevance my time there was!"

She sighed as Goff savored the ice cream on his spoon.

"But at least you have good feminine influences at home, Goff. Your sister . . . I thought at the Fathers Match how pretty she was."

"You must have been looking at someone else! Lucinda's quite ugly and frightfully bossy. All she thinks about is horses."

"And your mother. Mr. Lord told me she was a concert pianist before she married. Does she play still?"

"Not in public. Just when we have people to stay."

"I suppose your house is very big?"

"Marlwood? Quite big. We never use the east wing. My father has plans for it."

"Do you have lots of land?"

"Oh, a goodish amount. There's a lake and a wood," Goff said casually, scraping the last of the sundae from the sides of the dish.

"You're very lucky." Agnes looked pensive as she poured herself more tea. "And yet . . ." She leaned forward, staring at him over the rim of her cup, her eyes suddenly dark. "My own children will have different things. I shall tell them stories."

She smiled almost shyly.

"Your stories were always jolly good," Goff said.

"Not mine, really. Nothing new under the sun. Did you know I'd written a book? Well, two now. One published and one almost done."

"I could buy it," Goff said, thinking of the money in his wallet.

"Oh, my dear, I couldn't let you! Fortunately you needn't know what trash they are because I'm not using my own name. Still, they bring in some cash—Goff, be a love and eat the rest of the cake! Half was really ample for me."

He thought it undignified to wolf her leavings, but nevertheless he accepted the cake.

As he ate he sensed a change in her mood. She looked abstracted, and he didn't know why.

"I liked your teaching us," he suddenly said. "I liked the things you did. No one else ever does those kinds of things. I miss you."

She smiled, her eyes alight again.

"Goff, that's lovely. I'm so glad. But you'll soon outgrow anything I had to tell you. Would you like to see what I bought today?"

She reached down into a tote bag and took out a large book with a shiny blue cover.

"Fairy tales?" said Goff, disappointed.

"Perrault's. You know them? Sleeping Beauty, Puss in Boots—"

"We're going to the pantomime of that on Thursday."

"Here's the picture for it. These are lithographs by a man named Doré. Do you know what lithographs are?"

"Oh, yes. In my father's gallery . . ."

"But of course, your father's *the* Hillary Willoughby. I'd heard of his gallery in Mayfair, you know, long before I went to St. Fenrins. You can ask him about Doré. He'll tell you more than I know. Fairy tales and folk stories are the basis of all the literature in the world. They're incredibly exciting."

"I used to like them once."

"Everyone liked them once! Bluebeard here is my favorite. And look at this picture for Sleeping Beauty. Isn't it magical?"

It showed a flight of steps winding up through a very overgrown garden.

"Impossibly romantic!" Agnes said with a sigh. "And very beautiful! I wish everything could be as beautiful as a fairy story and as simple. You see the castle at the top? That's where the princess and the whole court have been asleep for a hundred years, waiting, just waiting . . ."

"It's a pity they're called *fairy* stories," Goff said, flicking the pages. "Really they're about magic, which is quite different."

"Take it, Goff," she said suddenly.

He stared at her.

"Take it, why don't you?" Her tone was almost sharp.

"But you've only just bought it."

"It doesn't matter. I know it by heart anyway. I'd like you to have it, really."

As he hesitated she scrabbled in her handbag, found a pen, and wrote rapidly on the first page. "To Goff, from Agnes Stratton with my love."

The name meant nothing at all. It seemed like the signature of a stranger. Yet he did recognize the handwriting from the time when, red instead of blue, it had chidingly bespattered his exercise book.

"You have to take it now," she said, holding it out.

Because she seemed elated, he felt he must be glad, too. Stammering his thanks, he put the book carefully back in the paper bag. Agnes was looking out the window with a dreamy smile that all at once turned bright.

"Look, there's Mr. Lord!" She waved vigorously. "He's seen us. We're over here, Justin!"

"Agnes, my love!" Lord approached theatrically as Goff rose to his feet. "You're *ravissante!* Not being at Fins suits you so well." Stooping, he pressed his lips to the cheek she offered. "But what's this? A clandestine meeting with another fellow? Hello, young Willoughby."

He ruffled Goff's hair irritatingly.

"Sit with us." Agnes was flushed now and very bright. "We've been having a delicious tea and a fascinating talk."

Goff was suddenly glum. All through tea he had felt himself her equal. Now, with the coming of Lord, the distance between them grew.

The History master took off his overcoat, drew up a chair between them, and called for tea and cakes.

"I'm only just back," he said to Agnes. "I intended to telephone you soon. What I had in mind was taking you and Harold to the Cock *ce soir*. Might it be a possibility?"

"Sounds lovely. We can catch him at the lab before he leaves. Oh, Justin, I'm glad to see you! I'm very up and down at the moment."

"How so?"

"I'll tell you all about it later."

Her eyes flickered toward Goff and away again.

The intimacy between these two disquieted him. He wanted to leave but didn't know how. In the end he cut in on their conversation abruptly.

"I have to go."

Agnes looked at him with the surprised expression of an adult who has forgotten a child is present.

"Oh Goff, must you?" she asked guiltily.

"I shall see you soon enough, worse luck!" Lord said. "Be sure you bring your wits back. These sportsmen are so bird-brained!"

"Don't forget your book," Agnes said.

"Been spending his Christmas money? A cricket almanac—or football? Which is it?"

"Neither. It was a present." Goff spoke gruffly, afraid that Lord might ask to see the book. He held out his hand to Agnes. "Goodbye," he said, "I can pay for the tea."

"Nonsense! It was I who asked you to come."

"I shall pay," said Lord, putting an end to the matter.

"That's an advantage of going out with men," Agnes said vivaciously. "They *always* treat one."

I would have treated you, too, Goff thought crossly.

"Thank you, sir," he said. "Goodbye Miss V—I mean, Mrs. Stratton."

"Agnes would perhaps be easier." She smiled. "Thank you for coming. Have a good term."

Goff hesitated a moment, then turned abruptly and marched off, clutching his parcel to his chest.

"He's gorgeous," Agnes said, as he passed the window and didn't wave to them. "So absolutely right, you know. That dark look that comes on him sometimes is irresistible. I'm glad I'm not the young girl who gets involved with him in five years' time." She shivered slightly. Glad—or is it that I'm sorry?

One rainy afternoon in the next holidays, Sandy Willoughby, switching on the light as she entered the playroom, was charmed by the picture of her two dark, good-looking boys, sitting with cheeks pressed close, poring over a book.

"Darlings," she said. "Are you having fun?"

Her elder son clutched the book and stared up at her, his eyes unfathomable.

"Goff's been reading to me, and it's ever so good," Fitz said, impatient at the interruption. "And the pictures are lovely."

"Are they, darling?" Sandy brushed back his springing hair. "What's it called, Goff? Oh, Perrault's fairy tales. But they're delicious! Wherever did you dig them up?"

"Mrs. Stratton gave it to me," Goff said grudgingly.

"Mrs. Stratton? Oh yes, she taught you at St. Fenrins. I met her once, didn't I? Rather a sweet girl. It was very kind of her to give you a book."

She looked puzzled, and Goff felt that he had to explain how it happened.

"Mr. Lord was there, too," something made him add. He turned to "Sleeping Beauty," and Sandy sat down between the two boys to look at it. "This is Miss V— I mean Mrs. Stratton's very favorite picture," Goff told her earnestly.

"It's certainly beautiful," Sandy said. "Very mysterious."

"Miss Vale liked things like that," Goff said. "She liked things to be enchanted in poetry and stories."

"She used to get some nice work out of Fifth," his mother said vaguely, putting her arm around Fitz and rocking him. "There was a piece by Arthur O'Higgins in the Fins magazine last year, rather original, I thought . . . A pity she couldn't stay on."

"Mrs. Stratton writes books," Goff informed her. "And she's having a baby, too."

(Tim Sergeant had mentioned that last term. Goff in the tea shop had never for a moment suspected it. When he'd heard about it he'd experienced a stirring inside similar to what he'd felt when he'd heard that she had married.)

"I'm glad," said his mother. "She's a sweet person."

Sandy in that moment was happy with her children, thinking how marvelous it would be if they could stay like this forever.

For a time Goff wondered about Agnes Stratton's baby, but when nothing further was said it went out of his head. Then one afternoon when he and Blount were hanging around Great Hall after lunch, Blount, right out of the blue, asked the headmaster's wife about it as she discussed menus with the housekeeper.

Susan Sergeant paused. She was harassed that day, and a lock of hair had fallen into her eyes.

"Mrs. Stratton had a little boy, Ben," she said, brushing it back. "But I'm afraid he died soon after."

Goff felt his stomach turn over.

"Oh I say, what rotten luck!" Ben's round face puckered in sympathy.

Susan Sergeant, who was possessed of a strong sense of her duties, laid aside her list and came toward them.

"These things happen sometimes," she said. "It's possible that a baby is sick and likely to suffer greatly. Then Nature, kindly, makes sure it doesn't have to do so. It's very tragic for us, but not for the baby. That's what we have to try to remember." Her face cleared. "I'm quite sure Mrs. Stratton will have other children, and they will be perfectly strong and healthy."

She smiled her confident smile and turned back to her work, conscious of one job at least efficiently executed.

As the two boys walked away slowly, they agreed that the right thing to do would be to go and see Agnes Stratton. Blount had been one of half a dozen boys who had taken down her address when she was leaving.

They cut rugby practice the following afternoon and arrived soon after two o'clock at a tall house that sat precariously at the top of a steep street known as Goose Hill in the Old Town.

"She said they had the attic, 'the garret,' she called it," Goff said, as they stared at the upper windows. "It used to belong to old Rosso's friend, the one that showed us the sculptures."

"I remember," Ben nodded. "We'd better go up."

"This must be it," Goff said, after they had toiled up about a hundred stairs and were faced by a dingy little door.

"Not a very good place for a baby," Ben remarked practically, still panting as Goff turned the handle and felt the door yield.

There was one more short flight of stairs. Halfway up Goff called out. A door opened, sending a shaft of light onto their upturned faces.

"Who's there?" called the voice of Agnes, and when they told her, "Good God! Come on up."

They found themselves in a long, low room with a skylight at one end and narrow windows the length of the other.

"Willoughby—and Blount!" Agnes exclaimed. "What a lovely surprise! Let me look at you properly."

Fearfully Goff raised his eyes. To look at a woman who had lost her baby filled him with dread. It was a relief to find that she looked very much as he remembered her.

"Darling boys!" she said, pressing their hands briefly. "Sit down and tell me things. What a treat!"

They placed themselves side by side on an old sofa and stared at her solemnly. She wore black pants and a flowered smock. Her hair was knotted carelessly on top of her head, and a pencil was stuck through the front.

Goff, allowing his glance to move to the room beyond her, had the impression of a great many books and much large, unmatching furniture.

"Did you have to get permission to come?" Agnes was asking.

"Oh, it was quite okay," he said quickly, before Blount had time to tell the truth. "We weren't sure you'd be in, though."

"I was typing. Deadlines, you know," she said. "I'm afraid all I can offer you to drink is tonic or lime juice."

They continued to sit in silence while she went to the kitchen and returned with tonic in tall glasses.

Goff nudged Ben.

"We, er, brought these for you."

Sheepishly he held out a package.

"Chocolates! Continental choice, too," Agnes said. "Very sophisticated! We must sample them at once. You know, it was nice of you to come and cheer me up."

"We only heard about the baby yesterday," Ben blurted before Goff could stop him. "Mrs. Sergeant told us. We're very sorry."

"My little boy?" Agnes's expression did not change. "He lived for only a couple of weeks. He was very damaged. Everyone assured me that it was for the best he went so soon. Rather a pity he came at all, under the circumstances."

She laughed abruptly and without pleasure. She had taken the pencil out of her hair and was turning it over and over in her hands, which were very white.

"But I'm over all that now," she went on. "I count my blessings, which are manifold. Isn't that a ridiculous word? What *can* it mean, manifold, manifold? I have my books, you see. And later in the year my husband and I are moving to the country. I shall keep myriads of lovely animals. Ben, you're the biologist. Tell me if animals are a good substitute for babies."

"I don't suppose they quite take the place of humans," he said seriously. "But I like them just as much."

"Of course you do, love. Now tell me all about Fins. Still skipper of the First Fifteen, Goff? Of course. And how are my little ones? Not so little now. . . ."

They talked for a while, easily enough. Agnes was cheerful, though she was very pale and there were dark smudges under her eyes. She appeared to Goff very vulnerable, far more so than at the time of the bicycle rides and in the tea shop before Justin Lord had come.

"Is that the Lady of Shalott?" Ben asked, indicating one of the pictures on the walls.

"That's clever of you. I'd forgotten we did the poem. How brazen of me to take on being your teacher! Do you still write those magnificent lyrical descriptions? Quite Wordsworthian, I thought."

"We don't go in for that stuff much now," Ben said deprecatingly.

"Is that woman from a poem, too?" Goff indicated a female who wore what appeared to be a black satin underslip and a preoccupied expression.

"Yes. The Beggar Maid. Her great humility won her the love of a king. Highly unlikely, I would have thought, but the Victorians were partial to moral tales. 'Her arms across her breast she laid, She was more fair than tongue can tell.'" Agnes, suiting the action to the words, had a pleasing air of humility. "The one there who looks as if she has a pain is the Blessed Damozel. They were all painted by the Pre-Raphaelites. Your father will know, Goff. Ask him about them."

After that Ben said it was time they were going because it was very important to be back by tea.

"Boys, it's been lovely," Agnes said as she went with them to the door. "Perhaps when I move Mr. Sergeant will let the old Culture Club come to a little party. We shan't be so very far from Fins."

She shook hands with them solemnly. Goff thought she was quieter than the Agnes of the bicycle day. It was sad to think she might never be like that any more.

"It'll be an awful sweat to be back in time," Blount remarked as they emerged from the house.

"Who cares? They can't do much about it. It was a good deed to come. She seemed more cheerful when we left."

"That would be the chocolates, I expect," Ben said and bounded down the hill.

". . . and the Grange at Tringham's gone at last," Goff's father remarked at dinner one night during the Easter holidays. "You remember the house, Sandy?"

"Yes. It's been empty for years."

"Hardly surprising. The position's damned inconvenient, and a place like Tringham, with neither pub nor shops, can scarcely be called a village at all."

"Must be a hamlet then," Goff cut in. "A play by Shakespeare!" No one else laughed at his sally.

"In that case it should suit the new owners very well," his father answered. "It's your literary lady, Mrs. Stratton, who's taken it on."

For the most part the adults' conversation swirled around Goff like water, but now he stiffened imperceptibly.

"What a coincidence!" Sandy exclaimed. "Mrs. Stratton used to teach Goff," she explained to her sister and brother-in-law.

"At Fins?" said the latter, a florid man named Rolf. "Wouldn't have thought the salaries there would run to country houses. You still a Governor, Hillary? Could there have been misappropriation of school funds?"

He chortled. Goff gave him a glance in which there was no enthusiasm.

"No chance," Hillary said easily. "Anyway Mrs. Stratton wasn't there long. She was one of T.S.'s experiments. Importation of a little femininity."

"Did it work?" asked Rolf, with a flicker of interest.

"Certainly it worked. Mrs. Stratton was a great hit with the boys. She took the younger ones chiefly, but she taught Goff's lot now and again."

"She married while she was there." Sandy's expression became sentimental. "Goff and all his form were awfully excited at the time, weren't you, darling?"

"I wasn't in the least excited," Goff said indignantly.

"Not bad looking, from what I remember, though I only saw her once," Hillary said. "No teaching qualifications, but she managed quite well without them. Kept you firmly in your place, eh, Goff?"

"So long as she didn't take him in hand!" Rolf said. "No harm in that, better than your bloody pederasts anyway," he went on with a grin as Sandy frowned at him.

"*Pas devant le garçon*, Rolf," she said quickly.

Goff scowled.

"Miss Vale—I mean Mrs. Stratton is a writer," he volunteered. "She writes under a—nom de plume." He cast a reproachful glance at his mother. "But really she's interested in more serious things, such as poetry."

"*Formidable! A bas bleu*, perhaps," said Sandy's sister, Ginevra.

"And she had a baby, but it died," said Goff.

He was aware that he was taking over the conversation but was unable to stop himself.

"How terribly sad!" said his mother uneasily.

"Oh, she's philosophical about it. She's decided to keep animals instead."

"Very wise!" Ginevra murmured.

"Ben Blount and I went to see her." There was no silencing Goff now. "She lived at the top of a very tall house at the top of a very tall hill. On her walls she had Pre-Raffles . . . ?" He looked at his father.

"Pre-Raphaelites," said Hillary. "Dead maidens and Dante Gabriel Rosetti."

"We took her a box of chocolates, continental ones."

"Did you really, darling?" said his mother, wonderingly. "Wasn't that kind of Goff, Ginevra? It was amazing, you know, how attached to her the boys became. And she gave Goff a book."

"It has illustrations by Doré," he said.

"She certainly seems to have brought a breath of culture into your hitherto Philistine existence," his father remarked.

"She knew loads of poems by heart," said Goff. "Mostly sad ones."

"Much of this is news to me," said Sandy amusedly to the others. "There are aspects of my elder son of which I obviously know nothing. All rather disconcerting."

"Now that you're to be neighbors, you'll have to be looking your Mrs. Stratton up one of these days, eh, Goff?" said Hillary jovially.

Goff frowned and looked down at his plate.

"I don't expect I will," he mumbled. "I shan't have time."

It was a relief to him when the conversation drifted on to more general matters.

⪗ FOUR ⪘

It happened that the spring half-term that year coincided with a pre-arranged visit to Ireland by Goff's parents and Fitz. Goff was to have had Karistides to stay at Marlwood, but at the last minute the Greek boy's father flew to London and sent for his son.

When Goff arrived home, he found that his seventeen-year-old sister Lucinda had invited another girl and two anemic youths to stay. The quartet regarded him with amused tolerance. They were quite prepared to have him with them on their various excursions, but he found the continual flirting and giggling and references to matters just on the edge of his understanding so little to his taste that he disdained the advances that were made and resolved to go his own way.

Yet this too proved unsatisfactory. He was completely unused to being left to his own devices, and by Sunday he was thoroughly bored.

It seemed to make matters worse that summer had arrived prematurely that year. The sky was a hot, unclouded blue and the air almost oppressively hot. Lucinda and her friends went off for a picnic, and Goff wandered aimlessly about the grounds all morning, thinking how different things would have been if Karistides had been able to come to stay.

By the time he had eaten a cold lunch that the housekeeper had put out for him, it was still only a quarter to two. Goff wandered up to his room. The pale curtains hung limp and unstirring, and the garden beneath the windows shimmered in a haze of heat.

Goff flung himself onto his bed and stared broodingly at the ceiling. After a while he took out his penis and rubbed it for the pleasure of feeling it stiffen. If Karistides had been there, they might have made comparisons. His friend had boasted that his own member was bigger than any boy's in the school.

Goff sat up and squinted down at himself. His own penis appeared mortifyingly small. He lay down again.

If Karistides had been present they might now have been looking at some of his sets of photographs. One of the sets depicted an incredibly "rude" woman with coarse black hair both on her head and between her legs, which in most of the pictures were wide apart. Her breasts were very large, with bright nipples so sharply jutting that they seemed like artificial adjuncts to her body.

There was nothing pleasant about the pictures, yet they engendered a strange, feverish excitement among those of the St. Fenrins boys who had been permitted to see them.

Lying back now on his bed, Goff closed his eyes and, thinking of the "rude" woman, continued to rub himself. When he looked up again the first thing on which his gaze focused was the blue-covered book given to him by Agnes Vale, which was still where he had left it on his bookshelf.

Idly, experimentally, Goff attempted to juxtapose the naked body of Agnes with the one in Karistides's photographs. He was unsuccessful. In thinking of Miss Vale, what came to mind was a statue of a nymph in the rose garden. The whole of its body and gently rounded breasts was very smooth. When he was about five Goff had pressed the knobs on the breasts to try to find out if they had any function and had concluded that they did not.

All at once, lying thus, he knew what he would do. He would go and see Miss Vale. Tringham was less than four miles away if one went by the Downs path. It was only just after two, and he could be there in an hour.

Hurriedly sitting up, he stuffed his penis back into his shorts and zipped them up. He jumped off the bed and ran from the room, down the stairs and out into the garden.

He paused only at the rose garden, where he seized a pair of pruning shears lying on a bench and snipped off half a dozen roses from a bed of Ena Harkness and wrapped the stems in his handkerchief. Then he set off.

As he walked, all the enervation of the last couple of days vanished. Physical exertion was always something in which he could lose himself quickly and satisfactorily. His mind felt suddenly keener.

An hour later the hamlet of Tringham lay below him. Everything seemed to slumber in the hot afternoon silence. He could detect no movement anywhere. Quietly, swiftly, he went down the hill.

Just beyond the church he turned into a lane and went past a deserted farmyard rendered ugly by a silo. He was approaching the Grange from the back. Soon he was on a fronded path that had been little used. No birds cried, and no small creatures rustled in the undergrowth.

The house when it came into view, very old and with its walls overgrown with ivy, had such a dilapidated look that it was hard to believe anyone lived there.

Suddenly Goff became aware that he was not alone. A large grayish dog was sitting on the shadowed step of a french window staring into space. On a sort of canopy above the window was perched a large white goose, likewise utterly immobile. Then, as Goff walked around the front of the house, he almost tripped over a red hen brooding in the long grass. Her little eyes seemed to wink at him, but she did not move. Finally, reaching the front door step, he was confronted by a great tabby cat, paws tucked into fur, malevolent green eyes gazing into middle distance.

The sight of the four immobile creatures and their complete lack of interest in him had a powerful effect on Goff. Together with the neglected house and the overgrown garden beneath the strangely still sky, they evoked in him a sense of ineffable mystery.

It was only with a considerable effort that he was able to break the spell that had fallen on him and bring himself to hammer with his fist on the big old front door.

The sound thundered into the silence, reverberated, died away. Goff's heart beat fast. He stared at the door, willing it to be opened. All at once it swung wide and Agnes Vale stood there.

As soon as Goff saw her, he knew with certitude that he loved her. It was not an idea that had occurred to him before, but now it seemed an immutable one. He felt for an instant a sinking, a kind of cold dread, as he realized how this love committed him.

Agnes stared at him, her expression for a moment as blank as that of the animals. Then her blue eyes seemed to focus, and life flooded into them.

"Goff Willoughby," she said, not moving.

"I brought you some flowers."

He held them out, but she did not take them.

"Goff," she repeated. She reached out. He felt her two hands resting on his shoulders, and her eyes met and held his for a moment. "But my dear, you're a magical boy," she said. "Come in. However did you know? Why are you here?"

Looking at her in the hall, he saw that she wore a long skirt of pale cotton and a loose white smock. Her fair hair was looped up carelessly as it had been at the house on Goose Hill. The realization of his love made Goff see her with new eyes. She was very beautiful. The length and paleness of the skirt gave her an appearance of slenderness and height.

"I don't know how you came or why," she said, holding out her hands and clasping his. "How did you find out I was here?"

He explained it all.

"You walked here?" she cried. "Goff, it's miles!"

"Only about four, if you come the short way."

"So near? I didn't realize we were neighbors. And these roses are for me?" At last she took them from him. "My favorite flowers! 'It was not in the winter our loving lot was cast, It was the time of roses, we plucked them as we passed.' Heavenly!" She sniffed the buds.

"They're very small."

"They'll last all the longer. Come into the kitchen and sit down." The first things he noticed in her kitchen were her typewriter and the papers scattered over everything.

"I'd better move some of this," Agnes said. "I've been incommunicado during the past week. There was something I had to do, so I cut myself off completely. Poor Harold's in Scotland. I'd be with him but for what I wanted to do. This morning I finished it. I felt like celebrating—and then *you* turned up!" She straightened the papers and pushed back her hair. "My head aches and my back aches. I'm completely disoriented. I haven't spoken to a human being for days." She laughed. Her cheeks were flushed and her eyes very bright. "Let's have tea and talk and talk. There's fruitcake. My sister sent it. First I must put the roses in water . . ."

Her compulsion to keep talking reminded Goff of guests at Marlwood similarly afflicted as a result of drinking too much.

"How pretty the buds look!" she exclaimed. "I wish I could arrange flowers artistically. Your mother can, I'm sure. Is she well?"

"Yes, thank you."

"And your handsome father. Does his gallery do well?"

"Oh, yes."

"Wasn't I reading some months ago about some marvelous plan to show pictures in your house—Marlwood, isn't it?"

"That's right. He's going to open the east wing and have exhibitions there."

"I think it's a beautiful idea. The London gallery's been in your family for generations. Your great-grandfather encouraged all the finest artists of his day. Do you think you'll go into the business, too?"

"I suppose I might," Goff said. "Really I'd rather be a cricketer."

"In summer, yes. When I was at St. Fenrins you were saying you wanted to be a footballer. How about an old Etonian soccer pro? Rather a novelty!"

Goff scowled.

"But you mustn't mind being teased," she said quickly. "Just my little joke. We'll go into the drawing room."

Except for a large chintz-covered sofa, there was little in the room into which she led him, and there were many clean spaces on the walls where pictures had hung. Agnes opened the french windows while Goff set the tray of tea things on the floor.

"We'll have to sit on the sofa together," she said. "Why hello, my love, come for your saucer of tea?"

A large, grayish animal had strolled through the window and was wagging a languid tail at them.

"I saw that dog earlier," Goff said.

"This is my Kashtenka. Poor love, she's very old. I got her from the Dogs' Home in Andham. They said there wasn't the slightest chance of anyone choosing her because her eyesight's failing. I had to take her. She gets on so well with the others, don't you darling?" The dog foolishly rolled its film-covered eyes at her. "You didn't come across Uncle, Goff? He's the fiercest of all cats. He bites, hard. He came with the house."

"I saw a cat, but he didn't seem to see me—and a goose and a hen . . ."

"The goose is Auntie. She's perfectly splendid."

"Your pets have funny names." Goff swirled the ice in the orange juice she had given him, noticing how fast it was melting.

"I filched them wholesale from a Chekhov story. Have you heard of him?"

Goff had not.

"He was Russian. One of the great writers of all time, and such a lovely man! I quite worship him. He wrote the story for children, come to think of it. You must read it."

"What about the hen?"

"She's sweet, but she isn't from the story. I call her Gertrude." Agnes caressed the dog's ears dreamily. "It's satisfying, living just with animals. It makes one feel rather good—innocent and pure." She patted Goff's hand. "Eat up your cake, love."

"They all sat perfectly still as I passed," he said wonderingly. "As if they were under a spell . . ."

"That would be the great heat. It will break. Now and then I hear a rumble far away. Goff, I want to know all the news. I love a good gossip."

They talked until the sun disappeared from the garden and twilight came. From the church the bell began to toll for evensong, sounding sweet as it stole across the overgrown lawn.

"So everyone just went off and left you," Agnes said at last. "How mean!"

"They couldn't take me to Ireland for four days. And it wouldn't have been so bad if Karistides had come. But Lucinda's so bossy, and her friends are idiotic. They giggle all the time over nothing."

He sighed self-pityingly.

"Poor Goff," Agnes's voice was warm with sympathy. "That's typical of the rich! It isn't only the working classes who have deprived offspring."

Goff knew he ought to have told her that his family never at any time neglected him. In fact, his father was fond of saying he'd dominate the household if given the chance. But he enjoyed the sensation of Agnes's sympathy. It was like being rubbed all over with oil. He sighed and looked as soulful as he could.

"Anyway, I'm grateful you decided to come and see me," she said. "Perhaps you'll stay to supper? I'm afraid it will be out of cans. I'm rapidly beginning to realize I'm not at all domesticated. Perhaps I should have stayed a spinster, forever teaching boys. I shall always remember that summer term at St. Fenrins. So beautiful, so simple."

It seemed to Goff that she needed no response to what she said. The big goose peered at them from the threshold of the window and stepped daintily into the room. When she found Goff there, she spread her wings and hissed.

"She's so intelligent!" said Agnes admiringly. "Of course, she won't be able to have the run of the place once it's done up. Little Gertrude wants to roost in the hall above the front door. Lord Byron kept a positive menagerie when he was in Italy, but then, he was an aristocrat. Anything is permitted of the ruling class."

Later, as they ate a haphazard supper, the fierce cat walked all over the kitchen table and consumed large chunks of cheese. The novelty of such outrageous behavior was deeply pleasing to Goff. While they ate, Agnes spoke animatedly of the "different" writing she had been doing.

"I've never been happy with the stuff I was working on," she said earnestly. "I've felt there was something else I ought to be tackling. Now I believe I've found it."

"What is it?" Goff asked. He was intrigued and flattered that she spoke as if he would understand everything.

She rested her elbows on the table and stared excitedly into his eyes.

"Harold and I were in Wales last year. We walked in the mountains, and there were sheep everywhere. I thought what an odd existence they have, just picking about the place until they die. I began to wonder . . . Suppose by some freak a sheep was born who possessed the intellect of a man . . ."

"It wouldn't be possible," Goff said positively.

"Of course not. Yet some sheep have faces that look quite human. Imagine one with a brain equal to Mozart's or someone . . . Anyway I've written a book about such a sheep. His name is Wolfram. He's medieval, and he has adventures . . ."

"What sort of adventures?"

"Incredible ones. There are castles, tournaments, a crusade . . . Wolfram is a good creature. He's definitely on the side of the angels."

"Can I read the book?"

"Not quite yet. I shall post it to my agent tomorrow. I did like writing it. If someone will publish it, I shan't use a pseudonym this time. I shall be plain Agnes Vale." She pushed back her chair. "Well, there it is. I'm glad you're the first to know about it. Now I'm going to find that Chekhov story . . ."

There was no suggestion of clearing off or washing up. Uncle fluffed himself up in the now empty fruit bowl, purring thunderously, a baleful expression on his face. The old dog lay at Goff's feet, and Agnes read aloud.

Watching how utterly absorbed she was in the story, Goff thought how much he had missed her. Yet it wasn't true. He had scarcely thought of her at all. It was only now, suddenly, that he needed her.

When it was eight o'clock, she broke off abruptly. She suggested that they telephone his sister and ask her to drive over and pick him up.

The idea of Lucinda and her vacuous friends breezing into this house—seeing Uncle asleep on the table and Auntie roosting in the hall, their loudness in the silence, the expressions on their faces—was so abhorrent to Goff that he found himself pleading to be allowed to stay the night.

"Stay here, Goff?" Agnes said doubtfully. "I'm not sure your mother would want—"

"My mother isn't here," he broke in petulantly. "You're the person who must decide. I could sleep very well on the sofa."

"We do have a folding bed. It's for when my sister-in-law comes over to help me."

"Then I'll sleep on that," he said quickly. "I'll phone Luce and explain I'll be back in the morning." He caught her sleeve. "Will you let me stay, please, please?"

He was reducing himself to a child by pleading, of course. But it was imperative that she say yes. He thought that if she acquiesced now, she always would.

"Of course you can stay, love," she said at last, mildly. "I'm sure it will rain heavily once the storm breaks, so it may be best if you do. But you must let your sister know at once. The telephone's in the study."

In a small room bare except for dozens of boxes, Goff looked out over the darkening garden and believed he could make out the hen Gertrude roosting in a bush. At his back Agnes was taking books from the boxes and laying them on the floor, murmuring to the dog as she did so about how much there was to be done.

When he had explained the situation to Lucinda, she at once began to raise objections, which infuriated him.

"Let me," said Agnes, gently taking the receiver from him. "We think it best if he stays," she said calmly. He thought it clever of her to imply that there were others in the house. He could hear Lucinda at the other end, gushing in the manner she had copied from her mother. "I'll see that he's home safely by lunchtime. No need for you to come over . . ."

As she replaced the receiver, he felt that they were conspirators.

Afterwards she led him from room to room, explaining all the plans she had for the house and the impossibility of executing them.

"It was pure chance we found it at all," she said. "We went for a drive one Sunday afternoon . . . the kind of thing the lower middle classes do, Goff." She gave him an ironic glance. "And we saw the 'For Sale' notice. I was drawn to it at once. It seemed such a forgotten place. We had to have a house, anyway; the doctors said it would do me good to have a change. This would have been completely beyond our means if it hadn't been falling to pieces and if Harold's father hadn't suddenly died and left him a little money and half a share in their house at Andham. As it is, we're mortgaged to the hilt till kingdom come. This is where you will sleep." She flooded a bedroom with the harsh glare of an unshaded light. "There are blankets but no sheets."

Goff said it would be fine.

"Rather narrow and hard. But at your age that doesn't matter. Let me show you the master bedroom."

At the end of a wide passage she flung open a door. The bed revealed was unmade, and a white bedspread trailed on the floor.

"This was very expensive," said Agnes with satisfaction, shaking the pillows and straightening the sheets. "Try it." She pushed him down. "Isn't it luxurious? I feel I should lie in it all day eating soft chocolates . . . Now we'll go down and look at the dining room. The thunder's nearer. Some rain will be a relief."

The dining room was long and smelled cold. Against the walls leaned a series of pictures that Goff recognized.

"My Pre-Raphaelites," Agnes said. "I hope the soulful ladies won't put people off their food. I shall hold elegant dinner parties to which you will be invited. And I shall also invite the loveliest girl, quite heartbreakingly young. I'll be wildly jealous."

"I don't like girls," said Goff, who pictured a series of Lucindas.

"No, but you will. And they'll certainly like you!"

He frowned. When she teased him, he remembered that after all he was only a boy to her. But he was mollified when they went back into the kitchen and finished "Kashtenka."

"That's a nice story," he said at the end.

"Yes. Wasn't it sad about Auntie? I very nearly cried."

"So did I. She was very clever. And the way he made the cat sort of bored was good. I don't think he would have done tricks at all, really."

"No, but it's still fun to think of it."

When it was time for Goff to go to bed, she gave him the top of a pair of her husband's pajamas to wear. The idea seemed to amuse her very much. As he lay in the dark the blankets were rough against his legs. Night sounds came to him through the open window. The goose exclaimed, and then there was silence. Goff fell asleep.

He was awakened by a great wind rattling the window frames, and as he turned over Agnes came in.

She was wearing a long, filmy nightgown in which she seemed to glide. She crossed to the window and secured it. Goff sat up as a great flash of lightning illuminated her.

"Go back to sleep," she said matter-of-factly. "It's certain to rain any minute," and she went softly away again.

Goff lay on his back and watched the lightning pattern the ceiling. With her flowing hair and her nightgown, Agnes had looked beautiful and strange. While she was at the window, in the flare of the lightning, Goff had seen the outline of her body beneath the thin cloth. As she stood by the bed he had wanted to reach out to her breasts that were so round, to touch them as he had touched the breasts of the nymph in the garden when he was a child.

He remembered the pendulous udders of Karistides's "rude" woman. In one photograph she had been gathering up her flesh in huge handfuls, and the bright red nipples had been squirming out between her fingers while she pushed forward her very thick, red-painted lips . . .

He jumped out of bed and padded to the window. In a flash of lightning he saw that it overlooked the churchyard. The old gravestones gleamed white in the livid light. The spirits of the dead could walk at any time between now and cockcrow. He shuddered.

Suppose the breasts of Agnes were like those of the "rude" woman and too big to be contained within her hands?

The garden, the house, shivered and trembled as the first rain began to fall. As Goff watched, it gathered force and dropped in a great releasing sheet, relieving a tension that had momentarily become unbearable. But what if he should see a figure, headless and white-sheeted, drawing on toward the house?

In a panic he fled the room, out along the passage. He arrived breathless at the master bedroom and without hesitating went in.

As he opened the door the first thing he saw was her hair spread over the pillow. The old dog, prone on the floor, raised her head and softly growled. The rain battered at the windows. Agnes, waking, switched on the lamp and blinked at him.

"Oh, Goff," she said. As she sat up, lifting her hand to brush the tumbled hair from her eyes, he saw the line of her breast clearly. "What is it, Goff?"

"I'm scared," he said flatly. "I want to get in bed with you."

"I'm so tired," she said, yawning. "You'd better sleep here if you're frightened. And after all, you're wearing Harold's pajamas!"

She giggled sleepily and pulled back the covers. In a trice Goff was beside her and she had turned off the lamp again.

"Poor little boy!" she murmured.

The sheets were soft, and the pillow into which his head sank was downy. Agnes pulled him to her so that he felt the warmth of her, and her breasts were nothing like the breasts of Karistides's woman. I love you, he said, but inside himself, not out loud.

Agnes uttered a long sigh and gathered him more closely in her arms. Beyond the window the rain lessened, although it fell steadily. Thunder rumbled, but the time between the peals was greater. The old dog snored gently. Goff felt himself sliding into the softness and smoothness of the bed and of Agnes and sleep.

In the morning he awoke to find that she was gone. Only the cat, perched precariously across his feet, growled and suddenly with surprising force nipped his blanket-shrouded toe.

"Fried eggs all right?" Agnes asked when he arrived downstairs in the kitchen. "There's honey for the toast. Isn't it a relief that the storm has cooled things down?"

This morning she wore the long skirt with a high-necked shirt tucked into the waistband. Her hair was bound up tightly and secured firmly on top of her head. She looked like an old-fashioned school-mistress, and her manner was cheerful and brisk. The radio was playing sprightly pop music, and Auntie stood in the middle of the floor muttering to herself.

"That bird is so clever," Agnes said. "Never lived with people before, yet she understands everything. Shift over, Auntie, there's a love. I don't want to trip over you."

Hissing gently, the bird moved its orange feet.

"Today I feel different," Agnes announced, placing orange juice in front of Goff. "Yesterday I was older than the Ancient Mariner, more aged than the rocks on which the Mona Lisa sits. I was Tithonus chained to life, not able to die. How *old* I was," she marveled, bringing over mugs of coffee and sitting beside him. "But today I'm young. The rain has washed me clean and new. I've loved having you here. I really believe you could be one of my best friends. Will you be my friend, Goff?"

"I am already," he said gruffly, dissatisfied, wanting more.

"Yes, I believe you are. And we shall stay close. We shall have an *amitié amoureuse*. I shall be a kind of adopted aunt . . ."

"No," said Goff sharply. "I don't want you for an aunt."

She was looking coquettishly at him over the rim of her cup. It hurt Goff to have her treating their relationship as a joke. His face darkened.

"Oh, you know I'm only teasing," Agnes said. "Now, if you'd like to hang on a bit, Harold will be able to run you back in the car."

"No," he said quickly. "I have to go this morning."

The idea of meeting the husband, whose image had been quite absent from his mind, was not pleasing. It occurred to him that Agnes's brightness this morning was probably due to the fact that this husband was returning to her.

The strident banality of the music was suddenly as offensive to him as the cheerfulness of her manner.

"Isn't there anything else on the radio?" he asked grumpily.

"You don't like it?" She switched stations. "Oh," she said, listening. "One of my favorites. *Pavane pour une Infanta défunte.* Poor little dead Spanish princess!"

The music chimed with the mood Goff was seeking, but he wondered guiltily if it might remind Agnes of the dead baby. To his relief, she apparently failed to make the connection.

While they listened he recalled, with a little prick of excitement, that he had slept with her. I shan't tell anyone that, he thought. Meanwhile he had to find a way of seeing more of her. He smiled as an idea began to form in his mind.

"Lovely," Agnes said, turning off the radio as soon as the piece was finished.

When he was ready to leave, she said she would go with him as far as the main road.

"Tomorrow you go back to school," she said. "Will you tell the boys who remember me that I was asking after them?"

"Of course. Shall I tell Mr. Lord, too?"

"Justin?" She laughed. "He knows where I am. Tell me, has he found himself a girlfriend yet?"

"No chance. I don't think Mr. Lord likes girls very much. Karistides says—"

"Oh, spare me the opinions of that cynical child!" Agnes said dismissively. "He isn't an oracle, you know. I'm always surprised you're such cronies. You're not at all alike."

"Andy's good fun. We have a laugh . . ."

"I'm sure you do. At whose expense, I wonder? I prefer nice, straightforward boys like you. I want things to be wholesome. Karistides seems to threaten that."

"There's nothing threatening about Andy," said Goff, not understanding. "He just likes things to be fun. I'm going to stay with him in Greece. My father says I can, when I leave Fins."

"I suppose you won't have much longer there now. Let me see, how old are you?"

"Twelve and a half."

"As old as that? I was thinking you were still ten. You were only ten when I first taught you. Soon you'll be grown up, and I'll be middle-aged." She sighed and shook her head.

"If I should ever be stuck with Latin," said Goff, carefully, reverting to something that had been in his mind earlier, "would you be able to tell me where I was going wrong?"

Agnes paused and rested her hand on the trunk of a beech tree. It looked very small and smooth against the rough, dark bark.

"I'm rusty," she said. "One never uses Latin . . ."

"But you'd know enough to get through your public schools entrance paper?"

"Perhaps, if I concentrated. But you have no problems. Mr. Godball is very sound."

"He's been on at me a bit. I've a feeling I may not do so well next half."

"I'm sure your father remembers enough to—"

"Oh, *he* wouldn't help me," said Goff. "It would be so nice if there was someone near I could ask . . ."

He assumed his bereft expression.

Agnes laughed and slapped the beech trunk.

"Oh, come to me if you're really stuck," she said airily. "I can always have a bash. I suppose I ought to turn back now."

When Goff put out his hand, she held on to it. Her pressure was warm and soft. Standing so close, he was suddenly aware that she would never tell anyone they had slept together. The realization gave him confidence.

"Mind how you go," she said, releasing his hand.

"Yes. Agnes?"

"Yes?"

"What was it you said we would have, at breakfast, when we talked about being friends?"

She laughed.

"An *amitié amoureuse*? Just my fun. If you can't work it out, your French must be even worse than my Latin! Go on, off you go."

Goff grinned and marched off. When he had gone a little way, he turned. He could see her pale figure at the edge of the trees with the gray dog at her side. She waved to him and turned her away, her long skirt sweeping the path.

"Of course something will have to be done," Hillary Willoughby said testily to his wife. "It's quite absurd. He came ninth out of ten boys, only managing to beat that silly Moss-Hemlock child—"

"But it was only in Latin, darling." Sandy Willoughby's eyes followed her husband uneasily as he strode about the room, Goff's reports sheafed in his hand. "He was fourth overall and easily top in History."

"That's why it's so bloody stupid to fall down on this," Hillary said. "Old Godball's obviously had it. Goff will simply have to be tutored."

"But we go to Ireland next week."

"I don't know if I'm going to be able to manage it this summer. The exhibition will never be ready for the opening unless I keep an eye—"

"But darling, you *must* come." Sandy looked panic-stricken. "It's all arranged. Ginevra and Rolf . . ."

Hillary shrugged. He knew the importance his wife attached to the traditional summers at her family's home.

"I may still make it," he conceded, soothingly. "But Goff will have to stay here, for part of the time at least." He sighed heavily. "How could he be so stupid?"

"He's awfully penitent," Sandy said. "Poor love, he knew he was falling behind but not what to do about it. He even mentioned it to that nice Mrs. Stratton—you remember he took himself off there while we were away—and apparently she offered to help him out."

"The Stratton woman?" Hillary paused in his pacing. "I thought she was some kind of a writer."

"Apparently she knows Latin. Old Erskine Fawcett actually mentioned that to me once. He seemed quite impressed with Miss Vale, as she then was."

"She couldn't tutor Goff, surely?"

"We could always ask her. Should I telephone?"

Hillary hesitated.

"Might be tricky. We could hardly offer her money."

"I doubt if she'd take it."

"It puts one under an obligation. All bloody complicated. Nothing's simple these days . . ."

"Let me at least talk to her. If Goff has to stay behind I'd feel happier if he went to someone we knew. The little boys loved her."

"I suppose he could always join us later, if he acquitted himself reasonably well. God, but this is inconvenient! Children are nothing but a burden. Damn Goff!"

How impatient he was becoming, Sandy thought. Of course, he had a lot on his mind this summer. Goff would be all right with Mrs. Stratton. She had seemed a sympathetic young woman.

The first thing Goff noticed on opening the gate and stepping into the garden was that the long grass at the back of the house had been roughly mown. He noticed also a space enclosed by wire netting with a chicken coop inside. He believed he recognized Gertrude among the brown hens within, but she looked very commonplace among others of her kind.

Someone had been working in front of the open french windows of the drawing room. There was a bag of cement and an empty wheelbarrow, and a few tiles had already been laid.

As Goff paused, Auntie came into view, picking her way daintily among the debris. With a rush of joy he hailed her. The goose lifted her wings in what he was sure was recognition, hissing gently, without animosity.

Hard on her tracks came a man Goff had never seen before, with a very brown exposed torso and cut-off jeans.

"Hello," he said. "Where've you sprung from?"

"I'm Goff Willoughby," the boy said, thinking that this was not Agnes's husband and realizing he had somehow imagined she would be on her own.

"Ag's ex-pupil," the man said. "She's going to help you with your Latin. Don't know any myself, but if you're stuck with Geography, call on me. I'm Jeff Miller, by the way. Why don't you go on into the house?"

Goff went into the kitchen. A figure at the sink caused his heart to leap, but it turned to reveal the face of a total stranger.

"Looking for someone?" The woman's voice had a sharp note.

"I'm Goff Willoughby and—"

"Ah, yes." The woman began briskly to peel off pink rubber gloves. "I'm Jennifer. Mr. Stratton is my brother. Maybe you saw my husband in the garden?"

"There's a man in shorts . . ."

"That's him," said Jennifer Miller with some satisfaction. "He and Harold are supposed to be laying a patio, but he never does much while Harold's at work. We're both teachers so we have long holidays, though not so long as you boys at St. Fenrins. We're on the staff at Andham Comprehensive. You won't have heard of that, I don't suppose."

"I don't believe we play them."

"Certainly you don't." She laughed curtly. "Anyway, I teach Math there."

Goff didn't know how he was expected to react to this information, which was issued in a challenging tone. He was relieved when the door opened and Agnes came in.

She was wearing a short, tight-fitting blue dress cut low at the neck. When she saw him, her face glowed.

"Goff!" She came to him and pressed the tops of his arms in what amounted to a half-embrace. "How tall you're getting! It's lovely to see you again."

"I've brought you these." Goff held out a big bunch of roses. "One of them's lost its petals, I'm afraid."

"Goff, how beautiful!" Agnes put her nose into them. "Divine!

Sniffing roses is like taking a cool drink. Look Jen, aren't they magnificent? I think perhaps I like roses better than anything in the world."

"I'll put them in water. You'll be wanting to get on with your lesson," Jennifer said without enthusiasm.

"I suppose we ought," Agnes said. "Let's take some lemonade into the dining room. It's cool there in the mornings."

"Have you still got Uncle and Kashtenka?" Goff asked anxiously as she took ice from the refrigerator and poured lemonade into glasses.

"Of course. Didn't you see the lad on your way in? He's out there pretending he's a tiger. Kashtenka's stretched out upstairs. She finds the heat trying. You'll be all right, Jen?"

"I thought I might lend Jeff a hand," the other woman said, beginning to roll up the sleeves of her blouse.

"Wonderfully practical girl!" Agnes whispered to Goff in the corridor. "So efficient she quite frightens me."

The dining room was now carpeted, and the Pre-Raphaelite pictures had been hung. The faces of the women looked sadder and more pensive than ever.

"What do you think of this table?" Agnes said as she drew out chairs. "It's very old. The wood's just like satin."

Goff would have liked to tell her how beautiful she was. She was tanned, and the dress clung to her figure excitingly. He was delighted to discover, as she pulled her chair closer to his, that her legs, like his own, were bare.

"I've a letter here from Mr. Godball . . ." Goff produced it from the pocket of his shirt.

"It only confirms what I know already," Agnes said when she had read it. "It's in the second paper that you're going adrift. Let's take a look at what I have here."

She leaned forward so that their heads touched. I shall most certainly tell her I love her, Goff thought, and it has to be done this holiday . . . The swell of her breast was delectable as she rested her arm on the table. He wished he could have the feel of it beneath his fingers . . .

". . . and probably not paying attention during class," she was saying. "It always amazes me how children can listen at all, especially in summer. Poor old Goff! It's beastly for you to have to spend your vacation like this."

"I don't mind. At least it means I can see you every day."

"That's a sweet thing to say, but what a poor compensation!" She shifted her leg, which was growing sticky from contact with his. "Are you really all by yourself at Marlwood?"

"Not quite. My father's not going till next week because of the new gallery."

"Well, that's something. Now I suppose we'd better get to work. Let's go over this. Caesar's describing the winter campaign . . ."

The pattern of their time together was established in the ensuing days. Goff felt that while they were working Agnes belonged to him exclusively. The rest of the world could be shut out. Often they would break off in the middle of a lesson to talk about things that interested them more.

"There's something frightening to me about the way roses burgeon," Agnes said to him once. "These will be huge before they drop. For the moment, though, they're perfect. On the verge of something lovely. *Jeunes filles en fleur.* Do you know what that means?"

"Roughly." Goff was fascinated when she talked thus. His incomplete understanding of what she said enhanced the attraction of it.

"*Jeunes filles en fleur,*" she repeated dreamily. "That's a very potent phrase, you know, in literature—and in life, too. How the girls will blossom when you're seventeen, Goff! All around you, so beautiful. When you're middle-aged, even when you're old, how your loins will stir at the beautiful, beautiful flowers of girls!"

None of the boys at St. Fenrins had ever been able to pin down precisely what loins were. That Agnes should refer to them was somehow exciting.

"My father's middle-aged," Goff said.

"Hardly. I'm sure I don't know how *he* feels." She sighed. "He's very strong. A totally masculine personality."

"Do you like him better than me?"

"I scarcely know him." She plucked a scarlet rosebud out of the glass. "His milieu is so very different from mine. I would never have encountered someone like you if I hadn't filled in for those few months at St. Fenrins."

"I'm glad you did," Goff said.

Yet he didn't say it then, didn't tell her what he meant to tell her, that he loved her. It was harder to do than he had imagined. The days slipped by pleasantly enough, and still it remained unsaid.

More people arrived at the Grange as the week advanced. Agnes's elder sister, Dorothy, came with two small children who spoke with an odd accent. The boy, Martin, was about Fitz's age. He formed a strong attachment to Goff on learning of his sporting prowess.

Goff began to stay on after his lessons, amusing himself with the children and the men and Agnes while Jennifer and Dorothy, who were interchangeable in his eyes, knitted and gossiped through the long, hot days.

Goff was used to large groups, but hitherto they had always been his groups. He was accustomed, both at school and at home, to being set against his own background. It was curiously satisfying to discover that he was able to take in his stride the unaccustomed role of outsider in which he now found himself.

The only cloud on the horizon of the summer days was the apparent inevitability of their ending with his mission unaccomplished. Darkly he brooded on how to bring it about. He wished he could get Agnes away to Marlwood. There on his home ground it would be easier, he was sure.

On an evening of unusual heat they were still playing "rounders" on the back lawn when all the color was draining out of the sky. As soon as he was run out, Goff looked for Agnes. He found her in a deck chair in the front garden with Kashtenka at her feet.

"You did very well," she said, as he flopped on the grass beside her. "Will you play in Ireland?"

"Sometimes we do. Too many girls, though. They won't stick to the rules."

"How about this young man of Lucinda's?"

"Hopeless, absolutely. She has him wound around her little finger. All they ever want to do is neck."

"Necking can be fun. You'll think so one day." Agnes smiled nostalgically. "I used to be something of an expert, but being married kills that sort of thing stone dead!" She laughed and stretched her arms high above her head. "How peaceful it is! The trees are as still as great paper cutouts. I love summer so much. You'll have a great time in Ireland, Goff."

"I don't want to go. I'd rather stay with you."

"You say such nice things. But your Latin's up to standard now. There's no need for you to be here."

"I shall miss seeing you every day." He plucked at the grass.

"Oh, once you get away you'll wonder how on earth you stood it!"

"It isn't like that. You never seem to understand."

Something in his tone made Agnes look at him closely.

"Never mind," she said. "We shall meet again soon. You know Harold and I have been invited to the Gallery opening?"

Goff's heart gave a lurch.

"I didn't know," he said. "No one ever tells me. You're really coming to Marlwood?"

He knelt beside her chair and stared at her keenly.

"I've accepted the invitation. The people will be rather grand for us, though. Are there to be lots, Goff?"

"Hundreds. My parents always give a party at the beginning of September anyway, when the weather's fine enough to be outside. This time it's going to be more than just local friends. There'll be lots of London people as well."

"It'll be something of an occasion for Harold and me. We don't have many of those."

"Will you promise to talk to me?"

"Of course. Who else? You'll be my only friend."

"But it's different when there are grownups there. Will you promise you'll be the same?"

He put his hand on her arm, the nails pressing into the skin.

"I shall be just the same, I promise you," she said gravely.

Carefully, as though disengaging a burr or an insect, she lifted his fingers from her wrist one by one.

"What are you two hatching with your heads together?" Jeff called, coming toward them with "rounders" bat in hand.

"Secrets!" Agnes said.

"You always look very serious when you're talking," he said. "What goes on?"

"We have an *amitié amoureuse*, don't we, Goff?" Agnes said.

"Come again?" Jeff squatted beside them. "I don't know how you manage it, Godolphin my lad." It amused him to call Goff by his full name since no one else ever did. "You get closer to Agnes than anyone except her husband. And I sometimes wonder if even he does as well as you."

"I'm not going to listen to such nonsense!"

Agnes jumped to her feet with a vehemence that disturbed the slumbering Kashtenka and stalked off. Jeff grimaced at Goff, but the boy turned away and stroked the dog's flank soothingly. He wanted to be by himself to think about her coming to Marlwood and what he would say to her then.

ᥱᥬ *FIVE* ᥱᥬ

Harold Stratton, caught in a press of well-dressed men and women, smiled vaguely and waited for it all to be over. It wasn't really his sort of thing at all, but at least Agnes was enjoying herself.

She was in her element, of course. The night, the people, the pictures all intoxicated her. Sandy Willoughby had received her with particular warmth, covering her with gratitude, ensuring that she met as many people as possible.

As it grew dark she wandered away from the crowd into a small, hedged garden. It was cooler here than inside the gallery, and she felt glad of a moment away from the exhilarating challenges of the night.

"What do you think of them?"

A gaunt, swarthy man who was following her around, catalogue in hand, indicated the modern sculptures that had been set about.

"They're interesting. Some of the shapes are very powerful, aren't they? Stark. And yet, you see that pale nymph over there? Eighteenth century, I suppose, not part of the exhibition. I have to confess that to me she's far more beautiful."

"Ah, a romantic! Very feminine." The man nodded, his smile saturnine. "And Ginevra tells me you're a writer."

"Ginevra? I don't think—"

"Sandy Willoughby's sister."

He gestured toward the terrace where a bold, dark woman was holding sway over a group of mesmerized males.

"Oh, yes." Agnes followed his glance. "Sandy introduced me to her. Yes, I do write."

"She said you were looking for an illustrator."

"For my children's book? That's right. It's more difficult than I thought it would be." Her expression lightened suddenly. "There's

Goff. On the terrace. How handsome he looks in that dark suit! Quite devastating!"

"Do you know him well?"

"Very well." Smiling broadly now, Agnes waved in the boy's direction.

"He's becoming very like his father," the man remarked unemphatically. "All the Willoughby men have a certain thrusting quality."

"Oh, Goff isn't like that. At school they used to say how stubborn he was, but I've always found him a sensitive child."

"Yes?" The man smiled. "I was right, you see. You *are* a romantic!"

Agnes frowned, but her face cleared as Goff approached them.

"Darling Goff!" She embraced him with a theatricality born of the occasion and of the wine she had drunk. "I thought I'd never see you!"

"Someone said you were in the sculpture garden with Mr. Forrester."

Agnes looked about her, but the stranger had melted back into the crowd around the house.

"Is that his name?" she said. "I don't know that I like him. He's very cold."

"He's an artist. My father shows his work," Goff said dismissively. "I want to show you the lake, Agnes. Will you come now?"

"And why not?" she said recklessly, taking him by the arm.

As she walked along with him, she noticed with amusement that he was carrying a champagne bottle and a glass.

"Such a crush inside, so hot," she murmured. "Oh Goff, it's a real lake!"

"Of course it is. Did you expect a pond? I think if we take a punt you won't have to do anything at all."

"I didn't think we were going to go on it." She turned her head toward the noise of the party. "I'm only here for the exhibition."

"Don't be silly," Goff said. "You're my guest, too. See, there's a punt tied up here all ready."

As she climbed in she wobbled on her high-heeled sandals and had to catch hold of his hand.

"How beautiful it is," she said as he began to pole to the middle of the lake. "And much nicer than being with all those people." She trailed her hand in the water. "I'm not sure I ought to have come to

Marlwood, Goff. Seeing you against your background makes me uneasy."

"Why? Aren't I the same person you knew at school and at your house?"

"Not entirely. All this makes what I want to do seem ridiculously puny and irrelevant."

"What rot!" Goff said.

He stopped poling, poured champagne into the glass, and handed it to her. Then he put the bottle to his lips and drank off the rest as if it were lemonade.

"At sunset this place must be like a landscape by Claude," Agnes said. "Utterly dreamlike! I feel as if I'm in a dream now . . . I'm glad we can be friends, Goff, even if it's only for a little while."

"Why should it be only for a little while?" he demanded.

"Because you have to grow up—"

"I'm not going to change," he said. "I love you. I always will."

There. It was said. He reddened and clutched tightly at the cold neck of the champagne bottle.

"Love me?" Agnes said lightly. "Well, I love you, too."

"No, really love. Not love like . . . liking. More than that. Something special."

"You have so much to love. Parents, family, your dog maybe, friends at school, sport—"

"Not that!" he said impatiently. "I *like* all those things. I'm talking about love. I love you."

Now it seemed easy to go on saying it. He thought he might repeat it a thousand times.

"I think of you all the time," he said. "I think you're really, really beautiful."

"That's because you've been very much alone lately. You'll feel differently—"

"No I *won't!* I don't want to." He was beginning to be cross. "It has nothing to do with now. I loved you even when I first saw you!"

"At St. Fenrins?" she said teasingly. "Impossible! I was a dragon of a schoolteacher, wholly unlovable."

"I didn't know I loved you then. I didn't know that what I felt was love. I only found out a little while ago. This is deadly serious, Agnes."

"It's most flattering," she said. "But do understand that you're quite free to love other people, too."

Goff leaned toward her. Her willful misunderstanding of the situation was profoundly irritating to him.

"I'm not going to love anyone else," he hissed. "I'm only going to love you."

"All right," she said equably, taking a sip of champagne. "You go ahead. There's nothing to stop you."

"But I want you to love me back."

His face was close to hers. The wine had made his amber-colored eyes glitter. She felt the force of him. The boat rocked dizzyingly.

"I do love you," she said, trying to dissipate the tension.

"I don't mean like your husband or Martin or Uncle or Auntie or Kashtenka." His tone was withering. "Or flowers! I mean a very special love."

"Believe me, Goff," she said seriously. "I have no other friend whom I regard as I do you."

"Then kiss me," he said urgently.

She smiled and, leaning forward, pressed her lips against his forehead.

"That's no good," he said vehemently. His hot face was very close to hers.

Agnes hesitated, then took it between her hands and kissed him lightly on the lips.

"There," she said, still holding him. "Because we're special friends. But you mustn't ask again. Now I want to go back."

Her hands dropped to her lap. Goff touched the knob of her shoulder where it emerged, smoothly brown and faintly shining, from the blue dress she wore. It wasn't enough, not nearly enough. With a sigh he picked up the pole.

It was completely dark as they walked back over the grass. The noises of the party came to them from a distance, but at the edge of the topiary hedge the garden was shadowed and still.

Agnes paused and looked up at the sky.

"It's all so lush," she said. "Tennysonian. Cypress waving on palace walk, gold fin winking in porphyry font. 'My dust would hear her and beat, Had I lain for a century dead . . .' Lush!" She laughed sadly.

"Agnes," Goff seized her suddenly around the waist. "I love you so much. I don't want to go back to Fins. Why can't things stay the same?"

He pressed his face against her body in its sheath of blue silk, clutching her tightly.

"Goff," she said. Seeing a garden seat, she pulled herself to it, half-dragging him with her. "Nothing ever stays the same, neither the good nor the bad, which is some consolation, isn't it?"

"Everything takes so *long*," he burst out. "I shan't be able to do as I like for years. I won't see you again, even, till half-term at least."

"Oh, come on, don't dramatize! You know you like school really. You do awfully well there. And I'm happy when you're gone because it's as it should be. You won't mope, Goff, will you? I shouldn't like that at all."

He shook his head and fingered the stuff of her dress where the warmth of her thigh pressed through it.

"I'll come and see you just as soon as I can," he said in a subdued tone.

"Yes, of course," she said brightly. "That's settled. Now we really must get back. Poor Harold, he'll be wondering what on earth has happened to me."

"Was it very dreary for you, darling?" she asked her husband solicitously as they drove away from Marlwood an hour or so later.

"Not really. You enjoyed yourself, anyway."

"Oh, perhaps." She yawned and stretched. "This sort of thing is all very well once in a while. But I have so much more. You're more understanding than anyone else would be. I'm lucky, very lucky." She patted his knee.

By the time they reached the Grange she was asleep.

In the autumn break Goff rode over to the Grange. He was fully aware of the theatricality of the action, yet found it irresistible. It was easy enough to saddle up Lucinda's chestnut gelding Russet, to call Flock, the red setter, and to ride away across the countryside. No one even knew he had left the house.

The woods through which he rode were silent and burnished; the late October air was still. At the Grange he found Harold sawing logs and was told that Agnes was in the little orchard at the end of the garden.

Goff saw himself as a young Prince come to the house of a humble peasant. That was Harold, sawing logs. For the purpose of the fantasy, Agnes was transposed from wife to daughter, the humble peasant's beautiful daughter.

When he hailed her, she peered at him from the top of a ladder. "You already?" she said. "It seems only yesterday you were here. I'm glad to see you. We're so quiet now that I feel old again. Aren't you splendid! What a noble steed!"

She scrambled down the ladder to talk to Russet, offering him an apple. Goff slid from the saddle with a trace of regret for his lost eminence.

"Your face is as bright as Keats's ode," Agnes said. "You remember how we used it as an example of personification? This is a beautiful dog. See, Kashtenka, what do you think of this?"

"Her name's Flock."

"What beautiful soft ears she has! Wouldn't it be nice if we could live, you and I, alone except for animals? Oh, I'm mad! Is that why you come to see me? Are you sorry for the poor mad woman at the Grange?"

"If it was moated, you could be Mariana," Goff said. "The women in your dining room remind me of her."

" 'My life is dreary, He cometh not.' How deliciously morbid! Perhaps I am Mariana, always waiting for you to come back. 'I am aweary, aweary, I would that I were dead.' "

"But I do come. You don't have to be sad. I always come."

He stared at her. A breeze ran through the trees, and apples gently fell. The horse and dogs had moved away. A bonfire crackled away to itself in a corner, the smoke heavy on the air. And all the while, in the background, was the steady sound of sawing.

"These trees ought to be pruned," Agnes said, as Goff squashed a rotten apple beneath his boot. "They're very old, and the fruit is impossibly high."

"I'll throw some down," he volunteered.

"Take care," Agnes said.

When she put back her head to look up, her long hair escaped its pins and tumbled halfway down her back. Goff shook the tree vigorously. He felt powerful and in command. The orchard was an enclosed and private place. Auntie came through the long grass, stepping high, picking her way through the fallen fruit.

"Stop!" Agnes called, as apples showered on her. "I feel like Danaë—well not entirely, fortunately. Come on down now."

Slithering from the tree, Goff picked up an apple, red and unmarked. He rubbed it slowly against his jersey.

"Who was Danaë?" he asked.

"One of the many Greek maidens Jove took a fancy to. Went to her as a shower of gold, coins I suppose. Must have been disconcerting . . . and not entirely satisfactory from her point of view."

"He went to Helen's mother as a swan, didn't he?" Goff said. The apple shone from its polishing, and he took a deep, satisfying bite from it. "But a swan couldn't really give a woman a baby."

"He was a god," Agnes said. "It didn't matter about the form he took."

"But they couldn't really have mated, could they?" he persisted.

"Better ask Ben Blount! How's the Latin now, by the way?"

"Fine now, thanks," Goff grinned. "I'm not kept in for extra work this term."

"Good. Not that I suppose I shall get any credit from that old misogynist Godball."

"What's a misogynist?"

"Someone who hates women."

"Then I must be the opposite." Goff hurled the apple core into the undergrowth.

"Quite right, too. Tell me, do you have a girlfriend yet?"

"Of course not."

"Oh, come on now! When there is one I hope I'll be the first to know."

"There's no one. I swear," Goff said.

He was irritated that she would treat the matter so lightly, as if their own relationship were not of that kind.

"Karistides—" he began, then stopped. "Arthur O'Higgins has a girl," he went on quickly. "They write to each other. And Moss-Hemlock's sister wants to date Ben, but he's too embarrassed."

"Is she pretty?"

"Livvy Moss-Hemlock? All right, I suppose. Better than her brother, anyway. I think girls are jolly boring."

"You prefer older women, of course."

"Age has nothing to do with it," Goff said sulkily.

"Ah, how often that must have been said! Shall we go in and have some tea? I want to show you the pictures for Wolfram. That man I met at the Gallery opening, Forrester, has done them. They're awfully good."

"I can't stay for tea. I have to go back now." He thought that inside, with Harold there, it wouldn't be the same at all. "But I shall come at Christmas," he said. "I shall come every day then."

"That will be lovely. It will cheer me up no end."

Goff gathered up the horse's bridle and they rounded the corner, where Harold still sawed with his sleeves rolled up.

"Darling, we shall be warm all winter," Agnes said, going to him. The goose fluttered up onto the log like a detail from a Dutch genre painting. "Goff has to go. But you and I shall have tea now."

She kissed his cheek. Goff whistled to Flock, mounted Russet, and rode away. If she had no husband, if she lived all alone, it would be better, he thought. All the same, it had been good in the orchard. Remembering the swan and the shower of gold made him smile. Biological impossibilities! It would be fun when Christmas came.

"Stack the logs later," Agnes said to Harold. "You deserve a break now."

He followed her into the kitchen and watched her put the kettle on the stove.

"You made quite an impression on young Goff when you did the Latin with him," he said. "Maybe you missed your vocation after all."

"I doubt it. There are quite enough teachers in this family anyway, with Jen and Jeff!"

Harold ran the water in the sink and immersed his arms up to the elbows.

"He's got a bit of a crush on you, that boy," he said.

"A crush? Goff? I don't really think so." Agnes raised her eyes from the teapot. "He's just a little boy who's very lonely at home."

"He's not a little boy. He's a big lad." Harold let out the water and took up a towel. "There's no reason for him to be lonely. He has everything a boy could want. He's not getting any smaller. You might have a problem on your hands one of these days, Agnes."

"With Goff? Never." She fetched a cake tin as Harold dried his hands carefully. "As soon as he begins to take an interest in that sort of thing, he'll get himself a girl. Lucky girl!"

"Your hair's coming down," Harold said. "It looks a bit untidy. If you want to put it up, I'll pour." Carefully he hung up the towel.

"Oh, what does it matter?" Agnes said, suddenly sharp. "There's nothing to put it up for, is there? Nothing happens here. Nothing at all."

It wasn't that Sandy Willoughby intended to pry. She came upon the diary quite by accident when engaged on a pre-Christmas cleaning of the boys' toy cupboards. It had been concealed at the bottom of a box of wooden soldiers that slotted into a tray. Ah, secrets, Sandy thought, amused, and sat down on Goff's bed.

It was a black, cloth-covered book of standard size. On the first page Goff had neatly printed, "This book is the property of Godolphin Hillary Willoughby and is strictly private," and then there was his signature scrawled in rust-colored ink—or it might even have been blood.

The entries for the first months of the year were factual and stark. Sandy thought how prescribed children's lives were, how like her own schooldays his seemed to be.

For the four days of spring half-term *"Karistides to stay"* had been crossed out, and beneath that was written, *"Bored, fed up, Luce impossible."* Poor child, not much of a half-term. She hadn't wanted to leave him anyway.

But the entry for the Sunday filled over a page, and the handwriting was suddenly more closely formed and intense. *"Today I went to the Grange. Came to a garden very overgrown. Saw a dog, a goose, a cat, a hen, like statues in the heat . . ."* Perhaps it's a story he's writing, Sandy thought; I never knew he wrote. *". . . saw AV all alone. She told me the names of the animals. The first three are in a story by Checkoff. It is a good story. At night in the great storm AV held me. I love her passionately. I have a sceme . . ."*

Sandy was frowning slightly as she read on.

For the summer holidays the entries were full of AV. *". . . the gallery opening, drank champagne and told her. It is all right. This is real love, not liking. . . . School again. Karistides understands . . . Forty, twenty-five, ten, three days to AV . . . In the orchard with her alone. Talked of Jove and babies being made . . ."* The final entry. *"I promise I will see AV at Christmas every single day."*

For several days Sandy was abstracted. Hillary noticed the almost painful ferocity with which her gaze tended to fix on the middle distance. He recognized the symptoms of stress but waited for her to come to him.

In his study one night he heard her at the piano. Wagner? Only when in one of her states would she play anything so heavy.

At last she crashed the piano lid down and stalked into his room. She wore a black skirt that swept the floor, and since she was always cold in winter she clutched a thick black shawl about her shoulders. Her face was drawn, but her eyes had a febrile glitter. She was a figure from the Greeks—Electra, Medea even.

"Something must be done about Goff." She confronted Hillary, twisting the rings on her fingers ceaselessly.

"What's he done now?" Hillary looked up tolerantly from the book he was ostensibly reading. His darkness, full, ruddy, and glowing, was in striking contrast to her drained look. "Everything all right at school?"

Since it was his study, he rose and motioned her to sit down.

"As far as I know he's doing all right there," Sandy said. "No, the problem is the Stratton woman."

"Goff's *littérateuse?*" Hillary looked amused. "She did a good job. His Latin seems well up to standard this term."

"That's hardly surprising," Sandy flashed, "since he never had a problem in the first place."

She began to tell him what she knew. Yet she couldn't bring herself to repeat the phrase that had been in her mind for days. "*I love her passionately.*" Instead she made much of the lies and deceptions.

". . . and took the best flowers every time he went there. I've spoken to Hatchard. He said Goff just hacked great armfuls. When Hatchard mentioned it to him, Goff said *you'd* said it would be all right. Lies. So many lies. . . ."

"Fairly harmless ones," Hillary said mildly. "It does sound as if he's rather smitten. Odd, I'd have thought he was the last kid for that sort of mooning, too much your team man."

"She played on his imagination. You heard about the book she gave him—oh, I don't suppose you were listening! Fairy tales. And poetry. Apparently they discuss poetry. Goff, of all people! Morbid poems!"

"She's been very decent—"

"But he's not a child." Sandy got impatiently to her feet, crossed to the window, shifted the curtains and stared out at nothing. "He's not Fitz's age. Then it might be quaint. Now is altogether different. He's practically an adolescent. When Karistides was here they had their heads together leering like a couple of old lechers! God alone knows what goes on in their heads. Have you talked to him about sex?"

"Nothing specific," Hillary said uneasily. "I thought when he leaves Fins—Maybe you're getting this out of proportion, darling. We mustn't see what isn't there."

"I want it stopped, that's all." Her tone was implacable. Her hands hung now at her sides. "I don't want him to see that woman."

Her nostrils quivered, and she began to fiddle with the fringe of her shawl. Hillary crossed quickly to her and patted her shoulder. It was always necessary to bear in mind that his wife was hypersensitive and that his mother-in-law, Lady Holder, had died insane.

"He's at a crucial age, Hillary," Sandy said. "Boys can be ruined for life at this age. I don't want my son—" She choked on the words.

"It probably would be best if he stopped going over there," Hillary said thoughtfully. "I'll have a word—"

"Don't expect him to take any notice." Her tone was bitter. "It's gone too far for that. So sly!"

"We'll make sure his time's taken up at Christmas. We'll have the Karistides boy over again. He and Goff seem to get on well."

"He mustn't see that woman. I won't have it."

"You're right. It would be as well if he didn't." Hillary put his arm around her and steered her from the study. "I'll deal with it. Don't upset yourself, for God's sake. It's so easy to get things out of proportion. Just put it right out of your head."

Agnes was curled on the drawing room sofa sipping whisky and reading *The Eve of Saint Agnes* when Harold arrived home, his cheeks chilled by December frost.

"Have a drink if you want one," she said, not stirring.

Harold shook his head. He was not in the habit of drinking in the evenings except on special occasions.

"Hillary Willoughby was here," Agnes said. "The mother's upset about Goff seeing so much of us—of me. She considers it unwholesome." She looked up at him challengingly. "You'd agree, of course."

"I only said he was getting to an awkward age," Harold said.

How unemphatic he is, Agnes thought. Always so fair, so judiciously impartial, always, to the end of my life . . .

"Naturally I won't see him again now. I looked on him as a child. I like children."

"They're not really our kind of people," Harold said evenly. "You couldn't really expect it to last."

"No. I used to enjoy Goff, though. I used to tell him things that

no one else wanted to hear. I suppose I was using him. Only that."
She got to her feet. "I'll start supper now—oh, the hell with it all!
I'll be glad when summer comes."

The tinge of unease Hillary Willoughby felt in facing his son was,
he told himself, irrational. It was the boy's first evening home. Best
to deal with the matter immediately and clear the air. No point in
spoiling the holidays.

When he was confronted with the situation, Goff's face flushed,
then darkened. He clenched the hands that hung by his sides, digging the nails into his palms.

"I don't see why I have to stop seeing her," he said. "Can you give
me one good reason?"

In his dawning anger he was handsome. He'll break a few hearts,
given time, Hillary found himself thinking irrationally. He experienced an odd, unwelcome pang of envy.

"Your mother and I both feel that under the circumstances . . ."
he began evenly.

"That's not a reason," Goff cut in rudely.

". . . and Mrs. Stratton is in full agreement with us."

"She hasn't told *me* that, and I don't believe it."

Hillary recognized the expression into which his son's face was setting. The argument ahead would be long and tedious.

"Nevertheless, she feels as we do," he said.

"Then I want to hear her say it. I'll go and see her and—"

"You will not see her again, Goff. No."

Hillary rested his hands on the desk. In the hot silence, resentment was palpable between them.

"You can't stop me from seeing her," Goff said at last challengingly.

"I can't?" Hillary's voice had a sarcastic inflection. "I'm telling
you not to do so."

"It's so sneaky, the whole thing, it makes me sick!" Goff burst out.
"What was Mother doing looking in my diary anyway? That's private property. And you, going to see Agnes behind my back. You
could have waited, you could have told me first. Sneaks!"

He turned and walked to the windows, although the drawn curtains prevented him from looking out.

"I'll bloody well do what I like." The words were muttered but audible.

"Oh no, you bloody well won't!" said Hillary, rising. "Come here. Look at me. That's better. Now listen, please. Enough time has been wasted on this already. Your mother—"

"Interfering old cow!"

"Goff!"

"That's what she is. A sneaky, interfering old cow! You know it, but of course you're on her side."

"Enough of this! You'll say nothing more about your mother. If you dare to disobey, you'll be beaten."

Hillary felt a thrill of shock as he uttered the archaic threat. In Goff's eyes he thought he detected a flicker of something that might have been triumph.

"And your mother is not to be upset any more over this," he said, striving to moderate his tone. "She's already distressed enough about how deceitful you've been. I don't intend to punish you for it. After tonight the matter's closed. Right?" He felt the anger and elation of a few moments before draining out of him. "Now, Andrew will be wondering what's happened to you. He's your guest, so you'd better cut along and entertain him. We're all going to have a happy Christmas, the way we always do."

He let his hand rest on Goff's shoulder, a conciliatory gesture that was a mistake. Goff returned his mild paternal gaze with one sharp with hate.

"You won't always be able to tell me what to do," he said witheringly. "The time will come when I'll please myself."

"Undoubtedly." Hillary strove to remain equable. "But that time is still in the future. For the present you must do as you're told, like any other boy."

"But every day I'm getting nearer and nearer to being able to do just what I want." Goff's eyes glittered. "And you don't have any control whatsoever over what I think. What goes on in my head belongs to me."

Hillary was chilled but forced himself to remain calm. He told himself Goff was a child still, a mulish child determined to have the last word.

"Don't be tiresome, Goff," he said wearily. "It's finished."

He turned away dismissively, and Goff left the study.

In the days that followed, his anxious, watchful mother found him curiously quiet and more or less amenable. But she feared that it would be a long time before he forgave her.

Agnes, answering a knock, found Goff on her doorstep. His cheeks were flushed, and his eyes shone. So vital and alive did he look that for a moment she forgot entirely the conversation she had had with his father.

"Goff!" She caught his hands, then, remembering, drew back. "You aren't supposed to be here."

It was a week into the new year. The Grange was quiet and the season dead.

"I had to see you." The conspiratorial urgency of the words involved her at once. "Karistides is covering for me. He's waiting by the road."

"You ought not to have come," Agnes said somberly. "But then no one ought to have told you not to come. It's absurd, really. Look, I'll fetch my coat and we'll walk."

Outside we might have met by chance, she thought, ramming a woolen hat over her ears, thrusting her arms through the sleeves of an old fur jacket.

The afternoon was cold and very still. The elms in the churchyard were stark and black. The hens in their run huddled and fluffed their feathers against the chill. Only Gertrude acknowledged the passing of human footsteps with a faint cluck.

Goff strode easily, cracking frozen branches with relish. He wore jeans tucked into boots and a long woolen scarf wound several times around his neck. He was growing fast. It would not be long now before their heads were level.

"Whatever did you write in your diary, Goff?" Agnes asked as they left the garden.

A deeper flush spread across his already reddened cheeks.

"I only said I loved you. Is that a crime? My mother's an interfering old bitch!"

He picked up a fallen stick and swished viciously at the hedge.

"Don't speak like that." Agnes put a hand on his arm. "She wants what's best for you. If I were your mother I should have acted exactly as she did. The very fact that you hid the diary so carefully—can't you see that suggests guilt? And I never knew you lied, Goff. Those flowers . . ."

"You said you liked them."

"I loved them. But they weren't really yours to give. And Goff, it *was* reprehensible to slacken off in Latin deliberately."

They stopped in their tracks to look at each other.

"It worked, though," said Goff with a grin.

"Has it been horrid for you these holidays?" she asked in quick sympathy.

"Pretty foul." He hunched his shoulders. "My father's been a sod, but it's her fault, really. I'm to leave Fins at the end of next term. I was supposed to have stayed till summer like everyone else. It's rotten to go at the end of Lent. People hardly ever do. Summer term's always the best to leave in."

"Yes. I remember. How awful for you. I feel it's all my fault."

"Of course it isn't. My father's like that. I've a good mind to make a complete mess of the exam papers and—"

"No. You know how easy it will be for you. Promise me you'll do your best."

"I suppose I might, for you."

They had reached the edge of the wood.

"If we go through here," Goff said, "we'll meet up with Andy on the other side. He'll hang about till I come."

"He'll be frozen," Agnes said. "We'd better hurry."

Yet as they walked among the trees their pace slowed. The wood was spiky and dim; the gray sky glimpsed through naked boughs seemed far away. Their voices sank, and their footsteps were deadened.

"In the Black Forest you might wander for days encountering no one," said Agnes, distracted as usual by images of the past.

"England was like that once," said Goff. "It must have seemed very big to people then, mustn't it?"

"Very big. The dark forests were trackless, eternal, full of whisperings . . ."

"Whatever happens, we'll still love each other."

"Yes."

"And I'll come to you whenever I can."

"No," said Agnes quickly. "That's been decided."

"But—"

"No. I don't want you to."

"But I must," said Goff. "I have to see you. Don't you know that?"

Glancing at him she saw that he was fiercely blinking back tears that glittered on his eyelashes.

"Oh, love," she said.

Stopping in a clearing, she pulled him down beside her on a fallen tree.

"Listen, Goff," she said. "We had a lovely time together, you and I. But it would be wrong to exaggerate the importance of it. You're at an age when things change very fast. At your new school fresh images and impressions and experiences will crowd in on you. Soon our friendship will be only a pleasant memory. You'll meet someone one day, someone young and pretty, and you won't want to think of me in the way you do now because . . ."

Goff twitched his shoulders suddenly and turned away from her.

"God!" he said. His voice was flat. "How stupid you are, Agnes, stupid, stupid, stupid! I love you and I always will, but whenever I try to tell you, you start saying these things about girls. Whenever I try to be serious you go on and on . . ."

His voice broke on an edge of hysteria.

"Goff." Agnes put her arms around him, held him against the soft fur of her jacket, and rocked him to and fro. "Don't be hurt. I can't bear it when you're unhappy. I do love you, of course I do."

She turned his head and looked into his face, the face of a child, with a tear already drying on his cheek. She kissed the cheek and felt the salt of the tear on her tongue with a curious poignance. Thank God there's no one here to see, a part of her was thinking; their worst suspicions would appear to be justified, but they'd be wrong, quite wrong.

Goff drew away from her and sat upright. He stared at the trees with their branches so knotted together that to unravel them would be a task fit only for the hero of a fairy tale.

"It's my being so young that spoils everything," he said. "I know that. But I'm changing. I can feel it. A time will come when—"

"It's like an old story," said Agnes abstractedly. "I'm a princess locked in a wood, deep. You go out into the world on some great quest. When it's done I'm waiting here still, your Aurora, your Mariana, your Lady of Shalott, your Penelope; your Annabel Lee . . . We are timeless, ageless, the world cannot touch us . . ."

She found peppermints in her pocket and gave him one. He sucked hard on it, then stowed it in his cheek.

"And when I come back to you," he said, "I'll do things I can't do now. Like Karistides, you know."

He looked ahead of him still, not directly at her.

"What's old Karistides been up to now?" she asked indulgently, sucking cozily on a peppermint.

"It happened last summer," Goff said. It was as if he were compelled to speak despite a curious reluctance. "Andrew went home for the summer, to his island."

"I remember he wrote about it once. Their house is white and very old and stands on a hill above the harbor, and there's a windmill further up the slope with cloth sails, and the sky is very blue and shimmers in the heat."

"It's very dull on the island when his parents are away. Every day is the same, the heat, the maids in the house chattering . . ."

"I can see it all quite clearly," Agnes nodded.

"It would be queer to see Andrew living a different life, speaking a different language. He speaks English very well, but his grandmother that died didn't speak a word of it. At home he only has his sister Katharine to speak English to. They got so bored last summer. Every day it was the same . . ."

"The mills creaking in the hot wind, the house in the dazzling heat, the doves in the white courtyard . . ." Agnes was entranced by her own images. "So beautiful . . ." She sighed.

"But boring," Goff persisted. He was encouraged by her enthusiasm for his story, yet he was still uneasy. "There's no cricket, you know," he said. "No other boys. Only Andy and his sister." He stopped, scowled into the distance, then said rapidly, "So in the end they just . . . well, they . . . did things . . ."

"Things?" said Agnes.

For the first time Goff looked at her directly.

"They had sex together." He spaced the words carefully, giving them equal value.

The dreamy look vanished from Agnes's eyes. A deep flush spread across her face. She stood up and put her hands over her ears.

"I don't want to hear this," she said in a surprised tone.

"They did it together." Goff addressed her back implacably as she began to walk about the clearing. "There was no one to stop them. At first Katharine said no, but Andrew kept on asking her. In the end she said all right because he wanted to so much. Maybe she wanted it as well."

Agnes turned to face him. She had taken her hands from her ears, and the flush had died from her cheeks.

"I expect he's making it all up," she said dully, without conviction.

"I don't think he is," Goff said consideringly. "It doesn't *feel* like a made-up story." He stared at the log and began to pick at the bark. "The first time it was awfully hard. Katharine begged him to stop. Then it was all over very quickly. And there was a bit of blood. He even saw spots of blood on his cock—"

"Spare me the details, please," Agnes said.

"She kept on crying, saying they shouldn't have done it. He was a bit sorry. But next day he felt different. He wanted to do it just as much as he had before. They did it every day. In the house with the maids in the kitchen and out on the hillside and once in one of the windmills. Not a working one, though the wind was shaking the sails. The dog lay on the floor while—"

"Don't," Agnes said.

"It didn't hurt Katharine in the end, though she was still crying and saying it was wrong. But it's only natural, Andrew says. He's the very first boy I ever heard of who did it with a girl. He's only just thirteen now. Last summer he was—"

"I suppose it's predictable." Agnes walked in a circle around the log. "Why am I so shocked? Andrew Karistides! There was always something about that child. I sensed it years ago."

She seemed almost to have forgotten Goff was there.

"He's not really bad," he said, shredding the bark with his fingers. "The way he tells it, you can understand. And he says he won't do it any more with Katharine, Agnes. Next time he says it will be another girl. You wouldn't mind that so much, would you, Agnes?"

"Wouldn't I?"

"He says it's no worse than what some boys do to each other at school."

"No, very likely not," she said bitterly.

"I didn't mean to shock you," Goff said quietly. "When Karistides told me—I felt I—knew how it would be. I felt it—down here." He pointed toward his groin. "And I knew that when I did it I wanted it to be with you."

"Oh, my God!" said Agnes, standing with her hands in her pockets at the foot of the fallen trunk.

"It's what they mean, isn't it, when they talk about love? It isn't like in stories, is it?"

Agnes slumped onto the tree trunk a little way from him.

"What a fool!" she murmured. "What a romantic, muddle-headed fool! Fairy stories, poetry, roses, magic, the Chanson de Roland, the Courts of Love. Of course you don't want *that*. Fool, fool, fool!"

Goff edged nearer to her. He insinuated his hand into her sleeve until she felt the coldness of his fingers against her wrist.

"It isn't *now*, Agnes," he said soothingly. "I don't mean yet. One day. I think it was wrong of Karistides to do it with his sister. But you and I aren't related. One day . . ."

"I feel very tired," she said. "You must go away from me, Goff."

"But you do still love me, Agnes?"

"I don't know anything . . ." She sighed and shook her head. "Yes. Yes, I still love you. Of course I must."

"Then kiss me, Agnes."

Their faces were very close. His was completely clear. No incipient beard, no hint of acne, the face of a beautiful child.

When he put his lips to hers, she felt the pressure of his teeth against her lower lip, caught on his breath the odor of peppermint.

"There," Goff said. "We belong to each other forever."

"We've been too long," Agnes said. "We must hurry now."

They began to walk fast along the woodland path, the dry twigs cracking beneath their feet.

"Dreadful boy," Agnes said, as if to herself. "To shatter my illusions . . . Oh, I wish I didn't see it all so clearly. The images will come back and back, and I'll not be able to wash them away. Curse Karistides! I knew he'd bring me harm."

"There he is," said Goff, who had scarcely caught the words. "We're here, Andy."

The Greek boy was stamping up and down where the wood bordered the road. Long tweed trousers and matching overcoat and a cap with earflaps turned him into a parody of a Victorian gentleman. Yet although he looked more mature than Goff, he seemed a child still. I mustn't judge him by my standards, Agnes thought. That wouldn't be fair.

"Hello, Andrew." She held out her hand. "It's ages since I saw you. Done any acting lately?"

"Hello, Mrs. Stratton." He shook hands. "We're doing *Treasure Island* next term."

"You're to be Silver, of course."

"Ah, Jim lad!" He nodded, screwing up his face and hunching his shoulders in a graphic parody of the sly old pirate.

"I'm sorry I shall miss it," Agnes said. "Have a peppermint. It might help to keep out the cold. Now you really must go or you'll both be in trouble."

"Don't worry, no one will find out," Karistides said, accepting the sweet. "I'm not going to say anything."

"I'm sure you won't," Agnes said. "Off you go, the pair of you, straight back to Marlwood. Take the rest of the peppermints, Goff. God bless you both."

She stood like some aged woman of the woods giving her blessing to two pilgrims. She waited until the boyish voices died away on the clear air, then turned and plunged once more into the trees.

She walked slowly, wishing she did not have to go back. But where else was there to go? When she passed the log on which she and Goff had sat, she stared at it with a kind of repugnance. A sense of her isolation overcame her. There was no one to whom she could talk, no one she could tell about anything. I mustn't see Goff again, of course not, she thought, and was at once overcome by a feeling of deprivation nonetheless real for being irrational, as she assured herself it was.

"I must pull myself together," she said aloud, as she left the wood. "My life at the moment is unsatisfactory. I ought to have another child, something to stabilize my existence. We need a family, Harold and I, if our marriage is to survive."

Uncle meowed to her from the fork of an apple tree as she went into the orchard, but she didn't even notice him.

Of course, after her first child had died, the doctors had advised a wait of three years at least. It wasn't yet two—but no matter, she had to do something now.

It's easily settled, she told herself, trying to be cheerful, as she crossed the frozen lawn. I shall make a new start. Everything will be different this time.

It was strange how leaden she felt as she left the garden for the sanctuary of the house, as if all the color had been drained out of her life.

Part II

◄§ SIX §►

At first Agnes, in the hall of the flat she shared with a television producer, was unable to identify the voice at the other end of the telephone. She thought it must be that of some friend of her roommate's young daughter, even though the caller had asked for her by name.

When he said he was Goff Willoughby, she colored slightly, with no one there to see, and gripped the receiver tightly. He sounded nothing like the child she had known but, of course, he must be turned fifteen now.

After she had murmured a few platitudes, she heard him explaining how he and Andrew Karistides were staying for a few days at his father's London flat and asking if they might visit her. They'd got her new address from "old Justin Lord." He said the name easily, as if it were that of a contemporary.

It was only after she had arranged a day and time and replaced the receiver that Agnes wondered if she had done the right thing. Dimly she recalled a promise made to his father not to see him again. But that can't be binding now, she thought, so much has happened since. The situation is entirely different.

And she remembered yet further back, in the green lushness of her summer at St. Fenrins, how she had said to the boys of Fifth, "You can all come and see me." Before Tringham Grange, before she had found marriage wanting, before the success of the Wolfram books. So simple and uncomplicated. "You can come any time."

Briskly, trying to shake off a faint unease, she went into the immaculate and tastefully furnished sitting room where her friend's daughter, on holiday from her convent school, was deep in a book.

"A voice from my past, Deborah," she said gaily.

"Not a sinister one, I hope?"

Deborah laid aside her book. She was a gentle child, refreshingly unaware of her own prettiness, with a permanently wistful expression.

"Quite the contrary." Agnes sat beside her. "It was a boy named Willoughby. A very nice boy . . . at least, he used to be. I taught him years ago at a run-down prep school in Hampshire."

"I can never imagine you as a teacher," Deborah said.

"Neither can I! Anyway, this boy—Goff Willoughby—was telephoning to ask if he and a friend of his, whom I also knew, could come and see me, though why on earth they should want to bother—"

"You're a celebrity," Deborah told her. "Or rather, Wolfram is."

"That sheep! I sometimes feel he has a life of his own."

"Everybody's heard of him, Agnes," Deborah said earnestly. "I've told you before how the girls at school simply can't get enough of him. I expect these boys want to be able to brag about going to see a famous authoress."

"From what I remember of those two, it's highly unlikely! Oh well, since they're coming to tea on Thursday, we'll have to do our best."

"Thursday's the day we're supposed to be going to the *Messiah,*" Deborah said. "If you'd rather not—"

"I've been looking forward to our evening out for ages. This won't affect it, my love. The boys will be gone long before we leave. You will help me to entertain them, won't you?"

Deborah blushed and tugged at her long brown hair.

"There isn't by any chance someone in London, some friend of yours, you might like to ask along, too?" Agnes went on quickly.

"There's Karin Schultz," Deborah said, after some thought. "She's not a close friend, but she's in London at the moment. I could telephone and ask her."

She left the room looking more cheerful at the possibility of having moral support. Of course it will be all right, their coming, Agnes thought. It will lay any ghosts forever.

She went to the window and looked out over the quiet Kensington Square. A woman crossed the road with a puffing Pekingese and let herself into the private gardens. For a moment Agnes felt the old regret for Tringham, although she rarely thought of it these days. The memories of her last months there, of the messy miscarriage and subsequent speedy deterioration of her marriage were not happy ones.

When the break with Harold finally came and he went back to live in his father's old house at Andham, she had been happy to let Jennifer and Jeff Miller and their baby move into the Grange and pay nothing more than the maintenance. One day, of course, Agnes would have to think about selling the place.

She thought now that her move to London, to live with Marcia Farrow, always cool and disciplined, had been the best thing possible for her in the state she had been in. At first, of course, she had desperately missed the old house and the animals she had been forced to leave behind in the freshness of the countryside. Now, however, time had tempered her sense of loss, and she was reconciled to a different way of life.

Deborah's friend, arriving on the day appointed for the boys' visit half an hour before they were expected, proved to be tight-jeaned and ultra-cool, with a pronounced transatlantic accent. Agnes was struck by the contrast between the two girls.

"Better fill me in, Mrs. Stratton," Karin said briskly. "Which one did you have in mind for me?"

"It isn't like that, Karin," Deborah said. "Agnes isn't pairing us off."

"People always do. It's only natural," Karin said, strolling about the room, examining ornaments. "Come on, I want to know all about them."

Laughing, Agnes told her.

"I'll take the Greek," she said at once. "I guess his family's loaded."

"Very likely," Agnes said.

"That's settled then. He can date me. If they want to double-date, Debbie, I'd like to catch the show at the Rainbow, so don't forget if your guy brings it up first. For eats let's say—"

"Karin!" Deborah cried, scandalized. "We don't even know they'll be interested. They're only—"

"What do you think, Mrs. Stratton," Karin said. "How do you rate our chances of a double date?"

"With you around, Karin, definitely good!" Agnes said, amused.

"Last vacation I dated this guy that was at Rugby. That's a good school?"

"Very good."

"But these two, their school's considered even better?"

"By some people, perhaps. It all depends how one's judging."

"Okay. Debbie, you aren't going to be a mouse this afternoon, I hope. We have these end-of-term dances, Mrs. Stratton, and she doesn't even come. She sits in the library and *works!*"

"I can never think of anything to say to boys." Deborah nervously wound a lock of fine hair around her finger.

"But they're easier to talk to than anyone," Karin said. "They don't notice if what you say is a load of crap. They're too busy just looking."

As the doorbell rang she tossed her hair and arranged her long legs becomingly across the sofa.

"Not roses, not at this time of year!" Agnes exclaimed when she opened the door and Karistides thrust them under her nose.

"Your favorites," Goff said.

She stared at him wonderingly as she welcomed them in. He was now about three inches taller than she and would obviously grow more. His complexion had darkened and he wore his thick hair brushed back off his forehead and reaching to his collar. As she took his hand she thought she detected a trace of sullenness in the look he gave her.

"Lovely to see you," she murmured, turning from him. "And Andrew, after all this time."

The Greek boy's appearance gave her the greater shock. He was little taller than herself, yet he might easily have passed for nineteen. His hair grew low over his broad forehead where the eyebrows met, and there was a marked line of hair on his upper lip. There was something farouche about his appearance, yet his manner was more urbane than Goff's. His voice when he greeted her had the beautiful modulation, the faint hint of un-Englishness, that she remembered.

"Come along in," she said, wondering what they thought of her, glad of the girls whose presence was sure to claim most of the attention.

All the same, as introductions and some polite conversation were made, she was aware of Goff looking at her, his expression morose still, while Karistides chatted away, seeming perfectly at ease.

As soon as she could, Agnes slipped away to the kitchen, refusing Deborah's eager offer of help.

She and Goff would make a beautiful couple, she thought, if only she weren't so shy. I hope he isn't smitten with Karin.

When she had switched on the kettle and set crumpets to toast, she found a vase for the roses. As she arranged the pristine buds she was overwhelmed by an aching nostalgia for the cluttered Grange kitchen and for Auntie's orange feet strutting over the broken tiles. Her eyes filled with tears as she stared into the velvety petals.

"Can I carry a tray or something?"

She looked up quickly and found Goff there. She turned to the grill with a sniff.

"What are you doing here?"

"I thought you might need some help."

"Everything's under control," she said shortly.

"Are you upset about something?"

He approached the stove and stood beside her.

"It's only that the roses remind me of the Grange."

"I hoped they would," he said, unsmiling.

"At first I missed Uncle and Auntie and Kashtenka unbearably. Even after all this time . . . can you understand?"

"Of course you must." Goff removed the crumpets from the grill.

"I wouldn't say that to anyone else. It sounds absurd. Let me butter those quickly. Do you like crumpets? There's honey to go with them."

"That will be nice."

"I thought it was the sort of thing boys liked. But you and Andrew seem very sophisticated."

"One doesn't eat as much in town as in the country," he said composedly.

"I hadn't thought of that. How are you getting on at school?" She was striving to dispel a certain sense of awkwardness, even disagreeableness, between them. "Are you doing very well there?"

"So-so," he said without interest. "It's a place to be until I can be somewhere else."

"Some of the old Fins crowd went too, didn't they? How's Marcus?"

"Moss-Hemlock? He's developing into a dreadful little poof," Goff said contemptuously. "I have very little to do with him. He's in another set altogether."

"And dear old Arthur O'Higgins?"

"Oh, he's all right. A bit wet. They're neither of them in our House, you know. Are these scones to go in, too?"

"Yes. Don't you have a good word for anyone these days, Goff?" she asked lightly.

"I might have, Agnes, given a little encouragement."

When he smiled she was struck almost electrically by the force of it. I always knew he'd grow up very attractive, she thought with a pang.

"I didn't realize your father had a place in London," she said quickly.

"It's just a pied à terre near the Gallery. He stays over during the week if there's a lot on. Andrew and I borrowed it."

"Will you stay long?"

"Until the end of the week. We're going to Marlwood for Easter. Is this everything for the tray?"

His manner was still cool. He doesn't like me any more, Agnes told herself. Absurdly, she could have cried again. Instead, with a brave smile, she followed him back into the sitting room.

Karistides was comfortably ensconced on the sofa, with the girls on either side of him.

"Crumpets!" he exclaimed. "Nothing like a bit of crumpet!"

As he began handing round plates, Agnes recalled his performance in the St. Fenrins Nativity. Now, as then, he seemed to be acting a role.

"We used to have marvelous homemade cakes at the Grange," Goff said, looking unenthusiastically at an expensive éclair. "Were you ever at the Grange, Deborah?"

It was the first remark he had addressed to her directly, and she blushed as she answered that she had never been there.

"You must have known Agnes a long time," she said.

"A very long time," he said, looking at her as she poured tea.

". . . and you're all off to the Festival Hall this evening?" Karistides was saying.

"Not me," Karin said at once. "I don't have anything to do. London is a drag when you're on your own."

"Absolutely," he agreed. "We're not doing anything either. Why don't we do nothing together?"

The pair arranged it between them. The boys and Karin were

going to meet Agnes and Deborah after the concert, and all five would have supper somewhere.

"I like them, they're real smoothies," Karin said, flushed with satisfaction, after the boys had left. "That Karistides, he's sexy. Wouldn't you say, Mrs. Stratton?"

"I suppose I would."

"The other one, Goff—that's a crummy name—is something else. Much better looking, but *very* superior. But he liked you, Debbie, I could tell," she added generously. "Didn't I say it would be okay?" She patted her friend's knee. "I guess I'll split now, got to look for something to wear. Mrs. Stratton, I want to thank you."

"She thinks I'm an awful stodge," said Deborah when the American girl had left. "Andrew really seemed to like her a lot."

"How about Goff? Did you like him?"

"He's very good-looking . . ."

"It's unfortunate that that's always the first thing people notice, about women and about men. Goff's more than just that, though. Years ago I'd been . . . ill, and he and another boy played truant just to come and visit me. Then when I lived at the Grange—you heard him mention it—he used to come and see us nearly every day in the holidays. I wish you could have been there, Deborah. We had such fun then . . . all the animals and the days so hot, like a beautiful dream . . . Goff always brought me roses. They were so lovely! I only found out later that he'd stolen them from under the gardener's very nose! He really is nice. I hope you get on well with him."

"He seems awfully good at games." Deborah carefully stacked dishes on a tray. "That sort of boy is always very popular. They tend to find me boring." She sighed.

"There's more to Goff than that, I promise you," Agnes said. "He's interested in painting, music, poetry. You'll find out as you get to know him. You won't see that side of him so much when he's with his friend, of course. I must confess I never cared much for Andrews Karistides as a child. He used to be very sullen. But he seems to have improved with age."

That evening when the concert had ended, Agnes and Deborah found Karin and the boys sitting overlooking the river, their dark heads close, like old friends. Karin has melted any awkwardness already, Agnes thought; an English girl couldn't have done that. I'm glad Deborah invited her.

"I'm so hungry!" the American girl exclaimed when she had greeted them. "Andrew knows a place for supper that we can walk to from here."

"If I can just manage to find a taxi," Agnes said.

When they all protested, she shook her head with a smile.

"I have to get back home."

"But you can't desert us, Mrs. Stratton," Karistides said.

He cast a mocking glance in the direction of his friend, who was frowning.

"We'd like to have you go with us, Mrs. Stratton, really," Karin confirmed.

"Children, I'd like it, too! But I've already taken a whole afternoon and evening off work, and there's a chapter I must finish tonight. Signal to that taxi, Goff. He's seen you. What luck!"

"Today's been fun," Karistides said as the car drew up. He had his arm around Karin, holding her close. "We're all very grateful to you, Mrs. Stratton."

"It's been marvelous to see you both." Agnes noticed how Goff and Deborah stood well apart. "I hope we can do something again some time, in the summer maybe, if you're around."

"At least let us see you home," Goff said.

"You mustn't think of it. You heard Karin. Feed the girl! Have a good time, all of you."

She closed the taxi door firmly. Deborah and Goff were still standing apart. She's a lovely girl, put your arm around her, unbend a bit, arrogant boy! she thought, leaning back and shutting her eyes.

Marcia Farrow, when apprised of what had occurred, was not altogether approving.

"Deborah's very young for her age, you know, Agnes," she said reproachfully. "She's not like some girls. I'm not at all sure she's ready for this sort of thing."

"She'll be perfectly all right. These boys are from very good families." Agnes wondered, even as she said it, what was meant by her own remark. "Anyway, in a foursome they can't possibly come to any harm."

"From all I hear about young people nowadays, that doesn't necessarily follow," Marcia said dryly. "Oh, I'm exhausted! I've never in my life worked with anyone as exasperating as this Prince man."

"I've still a lot to do," Agnes said quickly. "Let me wait up for Deborah."

Marcia agreed and went off to bed, still looking aggrieved.

Fifteen, is that too young? Agnes thought. If I had a daughter that age, how would I feel? But I'll never have a daughter now, nor a son either. If we'd had a family, would Harold and I be together still in the drafty old Grange, country people, children and dogs tumbling together?

But it hadn't worked out that way, and she must make the best of the alternatives. She picked up her papers and began to go through them with practiced rapidity.

Deborah was home before eleven-thirty.

"Did you all have a lovely time?"

Agnes pushed her reading glasses up onto her forehead to scan the girl's flushed face.

"Lovely. We went to a place that had a girl with a guitar. Folk songs, you know. You were right about Goff. He's very nice."

"I'm glad we agree about that."

"I wish I could be more like Karin. She makes it all seem so easy. She and Andrew were even necking in the restaurant! Goff just sort of looked . . . I don't think he likes me all that much. If he did, maybe . . ."

She flung out her hands helplessly.

"Neither of them is English, remember," Agnes said. "You and Goff have been brought up differently. Relationships that move so fast are often superficial, anyway. Are you seeing them again?"

"They want to take us to a party on Saturday night," Deborah confided excitedly. "Some cousin of Andy's. I'm sure it will be too old for us. Karin's keen, but she won't go unless I do. I do *half* want to go. I want to see Goff again. But there's Mummy to consider. She always says I've *years* to enjoy myself, and work must come first at the moment . . . Oh, it's all so complicated!"

She spoke rapidly, almost incoherently. Have they been filling her up with drink? Agnes wondered. I've never seen the poor child so animated.

"I don't see why you shouldn't go," she said. "You may as well see the boys while you have the chance. Perhaps I could have a word with your mother."

"Oh Agnes, would you? Your knowing the boys makes all the difference. Mummy will listen to you."

"We'll talk about it. Off you go now. Sleep well, my love."

Agnes could feel the rapid beating of the girl's heart as she bent to kiss her cheek.

"You and Mummy must be about the same age," she said. "But you seem so young, more like my big sister. I wish you were!"

"Go to bed, child," Agnes said with a smile. "I'll talk to your mother in the morning."

Goff had never at any time regarded his relationship with Agnes as being at an end. He had gone back to the Grange as soon as he could, of course, but that was not until the summer holidays, and by that time she was gone.

It was a shock to him. He saw it as an act of betrayal on her part, a desertion at the very time he needed her most. His first term at Eton had not been easy. He'd gone there quite alone. The weight of numbers and of his newness oppressed him. He needed Agnes to renew his confidence in himself. And she wasn't there.

At the same time he knew that really he was already over the worst. In the Christmas term other St. Fenrins boys joined him. Karistides was in the same House, and they were able to pick up their friendship where it had been left off.

The sense of Agnes's betrayal faded as his new life became more absorbing. A boy with his sports abilities could not fail to be popular, and he found the work surprisingly easy once he put his mind to it. During the next two years there was no urgency about his feelings for Agnes. Although she remained somewhere in the back of his mind, he was reserving her for later.

He might have let things drift for a couple of years more if he hadn't run into Justin Lord during the Christmas holidays and learned something of her circumstances. That started up a restlessness within him, and by the time he and Karistides arrived in London three months later it had grown into a need to challenge his own developing powers. He decided that the time had come, after all, to take her up again.

Confronted with the two girls at Marcia's flat, he was initially irritated. It was all so obvious. Yet he soon saw that it was a way in which the reestablished contact might be maintained. Tedious though he found it, he decided to play along with what was expected of him.

"Decent of old Vale to set that up for us yesterday," Karistides remarked next morning as he smoked in bed. He had been wakened prematurely by Goff, who had suddenly felt the need to train and was in the process of donning a track suit.

"I could have done without it." Goff hunted for socks. "Deborah's a pretty gauche kid."

"You go for older women, of course," Karistides said sardonically. "But what do you think of little Miss America? Can't be too soon for her, I reckon. She made a grab for my cock in the taxi."

"Did she?"

Goff paused and regarded his friend with interest.

"She's eminently fuckable," Karistides went on dreamily. "And after all, why push away what's offered on a plate? You noticed she wasn't wearing a bra?"

"Can't say I did."

Goff had found his socks and was now lacing his track shoes.

"She'll drop her pants before you can say knife. Some cunt! Toss the rest of my cigs over on your way out."

"What do you want to do today?" Goff paused in the doorway. "We might play squash later. We can use my father's club."

"I suppose I ought to show myself at my aunt's hotel so she can report back to the parents that I'm being a good boy," Karistides said. "Are you seeing Deborah before the party?"

"I hadn't made any plans. Why should I?"

"You do realize she's a virgin? That makes two of you, doesn't it?"

"Shut up, Karistides," Goff said warningly.

"Okay," said the other boy mildly. "Only here's your chance to do something about it. Doesn't do to keep seeing this thing like a visit to the dentist." He grinned. "When you've finished with her, you can always pass her on to me."

"You fat oaf!"

Goff flung the cigarette package at his head and went out, slamming the door.

Jogging through the crisp morning, falling into the old routine, he soon recovered his good humor. To have a pretty girl displaying interest in him could not fail to be flattering, though he cared not a jot for her. And there was still Agnes . . .

Goff gulped in the sharp air that stung his nostrils and lightened his head, his body settling into its stride with all the lithe grace of a young predator.

The two girls had arranged to come to Hillary Willoughby's apartment on the Saturday evening. When they arrived, Karistides insisted on pouring generous measures of whisky despite Deborah's protest that she didn't drink liquor.

"Nice place your daddy has, Goff."

Karin kicked off her high-heeled slippers as if settling down for a long stay. Deborah perched primly on the edge of an armchair, long skirt pulled tight over her legs so that not even a glimpse of ankle showed.

"What's Agnes doing tonight?" Goff asked. "Is she out, too?"

"No, she's just finishing another book about Wolfram, her fourth. It's keeping her very busy."

"That sheep, he really knocks me out," Karin remarked. "I know he's meant for kids, but somehow you can't leave him alone once you get started. It's a shame Agnes is staying in, though. On Saturday night, too! She ought to have some guy take her out."

"She could if she wanted to. Lots of men are interested in her," Deborah said loyally. "It's just that her work matters more to her."

"What remarkable dedication!" Karistides murmured.

"Not everyone has your inexhaustible interest in the opposite sex, Andy," said Goff witheringly, at the same time flashing Deborah a glance that surprised her by its warmth. "Well, isn't it time we were on our way?" he added briskly.

"What's the hurry? Things never get going till after ten," Karistides protested.

"Deborah and I want to see some action. Isn't that right, Debbie?" Goff patted her shoulder.

"I'm ready any time," she said, setting down her untouched drink with relief.

The party was held in the penthouse of a modern building overlooking Regents Park. Karistides's cousin, a curly-haired youth in a silk shirt open to the waist, greeted them affably.

"The people out there look awfully old," Deborah whispered, peering at herself in a peach-tinted mirror in one of the bedrooms. "We'll easily be the youngest."

"Relax, hon." Karin sprayed herself liberally with French cologne. "We'll be perfectly safe. No one's going to rape you!"

"All right?" Karistides's cousin said, clapping Goff on the shoulder as he stood moodily surveying the gathering guests.

"Fine, thanks," said Goff in his careless way.

"Feel free to dance. I'll turn up the stereo. Sometimes I think, you know, that this is the best part of a party . . . while you can still hear yourself talk. All the booze you want in the kitchen. Help yourself."

He grinned amiably and turned away.

"Motown!" exclaimed Karin, who had emerged from the bedroom leading Deborah firmly by the arm. "Didn't know anyone still played the stuff. Come on, Goff. We'll show these old stuffed shirts how to get things moving."

She seized his hand and led him off.

"Better give them a bit of support, Deborah," Karistides suggested politely, draining his glass and ushering her in their wake.

As a result of their efforts, general dancing was soon under way. Karin swirled and twirled tirelessly. Goff, going to fetch more drinks, left his jacket and tie in the hall. Few of the men were wearing ties anyway. He opened his shirt and gulped a glass of white wine in the kitchen before taking a bottle and glasses back to the dance floor.

"Hi, handsome, fill me up!" Karin said, appearing suddenly as he crossed the hall.

Laughing, she turned her face toward him and kissed him hard on the mouth. He responded before he had time to think. Karin slipped her hand inside his shirt. The fingers that had been holding a glass were deliciously cool against his skin.

"Nice!" she murmured.

He opened his eyes. Her own, inches away, glittered wickedly.

When he had managed to disengage himself and return to the dance floor, he found it hazy with tobacco smoke. Someone put on a slow record. Karin entwined herself expertly around Karistides. He whispered something in her ear that made her giggle.

Tentatively Deborah put her arms around Goff's neck. When she looked up into his face, he found himself kissing her slowly and as he ceased felt her settle more closely against him. The sensation was more pleasurable than he wanted it to be. There was a temptation to drift mindlessly.

With an effort he forced himself to look at his watch over her shoulder. It was not yet half past ten. He led her to a sofa.

"Wait for me," he whispered, as she looked trustingly up at him. He kissed her cheek. "I'll fetch you another drink."

In the hall he met Karistides.

"I'm going out for a while," Goff said coolly, picking up his jacket. "Keep an eye on Deborah for me. She needs some more wine."

He shrugged into his overcoat and stuffed his tie in the pocket.

"Where the hell are you going?" Karistides asked, astonished.

"Just out. I'll be back. See she's okay, Andy."

"I have my hands full as it is." Karistides shrugged. "You're mad."

But Goff had already gone.

It was cold in the street, and frost glimmered on the roofs of cars. Goff's head felt wonderfully clear, but every now and then his heart lurched with excitement. At the corner he hailed a taxi and gave the address of Agnes's apartment.

After he had spoken to her through the intercom, he found her waiting for him upstairs in the open doorway. She was wearing a long, loose cotton robe that might have served either as a dressing gown or as a dress.

"Is everything all right, Goff? Where are the—"

"Relax. Nothing's wrong," he assured her. "The others are having a whale of a time. It's all right. I promise you."

Standing beside her in the hall, he put his hands on her shoulders reassuringly. Barefooted, she had to look up at him. Her eyes were bright with bewilderment.

"Oh, how handsome you are, Goff!" she exclaimed inconsequentially.

She stared at his flushed face and shining eyes, at his gaping overcoat and the buttons of his shirt undone. He laughed and stalked into the sitting room. It was softly lighted, and low music came from the stereo. There was a half-filled glass on a marble-topped table in front of the fire.

"Cognac," he said, looking into it. "And what's this you're playing?" He listened. "Something folky. It isn't English."

He laughed again and began to pace about the room, still in his overcoat.

"I don't understand why you're here," Agnes said, sitting down warily on the sofa.

"I suddenly thought of you all by yourself. I had to come and see that you were all right."

"But the party. . . ."

"I've never cared for parties much. Karistides, you know, he's well away with the American girl."

"And Deborah?"

"Deborah is having rather a good time. She never even noticed my departure. I said I'd look back later, but there's no need. No one will miss me."

"Poor Goff!" Agnes said sympathetically.

"I find it all so shallow." He took off his coat and threw it across a chair. "I'd very much rather be here, talking to you. You're not all alone, surely?"

"Yes. Marcia's gone to some official do and will be back late. I'm putting the finishing touches to the latest Wolfram."

"What's he up to this time?"

"Oh, I've set this one in the Roman era, 52 B.C. I don't tie him to any specific time. He roams up and down history. The universal sheep! How absurd it all is. I wonder anyone takes it seriously for a minute."

"You didn't talk like this at the Grange, when you'd just invented him. I've never forgotten how excited you were then. You'll never be allowed to drop him, you know."

"That's a miserable thought. I did rather like him for a while, I have to admit. But it's all very trivial, isn't it?"

Rising she crossed to switch off the record player.

"Don't do that," Goff said. "The music's nice."

"It's one of my favorites. A Spanish soprano singing songs of the Auvergne. I've never been there, but I can visualize how it must be. I don't listen when other people are around. It's very tedious to have to hear someone else's favorite music."

"Turn it up," Goff said. "I want to hear it."

Agnes did so and sat down again doubtfully. The music soared and swirled around them.

"It's very beautiful," Goff said, when it was finished. "How could you have been so mean as to want to deny me the pleasure of knowing it, too?"

"Not mean," Agnes said. "I simply don't see how it could have anything to say to you. It's so remote and rural—and so young! How *young* folk songs always seem to be. How could that mean anything to you?"

"Do you know what she's singing about?"

"Oh, a Prince's three daughters are sitting under a cherry tree. The first two laugh and sing, but the third, who's called Pernette, cries all the time. When her father asks her why, she says she's crying for all the poor souls who died to gratify love. I suppose it's rather silly."

"No," said Goff. "Let's hear it again. I want to remember it."

They sat side by side, listening gravely.

"There," Agnes said when it ended. "That's how I feel, you see. Like the Prince's third daughter, fated always to cry over the sorrows of love."

"You could be one of the first two," Goff said reasonably. He saw that her eyes were filled with tears and felt a resurgence of the pity he had felt for her at times when he was a child. "The ones who laugh and sing."

She shook her head.

"No, I'm better suited to be the third princess, I think. I don't understand, Goff, why you should leave a party to come to me, leave *toutes les jeunes filles en fleur . . .*"

"A flower is most beautiful when it's full."

"Is it?" She sighed. "That's only because it's gathering itself for one final burst of glory before it droops and dies."

"And you," he said carefully, "are more beautiful to me than any young girl can ever be."

She stared at him, the tears still shining in her eyes.

"Hold me, Agnes," he said. "Won't you do that, please?"

She sighed again and put her arms around him. He let his head rest on her shoulder, and she stroked his hair in a gesture that might have been maternal.

Though he appeared quiescent, Goff's mind was racing. All the circumstances of the night—from the whisky and the wine he had drunk, from Karin's kiss and Deborah's kiss amid the insistent throb of the party music, to the fluid notes filling the quiet room and the proximity of Agnes's soft melancholy—had elated him to a point where he believed anything to be possible. In his confidence, in his intoxication with himself, he had become a Colossus. Never again would he feel so totally in command of a situation.

After a while he took Agnes's hand in his and kissed it, then let it fall again to her lap, then took it up and kissed it again, and then began to cover it with kisses so that she took it away with a little stifled sound.

Goff sat up and drew her face toward him. For a moment their eyes met and held, and then he kissed her. She tried to pull away, but he put his hand firmly behind her head and went on kissing her until all at once she was kissing him back. Then he knew that he had won, a realization so heady that it overwhelmed him.

As he showered kisses on her face and neck, he fumbled with the buttons of her robe. When it fell open, revealing her breasts, he thought his desire would choke him and pressed his face into them with a groan.

Again, Agnes pulled away. Her eyes were black and her hair was tumbling as she clutched the robe about her body.

"No," she said. "No. No. No. No."

But Goff was pulling at her hands, jerking the robe from her shoulders again.

"Darling, darling Agnes," he said. "You know you must."

Some small part of him, looking on detachedly, was excited afresh by the realization that it was all much more intense than any of the books about it suggested. It was glorious!

"Not here . . ." she said. "In my room . . . The door must be locked . . ."

Before anything could change, he pulled her quickly across the hall to a door she indicated, drew her inside, turned the key in the lock.

His awareness of what happened next was superseded by the throbbing of his own senses. They precluded everything else. He felt himself swelled to unbelievable size.

Yet by the time he was inside her it was already too late. There was an explosion, then all the bright stars dimmed. As the great balloon of his exhilaration was pricked, misery and humiliation swept him.

"Hell!" he said. "Hell, hell, hell!"

But Agnes would not let him go, prevented him from pulling away as he might have done. She held him for a long time until his heart ceased to flutter and he slipped easily out of her.

"We've done it now, Goff," she said a little sadly, resting on her elbows and looking down at him. "You should have left me alone. What's going to become of me?"

"I love you," he said. "I've wanted you always, and as far as I'm concerned you can take all the flowering girls and dump them in the sea."

"Don't say pretty things." She put her hand over his mouth. "I can't resist them. If you hadn't said them, we wouldn't be here now. I love you." She kissed his shoulder.

"I know that," he said without complacency. "Everything will be all right."

"Goff, how could it be?" she said. "But I don't want to think of the end of it. I'm dull and staid, really. Nothing untoward ever happened to me. And now . . ."

"Agnes," Goff said. "Kiss me again."

It was better the second time, although still much too quick. Over before you get started, Goff thought, aggrieved. How can you savor it when all you feel is yourself going off? I shall have to work at it.

He wanted to try again, but Agnes said he must go.

When she came out to say goodnight she looked amazingly composed, with her hair tidy and her robe buttoned to the neck. He had a sudden panicky thought that she would try to go back on an arrangement they had made in the bedroom, and flung himself upon her fearfully.

"Go straight back to the party," she said, kissing him. "Bring Deborah here and don't come in, even if she asks you. I don't want to see you again tonight."

"But about tomorrow. You promised—"

"Of course. That's arranged. We've discussed it all. Just go now, for God's sake."

She pushed him out the front door and shut it firmly behind him.

I shall not think, she told herself; later I shall have to think, but not now. She busied herself with mundane things, changing the sheets on her bed, washing the tumbler from which she had drunk, taking the record from the turntable and replacing it in its sleeve.

"Ah, Pernette the Prince's daughter, you have a lot to answer for!" she said aloud, looking lovingly at it before she put it away in the cabinet.

She had not long finished when Deborah came in, explaining how Goff had left the party suddenly, hours before, and that Karin and Karistides had brought her home.

"How odd of Goff!" Agnes said. "Never mind, my dear, you've had a lovely time."

She thought her own voice must crack with insincerity, yet it came out bell-like. Deborah, sitting quietly on the sofa, looked so submissive, so passive, that despite herself Agnes was faintly irritated.

"Maybe young Goff isn't such a good idea for you, after all," she said brightly, despising herself for the hypocrisy. "Oh well, there are lots of other very nice boys around."

"But I don't want anyone else," Deborah said. "Anyway, he's easily the nicest."

"I expect when he thinks about it he'll feel the same about you. I'm sure he'll telephone some time," Agnes said briskly. "I'm off tomorrow, by the way. I'm going to Tringham for a couple of days. I simply must have some country air."

Her own manner was hateful to her in its plausibility.

"How lovely," Deborah said. "It's very near where Goff lives, isn't it? He talked about it. He and Andrew are going to Goff's house tomorrow. You might even see them." She looked wistful.

"I doubt it," Agnes said. "I'll take you to Tringham some time, if you like. I can't ask you to come tomorrow. I want to get away from—"

"I understand," Deborah said. "A writer needs to be alone a lot. I suppose I'd better be going to bed." She got to her feet slowly. "It's funny, isn't it, how you look forward to something very much and it comes and then it's over and there isn't anything any more? They don't last long, the nice things." She sighed.

"Don't worry about Goff," Agnes said, after a moment's hesitation. "You're so young, all of you, and have so far to go."

"Yes." The girl nodded. "Agnes, he kissed me," she added suddenly, reddening. "He kissed me tonight."

"Goff did?" Agnes smiled at her. "How could he resist it? You're very sweet. Lots of boys will want to kiss you from now on, you'll see. Goodnight, darling, sleep well."

When Karistides switched on the bedroom light, Goff groaned and pulled the pillow over his face.

"You're here!" Karistides came and stood over him. "Where the hell did you get to?"

"Was Deborah all right?" Goff asked. "I went back to the party, but your cousin said you'd all left."

"If she was, it was no thanks to you, you bastard! I had quite enough on my plate without playing knight errant to the little mouse."

"Was she cut up when I left?"

"How should I know? She seemed okay. Where did you go, Goff?"

"I went to see Agnes." The reply was muffled by the pillow.

"But I don't see . . ."

Goff lifted the pillow and stared at Karistides. It gave him enormous pleasure to watch the variety of expressions that passed in quick succession over the Greek boy's face.

"You didn't—You couldn't have—You didn't by any chance *screw* her?" he said at last, almost fearful in his incredulity.

For Goff it was a sweet moment. Under different circumstances, it might have been the sweetest moment of all.

"If you must put it so crudely, yes, I did," he said.

Karistides seized the pillow and dragged it away. Delight suffused his face. He looked as if he were about to kiss his friend.

"You old bastard!" he shouted, sinking onto the bed and pummelling Goff's shoulder. "You *fucked* our Miss Vale! Fucked old Big Tits Vale . . . 'If only you would *try*, Karistides, to instill a little *life* into what you write . . . This is all rather pedestrian, Karistides . . . I never find myself getting very *excited* about your essays, Karistides . . . Karistides, *do* get on with your work and stop looking out of the window. I know the view of the gardener's boy tossing off is infinitely more interesting than parts of speech. I think so, too, but unfortunately it isn't in the exam syllabus . . . Now, Karist—' "

Goff sat up, his hair tousled, his eyes glittering.

"We'll drop it now, Andy," he said quietly. "No more puerile cracks. And if ever I hear so much as a whisper of this outside, I shall wallop you within an inch of your grubby little Levantine life. You do understand what I'm saying to you?"

Karistides looked hurt.

"Look, we're friends, aren't we?" he asked. "Friends from way back? You know you can trust me."

Goff stared at him with the unwavering gaze that always seemed to hold a hint of hostility. Karistides's own little eyes winked in an effort at sincerity. He tried to keep his gaze fixed, but in the end it flickered away.

"Only tell me," he said, looking at the wardrobe. "Where do you go from here?"

Goff sat up with his knees under his chin, elation lighting his face.

"It's all working out remarkably well," he said excitedly. "We go to Marlwood tomorrow, right? You know Agnes still owns the Grange at Tringham, though some relatives of her husband live there? It just so happens they'll be away over the holiday, and Agnes keeps a key . . ."

Karistides looked at him admiringly, bunching his fingers to his lips and kissing the tips.

"So you will see her again?"

"Tomorrow night." Goff was unable to keep the triumph out of his voice. "It's imperative that the family knows nothing, of course. I may need your help."

"But of course," Karistides said blandly, his eyes glinting at the prospect of conspiracy. "I say, this has real style, you know?"

Goff lay down again.

"I'm absolutely bushed," he said. "Would you mind coming to bed at once?"

"Certainly," Karistides sang out, beginning to drop his clothes on the floor. "Shan't bother to clean my teeth. No one to notice now. What a night, eh?"

"How did you make out with Karin, by the way?" Goff asked politely.

"Oh, I'd completely forgotten that." Karistides, in his shorts, stood square on his thick legs and placed his hands on his lips. "It was okay. Routine stuff compared to yours, though." He let the shorts fall and surveyed his body critically. "Sling over my pajamas, will you?" He scratched his testicles with gusto. "You know, I'd never have dreamed of fucking Agnes Vale," he said wonderingly. "One of the few fantasies I didn't have. Not that she wasn't fanciable. She'd never look at *me*, though. Likes your clean-limbed, sporting, English boy. No, you were always the one there. You have a way with you . . . you've had your way with *her*, all right!"

Chuckling, he jumped into bed, making the springs bounce.

"Tell you what, Goff," he said, winding his wristwatch. "Doesn't it beat wanking every time?"

"If you must put it like that," Goff winced. "All right. Yes, yes it does. Now go to sleep, for God's sake."

He reached over to turn out the light. There was an interval of silence in which they lay side by side, their bodies not touching.

"It wasn't all that—Andy—you know . . ." Goff suddenly said. "I mean it was okay, but the mechanics of the thing . . ."

"It'll get better," Karistides said reassuringly. "These things are usually a bit of a letdown the first time, you know. You remember me telling you when . . . Of course, it will improve."

"It's only . . . I wish I didn't *care* so much."

"Give it time."

Karistides patted his shoulder almost paternally, then turned on his side and immediately fell asleep.

♣§ SEVEN §♣

" 'The stars were dim, and thick the night,' " Agnes said. She opened the french window at Goff's knock and stepped onto the patio. "How still it is in the country—and the air's so sweet!"

"That about the stars is from *The Ancient Mariner*," Goff said. "I remember it from Culture Club."

She was beautiful tonight, he thought, as she led him inside and they stood in front of the log fire. He could never remember her looking so beautiful. Though she wore pants and a shirt, femininity emanated from her hair and her eyes. Goff had never noticed before how big and luminous her eyes were.

"I couldn't be certain you would come." She held both his hands tightly. "I wasn't sure you'd be able to get away."

"It was easy." They spoke softly, in the manner of conspirators, though there was no one to hear. "When supper was over at last, Andy and I said we'd like to play records. Mother let us take some beer upstairs. Awfully decent." His lip curled as he sat beside Agnes on the lumpy sofa. "Half an hour later I slipped out. Luce always leaves the keys in her car."

"You drove here?" Agnes looked at him in horror. "That's terribly dangerous!"

"I drive as well as anyone who's passed a test. I've been doing it around the grounds since I was eleven."

"You're under age. If you were stopped—"

"I won't be stopped. Not with the police around here!"

"If anyone should find out—"

"Who would find out? My rooms are pretty well sacrosanct now. It's a far cry from the days when people went grubbing about in my personal belongings." As his mouth tightened, he looked momentarily vicious. "They're encouraging me to lead my own life. Magnanimous of them, isn't it?"

"Don't be so bitter. They only want what's best for you."

"They want what's convenient. They make me sick. I wish I could get out. School and home shut me in. I'm nearly old enough to leave."

"Don't be childish. Your education's nowhere near complete."

"No. I take my main block of O levels this summer—I've already got a few. Then it's A levels and university, then the business. All planned. Fitz too, poor little sod! Mayfair Gallery for me, Marlwood Gallery for him. Mapped out from the moment we were born."

"Consider yourself lucky. Think of the security."

"Who needs security? I want to do something. I will one day, I'll show them. They're in for a rude awakening."

"I don't like you when you talk like this," Agnes said. "Bitterness is corrosive. It will poison your life, and you'll never be happy."

"I am happy." He put his hand to her cheek and held it there. "Last night was simply . . ." He touched her breasts as his feelings overwhelmed the words.

"Don't take risks, Goff," she said. "You know if anyone finds out . . ."

"No one will, Karistides will cover for me. He's a resourceful chap."

"I'm sure of that. But I don't like to think of your having to rely on him."

"Karistides is all right. You've never understood him, have you?"

"Do he and his sister still . . . ?"

"Oh, that was all over years ago. He's had any number of women since then."

There was a note of admiration in his voice that Agnes noted with unease.

"That sort of thing is very important to boys of your age, isn't it?" she said. "Any woman will do."

"I know what you're thinking," Goff said quickly. "But this is different. I promise you. I faithfully swear it."

"In a few months, a few weeks, that will change. How little time we have! Why must I love you so much?"

"Don't be afraid." His arms tightened around her. "No one will ever take your place. We have tonight and tomorrow. After that . . .

Oh Agnes, I feel so randy always! Agnes, can we go to bed now, please?"

When he came back the next night, when they sat in the firelight before the shifting logs, she wished that there need be nothing more than what they had there and then.

"Won't you recite a poem?" Goff urged her. "You used to recite them all the time."

"They were all I had in those days," she smiled nostalgically. "Huge cloudy symbols of high romance."

"Now you have me," he said complacently. "But you had me even then."

"The old school, the abandoned places, images of the past," she murmured abstractedly. "After that, this mossy, mouse-haunted Grange! Always I seemed to be waiting, waiting, filling my head with the cloudy symbols . . ."

"When I was a child, I never used to know," said Goff, "which were your own words and which were out of some book."

"A child? I suppose you were. Oh, those roses! Hood, Landor, Yeats. Why do I know so many poems about roses?"

"'Roses roses all the way/And myrtle mixed in my path like May.'" Goff looked pleased at his remembrance of it. "What's the matter?"

She looked pale suddenly, Pre-Raphaelite tonight in a plum-colored robe, with her hair in disarray.

"I don't know why you should remember that now, Goff."

"'The rooftops seemed to heave and sway, The church spires flamed . . .' It gave me a feeling of—of everything being very fine and fresh . . ."

I do love him, Agnes thought, God help me, I do.

". . . and you told us it was Browning. *My Last Duchess, Porphyria's Lover*—you read them to us, too."

"Terrible poems to read to little boys! But you all *wanted* to hear about death, always. Why do you remember that poem now?"

"The way you talked about it was—is—so typical of you! You said it filled you with a fearful pleasure, it gave you a frisson, you said." Goff frowned in the effort of recollection. "You liked words like that. Blount took them all down in a notebook. 'Things change so quickly, boys,' you said. 'Look how this man goes from the pinnacle of triumph to the nadir of humiliation' . . ."

"I didn't say, 'nadir,' did I?"

"Certainly. We all used it for a while. In the end you said there were too many nadirs altogether."

"You know, it chills me even now, that poem. Such power, such heady, dizzying certitude—and then—"

" 'A year ago on this very day!' "

Goff was young and laughed at shadows that frightened her.

"I don't recite poetry any more," she said soberly. "It's not as I thought, Goff, any of it. Reality can never be anything like a beautiful work of art."

He gathered her to him. She was lovely in her unease. At times like this, he felt that she was younger than he was.

"I have a plan," he said, to comfort her. "The Millers will be back on Thursday, yes? Tomorrow will be our last night. Therefore we shall go out."

"Out?"

He held her at arm's length, the better to enjoy the doubt in her face.

"I shall come for you at eight. We'll drive in to Andham and have a good meal. You haven't had a proper one for days."

"It would be sheer lunacy! If you should be stopped . . ."

"I won't be. I easily pass for seventeen at least, everyone says so. It will be fun to go out. We're not going to hide in the shadows forever. I don't care for that sort of thing. It must be done. I've decided."

Perhaps he needs an element of danger, Agnes thought, an added frisson! She felt suddenly tired, too drained for a confrontation with him. Maybe this is how it must end, she thought fatalistically. He may kill us both! How very nasty for the people left behind—but how beautifully simple for us!

"So it's all fixed and you're not going to argue," he was saying. He tugged at her sleeve. "Bed now, Agnes."

Goff stared moodily around the half-filled dining room of the Cock. As usual when things did not go as he had planned, he felt a tingle of something vicious pulse through him.

When he and Agnes had arrived in Andham for their last evening together, they had found the discreet little restaurant where he had planned to eat closed for annual holidays. The Cock had been the only alternative, and he considered it a poor one. In the midst of its plebeian respectability, Agnes was watchful and ill at ease.

Small things irritated him tonight. First she refused a drink in the bar, so that headwaiter had to seat them at once. Then when Goff was presented with the wine list, she said she only wanted a beer. His eyes shot arrows of anger at her as he ordered a bottle of good burgundy.

"Look, we have to discuss what we're going to do," he said, when they had finished eating and were having coffee.

He resented her evasiveness whenever he tried to raise the subject. I have to do all the planning, he thought indignantly, she never even tries. Then he remembered how she looked naked, and his guts gave a kind of lurch.

"Not here, darling," she said, her eyes flickering in the direction of a stout woman at the next table.

Goff's heart reeled at the endearment, meaningless as it was.

After dinner it was early still, and they walked toward the river. He took off his jacket and draped it around her shoulders. There were other couples in the darkness, walking close, sitting on benches, locked in embraces down by the water.

"It's all so complicated, Goff." Agnes stared into the darkness. "You can't possibly come to Marcia's."

"We can use my father's apartment."

"Never! If he found us there . . ." She shuddered.

"It's essential that you get a place of your own as soon as possible," he said, stroking her arm. "And in the summer we must get right away."

Suddenly he pulled her toward him. He kissed her with his mouth open, his tongue thrust between her teeth. He savored the lust in his mouth and in his body until she pulled away from him.

"Shall we go home now?" he asked, his voice thick.

"I think we'd better."

She took out a handkerchief and wiped his saliva from her mouth. It wasn't straightforward as in Karistides's books, Goff was beginning to see. The women in them were always completely consumed by desire. It worried him that Agnes must compare him with other men she had had. He wasn't very adept yet. He needed to spend more time with her. She loved him very much . . . But what kind of love? It would be abhorrent if she should be loving his child self still . . . He placed his arm about her proprietorially.

She pressed companionably against him, and that contact soothed him. He was scarcely aware of a couple approaching until they drew level and he heard the woman speak his name. Then when they had passed the man bluffly called out goodnight.

Agnes drew away from Goff and pulled his jacket more closely about her.

"Who was that?" Her voice was suddenly cold.

"They're friends of my mother's. Well, more acquaintances, actually. She's on some sort of charity committee with the woman. I don't like her much."

"Oh, my God!" said Agnes. He saw under the street lamp that she had turned white. "She'll call your mother first thing in the morning, if not sooner."

"Why should she?" He was alarmed at the change in her. "It isn't important."

"It was quite evident you weren't with a girl your own age. She looked so hard at me. I'm afraid."

"I tell you it doesn't matter."

"But it does. I have a horrible feeling I was introduced to her at the Gallery opening. She was part of a group when your Aunt Ginevra was discussing my book. Yes, I'm sure she was. Don't you see? If she mentions me by name, your mother will . . . Oh, how messy! I know we should never have come. Shitting on your own doorstep is the crude colloquialism for it where I come from. How well it fits! You must take me home now."

Her footsteps tapped smartly on the pavement, and her face was set. On the way back she said nothing. Goff was a little afraid of her. She seemed so far away.

As he drew up in front of the Grange, she said, even before he switched off the engine:

"Now you will go home."

"Agnes . . ."

"You mustn't argue." She spoke quietly. "Go straight home, and don't try to get in touch with me again. I'm going back to London as soon as it's light."

"Let me stay with you tonight. It's our last chance. It would be silly not to."

"It's always a mistake," she said evenly, "to believe there's a point where it's too late to stop. That's a kind of self-blackmail. I won't submit to it. I've made a mistake. The blame is entirely mine. Now I'm telling you to go."

He saw that even his famous stubbornness wasn't going to help him now. He felt a moment's panic. Already she had climbed from the car and was walking toward the door. He scrambled after her.

"Agnes." He took hold of her arm. "Don't be so upset. Nothing we've done has been your fault."

She turned and stared at him.

"Who would ever believe that?" she said ironically. "I suppose I ought to be thankful I'm not a man. It's corruption of a minor then. For some reason these things are ordered differently for women. Though it's fortunate I'm not your teacher still. That would have been good meaty News of the World stuff."

"Agnes, we're not the first people ever to—"

"No, oh no, I know we're not the first. No one ever is. Karistides wasn't the first boy to poke his sister. Do you think that makes it any better?"

She inserted her key in the lock and opened the door.

"Agnes," Goff said urgently. "Listen a minute, please."

"There's nothing more to be said, my dear. We always talked too much anyway . . . until the time came when we talked too little . . ."

"Let me come into the hall, just for a moment, please. I promise you I'll leave. Only I must ask you something first, please."

He thought she would bar his way, but she let him follow her in. They stood in the darkness without turning on the light.

"Agnes," Goff said. "Tell me that you haven't been using me."

"Using you? *Me?* I don't see how—"

"I'm very much afraid that's what you've been doing. And I can't bear it. You never really loved me."

"What a terrible thing to say! Oh God, if I didn't love you, would we be in this mess?"

For some reason they would not raise their voices but stood hissing at each other in the darkness where he could just make out her eyes flashing at him.

"I don't think it's real to you," he said. "I think it's all just a game in your head. But it's real to me, Agnes, all of it. It always *has* been real, and it hurts!"

At last he seemed to have reached her.

"Oh Goff," she said. Her voice was weak. "My darling boy. How can you think it? Goff."

She took hold of him in the darkness, and it was sweet to him to feel the tears on her cheeks that mingled with his own.

"Not love you?" she said brokenly. "You're all I have."

"Then don't send me away without anything," he said. "At least tell me that when you get back to London I can call you. Then we can make arrangements."

He felt her hesitation, then her yielding with a soft little sigh.

"Perhaps. Go now, darling, please go."

"Yes."

But holding her, the desire that had lain quiescent for the past half hour suddenly burst upon him afresh. He wanted her more than ever before.

"Oh, I do want you," he said, covering her face with kisses. "I want you so much! Feel me, Agnes. Oh, dearest, darling Agnes, let me love you. Now. Here. Please. I promise I'll go—but first—please."

She didn't put up a very strong resistance. What was the use of that? He might have forced her anyway. He was completely consumed by what he felt. There in the hall, pressing her up against the wall, pausing to remove only the minimum of clothing, he possessed her with a sensation keener and sweeter than anything he had known. He thought as excitement nearly choked him that there could never be anything to equal this.

"You see," he said, gasping, when it was over, his hair plastered against his head, his face drenched with sweat. "It *is* right. It must be. Because it wouldn't *be* like this if it wasn't right. You know, Agnes, you know."

"Goff."

There was all the love in the world in the word. Now that his eyes were accustomed to the dimness of the hall, she looked small to him.

"I'll go now, as that's what you want," he said, briskly buttoning his clothes. "I'll come to you in London, as soon as I can. Don't worry. No one is going to hurt you. You're wonderful, beautiful. You belong to me."

On the drive back to Marlwood he felt purged, elated. He whistled as he drove. There isn't anything to it, this love, this sex, he thought. He was looking forward to seeing Andrew Karistides again. Tonight had been the best ever for him. He wanted to talk about that.

Agnes, in Marcia's flat, waited and wondered what she must do. She felt curiously passive, incapable of action.

She was alone on Friday afternoon when the doorbell rang. It may be Goff, she thought, quite composed. I shall offer him tea. The bell rang for a second time as she went slowly to answer it, patting her hair tidy.

To see Andrew Karistides cut cruelly into her passivity, giving her a nasty kind of jolt.

"Why, Andrew . . . Come in," she said brightly.

How foreign the boy looked!

"I have a message from Goff," he said as he stepped inside.

Hermes . . . the go-between . . .

"Some tea?" she said, sounding calm though her stomach churned. Something wicked this way came, she was sure of it.

"That would be nice, thanks."

When she came back from the kitchen he sat a little forward, broad hands clasped in front of him. As she poured the tea, she realized uneasily that she had never before been alone with him.

"Goff couldn't make it?" she said in a conversational tone, offering him a cup.

"He's in Ireland. He went yesterday. With his mother and Fitz."

"Yes?"

"There was a bit of a bust-up," Karistides said mildly.

"Really?"

Agnes set down her own cup carefully so that it wouldn't rattle against the saucer.

"Yes. Some fool of a woman called Mrs. Willoughby on Thursday morning. Ostensibly it was about some committee. She seemed to have seen Goff in Andham the night before."

"You know everything, Andrew?" Agnes cut in.

"Absolutely everything, Mrs. Stratton."

"Call me Agnes. Tell me what happened. All of it."

"There was a real upper-and-downer." His eyes gleamed at the recollection of it. "The woman said Goff was with someone she remembered meeting. Mrs. Willoughby reached her own conclusions. I think myself her nerves are in bad shape. The menopause, would you say?" He looked at Agnes alertly.

"Possibly. What happened?"

"She confronted Goff. Voices were raised. I couldn't help overhearing. Of course Goff told her to mind her own business. Later she started on me."

"On you?"

Karistides put down his cup and stood on the hearth rug. Absurdly, Agnes was reminded of the time she had seen him act. He looked very alive today. All of him, skin, hair, eyes, postively shone. He was glossy with vitality.

"She got me by myself," he said.

"And you said . . . ?"

"I told her everything, of course."

"Of course," Agnes said in a hollow voice.

"Everything. I was reluctant, but I felt it was for the best." His eyes were dancing now. He could scarcely keep the laughter out of his voice. "In Goff's interests, to tell her what he wouldn't. As his friend. Of course, I made it clear that I was jeopardizing our friendship. She didn't seem to care. People are singleminded, aren't they, when you have something they want?"

"What will happen now?" Agnes said.

I will have to leave the country, she was thinking. But will there be any scandal? Surely they'll want to keep it quiet? All the same, I must get out. I wonder if that offer Levy spoke about would . . .

There was no question about how much Karistides was enjoying himself. Standing over her, he had her at a disadvantage. She ought to get to her feet but didn't feel she had the strength required, so he would keep his advantage . . .

"I had to tell her about Deborah," he was saying.

"Deborah?" Agnes repeated dully.

"About this thing that's developed between her and Goff. How hard it's hit him, his first real love affair. It's crap, isn't it, Agnes? But you have to give people what they want. I told her about your friend, Deborah's mother, believing that she's far too young for anything serious, and how she won't let her daughter see Goff again, and how he's been more cut up than he's shown. That's where you came in."

"Where I came in?"

Agnes was feeling very weak. Karistides spoke so smoothly that the words rolled from him like oil.

"Goff having met the girl through you. His feeling you might have some influence with the mother. Your happening to be at your Tringham house over the holiday. Goff's begging you to meet him in

Andham to talk about it. To ask you to use that influence. Of course it was wrong of Goff to borrow Lucinda's car. His mother's angry about that. All the same, I think she's ashamed now of her first suspicion. Such a nasty thing to think about your own son! The idea that you and he . . ."

Agnes found she now had the strength to rise to her feet. It brought them exactly level.

"You did this?" Her voice had a crack in it.

"Goff's furious," Karistides said ruefully. "He'd much prefer the real truth to be told. Yet this is so much more—satisfactory—from everyone's point of view, don't you think, Agnes?"

He gave her a smile of transfiguring sweetness.

"Yes," she answered faintly.

"So if she should get in touch with you—which I rather doubt in view of her first thoughts—I would suggest that you tell her how you tried to point out to Goff, tactfully, that he and Deborah were far too young for any serious involvement. I'm sure Mrs. Willoughby will be very grateful, whether she admits it or not."

Karistides put his hands in his pockets and took a turn about the room, moving with a spring in his step. At the window he turned.

"The upshot of it all is that Mrs. Willoughby has taken Goff to Ireland. She was going there with Fitz anyway for a couple of weeks. She tried to get in touch with Mr. Willoughby, but he wasn't available, so she had to act on her own initiative."

"And you, Andrew?"

"There didn't seem to be any place for me there any longer. Goff's thoroughly fed up with me anyway. It's understandable." He shrugged. "I won't be persona grata at Marlwood for a while."

"What a shame," said Agnes. "After all you've done. Oh, Andrew!" She put out her hand to him briefly. "How clever! To turn the tables like that. It was Machiavellian."

He bowed his head in acknowledgment of the compliment.

"It's best for Mrs. Willoughby to see it this way. The other would upset her too much. People are very narrow, aren't they, Agnes? It's something that never ceases to surprise me."

Standing very close to him, looking into the bland face bisected by the one straight line of his eyebrows, Agnes felt a moment's fear. In a wild instant she thought that he would demand as his recompense just what Goff had had.

The moment of insanity passed. Still looking directly at the boy, she was aware that whatever he wanted, a share in her body was not part of it.

"You're masterly," she said. "Goff's fortunate to have a friend like you. He'll appreciate what you've done, once he's cooled down."

"I don't know about that," Karistides said. "We'll have to wait and see."

"He thinks a lot of you. He always has." Agnes could see that the reassurance flattered him. "I wonder, is it too early to have a drink? I don't think so. I certainly need one. What will you have, Andrew?"

He asked for vodka, and Agnes poured it. She very much wanted to be alone but knew she must set herself to entertain this boy in whose debt she stood.

It was very odd to her to be with someone so close to Goff in age and yet so different from him. Now that he had told his story, the animation and vitality in him, the sense of an actor projecting himself, had vanished. The light had died from his face; once more it was heavy and morose. Agnes had to do all the talking while, sipping his drink, he listened.

It was a relief to her when Deborah came in. The girl had been skating. She still wore a brief, swirling skirt edged with white fur. Her face was flushed, and her long hair had gathered into clusters. How pretty she is, Agnes thought. If Sandy Willoughby were to see her now, she would believe the story of her son's infatuation. How simple and beautiful and innocent if it were so!

After a quarter of an hour of platitudes, Karistides left. In the hall he murmured to Agnes that if she wished to write to Goff it would be advisable to send the letter through him. So they were to be conspirators still; there would be no escape. Thanking him again, she shook his hand warmly.

When the door closed on him, she leaned against it, feeling very weak. But she took a few deep breaths and forced herself to return to Deborah.

"Did Andrew mention Karin before I came in?" the girl asked.

Agnes replied that he had not, thinking how trivial it all seemed when set against her own problems.

"It's marvelous the way people—boys—talk to you so easily," Deborah said. "They don't do it with me."

"I've had a lot of practice," Agnes said grimly.

"Yes." Deborah was inhibited by something in her tone but ventured at last, "Goff's in Ireland, isn't he?"

"I believe so."

"I wonder if he would have come with Andrew if he hadn't been?"

"Perhaps."

"Andrew telephoned Karin this morning. He wants to take her out, but she isn't sure. She's arranged to meet him for coffee. That doesn't commit her to anything. Karin's so confident about these things. Andrew's very sure of himself, too. He's so worldly. I feel all the time I'm talking to him, he's smiling at me inside."

"If you had wanted to, you know," said Agnes, whose nerves were being stretched taut by all this gossip, "you could have had him ask you out this afternoon."

"He isn't interested in me." Deborah grew pinker. "I'm not his type."

"A pretty girl is every boy's type," Agnes said cynically.

"If it were Goff . . . Agnes, if you had a choice of the two, you would pick Goff, wouldn't you?"

"I suppose I would."

Agnes turned away. Is it so clear, even to this child? she thought.

For hours that night, sleep eluded her. Constricted, she paced her bedroom, afraid of waking Marcia or Deborah, while wild thoughts chased one another around in her mind.

She was fortunate to have come out of it all so well. That was due entirely to the Greek boy. But Goff . . . No, she mustn't dwell on that. It had to be over now. His hurt would be less deep and lasting than her own. He had to lose his virginity sometime. Weren't there certain primitive tribes where initiation by older women was the natural order of things? And in literature, particularly the French, it was common enough . . . Dumas . . . Colette . . . But they were not members of a primitive tribe. And literature was not life.

How beautiful Tringham had been! Safe. A child's admiration. Homage of roses. Pretty fancies. But all exacting their price. Goff deserved better. The girls he had in the future would be beautiful and right, and in time he'd forget what he felt now . . .

She must go away. Another Fresh Start. How many more? Nothing fresh about her now. She felt too expended to put this down as another one. But at least a decision had been made. It was over.

In her disordered dreams, it was not the face of Goff that came to her, but the smiling, simian features of Andrew Karistides, her ironic, sardonic savior.

⊷§ EIGHT §⊷

It was at the end of the following winter that Agnes made her first television appearance. An interview with her formed part of a program devoted to children's books. She and her illustrator, Conrad Forrester, talked informally about their partnership, and some of his Wolfram drawings were shown.

Everything went well, and she and Forrester left the studios euphoric with relief at about ten o'clock in the evening. They were accompanied by a visiting American producer who had been sitting in on the broadcast and with whom they were to have supper.

It would seem to Agnes later that there was something cinematic about what happened. She could envisage it as a series of shots from a script. Herself a slim, fashionably dressed woman, escorted by two good-humored, worldly men. A very metropolitan scenario.

As they left the elevator, a figure that had been standing with its back to them stepped forward and placed a hand on her arm.

A dark figure, half-man, half-boy. Her past taking her by the arm . . .

"Andrew Karistides!" Agnes said. "Whatever are you doing here?"

A small, chill wind blew into the warm, perfumed, gin-scented cloud of security in which she had been moving for the past few months.

"You know this boy?" Forrester asked, looking hard at him.

Agnes's first thought was tinged with hysteria. He's come for me. Like the legend of the appointment in Samarra, no matter where I run he'll be waiting for me. A year ago to this very day . . . Not quite a year, but near enough . . .

"May I have a word with you, please?" the Greek boy said in his beautiful, clipped, not quite English voice.

Agnes hurriedly excused herself and moved away from her escorts.

"Will you come with me now?" Karistides asked, speaking rapidly and low. "Please. It's important. It's Deborah."

Deborah. Agnes had seen nothing of the child since she'd moved out of Marcia's flat and away from London the previous May.

"Is she in trouble?"

"It's all a bit of a mess. I'd be grateful if you would come."

As she met his gaze, Agnes saw that his eyes were alight with the odd excitement she recognized from other times. Hiding her agitation, she returned to the two men and explained that she must leave them.

"I have a taxi waiting." Karistides was unabashed by the sharp looks they gave him. Such aplomb, Agnes thought, one of the benefits of an English public school education . . .

In the taxi he leaned back, offered her cigarettes from a silver case, lit one himself, very composed and not yet seventeen.

"There was no one I felt I could call on," he said. "When I discovered that you were appearing on the program tonight, it seemed providential."

"You said Deborah," Agnes prompted curtly, remembering the pleasure it had always given him to play with people. "What has happened?"

"She tried to kill herself." His enunciation was meticulous. "Oh, don't worry, it's all right. She slashed her wrists, very clumsily. Some blood, but it amounted to nothing major. My cousin knows a girl who's a nurse. She fixed her up. It'll be quite okay."

"Is she in a hospital?"

"No, she's at my cousin George's place." His eyes flickered past her. "That's where it happened. He's away now."

"But what was Deborah doing there?"

"Staying. She has before, lots of times. We first went there when my cousin invited us all to a party, it must have been nearly a year ago."

"I remember," Agnes said.

She felt cold and afraid of what was ahead. As the car drew up, she fumbled in her handbag.

"You must let me pay for this," she said. "It will be a lot with the waiting."

"I've plenty of money," Karistides assured her.

They entered the luxury apartment building, plush and anonymous, and an elevator bore them with silent speed to the penthouse.

"We're here, Debbie," Karistides called as they entered the apartment.

He flung open white double doors and revealed a long, expensively furnished room; Deborah was almost lost amid the cushions of a great sofa.

"See," Karistides said in an avuncular way. "I said I'd bring Agnes to you, didn't I?"

The girl sprang to her feet.

"Deborah, love." Agnes, enfolding her, felt the young body beginning to shake. "Hush, darling, it's all right."

"I'll go out for a little while." Karistides poured them drinks while they sat down together. "That will make it easier for you to talk."

"Andy, don't," Deborah began.

"I need to go out, anyway." He looked down at her. "I won't be long."

As he left, closing the doors noiselessly, Deborah took a sip of the fruit juice he had given her.

"Poor Andrew," she said. "It's all very tedious for him."

Agnes looked after him with distaste.

"Whatever are you doing here, child?" she asked. "Does your mother . . . ?"

"Mummy knows nothing." Deborah shied away with a nervous movement. "Anyway, I'm all right now."

Agnes noticed the neat bandages, like cuffs to the flowered dressing gown she wore.

"How did this thing happen?" she said harshly.

In a familiar gesture, Deborah pulled at a lock of her long hair.

"I keep getting depressed," she said. "Or rather I did. It's quite usual, lots of people will tell you, after an abortion."

"Deborah!"

"You aren't shocked? I wanted to see you because I thought you, of all people, wouldn't be shocked . . . I've always felt that you didn't judge people. Andrew says I must tell you everything. When once it's out of me it won't hurt so much, it won't matter. Cathartic, he says."

"Quite the amateur psychologist!"

"Don't blame him," Deborah said. "He was dragged into it. He's very good, really, when you get to know him."

"You'd better tell me all about it," Agnes said with a curious sinking in her spirits.

"It was last year at the beginning of May. A Friday evening. Perhaps it didn't really start then, but for me it felt as if it did. I was home because I'd had a dental appointment in London and wasn't due back at school till next day. I was in the apartment by myself when Goff came . . ."

"Goff?"

"Yes. He came looking for you. It had been raining. His jacket was all wet, and his hair was plastered down. He must have walked a long way." She bit her lip. "I told him I couldn't give him your address because you'd only left us Levy's. I offered him that, but he said it didn't matter."

"Surely he should have been at school?"

"He said he'd come up specially. He stayed a while and we talked. He must have found it rather boring, a wasted journey and everything . . .

"When I got back to school and told Karin, she said it proved he was interested in me after all, that asking for you was just an excuse . . ." Excitement rose for a moment in her cheeks, then died down again. "But if she'd seen us together she wouldn't have thought that," she added a little sadly.

"And yet, somehow Goff got into the habit of looking in at home in the holidays, always when I was alone. I never knew why. He didn't seem to enjoy it particularly. Sometimes he had such a strange look, as if he didn't know what he was doing there. He talked about you a lot, Agnes. I always felt that was the only thing we had in common, us both liking you so much.

"After he'd been a few times he kissed me. He'd kissed me once before, you know, at a party here. But this time it was different. It all began to get rather rough and wild. The first time it happened, I stopped him. He went off very quietly. I thought that would be the end of it. Yet he did come back. And he kissed me, not as if he were beginning again, but as if he were carrying on from where he left off." She looked at Agnes. "I didn't stop him. I didn't want to stop him by that time . . ."

The old cliché, Agnes thought wearily, and you can't blame her. Look what you did when the same thing happened to you . . .

"It never seemed to be right," Deborah said dispiritedly. "That was my fault, of course. Goff was much more experienced. Really, you can't blame him for being so disappointed. We did it five times altogether. We could both see it wasn't any use, but I kept hanging on. I felt it was something, you see, just to have him. I even thought in time he might get so used to me . . .

"In the end he had to tell me it would be better if we finished it. The night he said that, we were to go on to a party. It was the only time we'd ever gone out together. I'd been looking forward to it . . .

"When we got to the party, Andrew was there. Goff didn't stay. He just looked around with that way he has of not caring very much for what he sees, and left. Andrew was very nice to me after he'd gone. By the end of the evening I could see he was wanting to make love to me, too. It's very odd, having two boys want you, yet neither of them caring at all. I could see that Andrew didn't really care, and yet he was nice, in his peculiar way."

Deborah stared wonderingly into her glass. Agnes lit a cigarette, though her mouth felt dry.

"I began to go out with Andrew. After a while, there didn't seem any reason not to have sex. 'It isn't as if you're a virgin,' he said. I thought if I just closed my eyes and held him I could pretend it was Goff. But it didn't work like that. It was always Andrew.

"He was so very different. Goff had only wanted it over and done with. But Andrew liked it to be a long time and was always wanting to know how it felt to me. He said I had to relax. He said a little pot and a few drinks would do me no harm at all. The things we did then, odd things, began to seem quite far away. I didn't mind them. Though he wasn't Goff.

"When I found I was pregnant, I knew it must be Goff and not Andrew because of the timing. But it was Andrew I had to tell. There was no one else."

"Your mother?" Agnes found the taste of the cigarette unbearable and stubbed it out.

"Mummy never suspected for a minute I'd . . . I half thought Goff would get in touch when he heard, but he left it all to Andrew . . ."

"You mean he knew and did nothing at all?" Agnes said.

"You can't blame him," said Deborah. "He'd never wanted me. I was just there. Anyway, Andrew didn't mind. He was awfully cheerful about it. He's been such a good friend to Goff."

"Yes. He was always a good friend to Goff!"

"They share everything."

"Not quite everything."

"But they tell each other things. They don't have secrets. It must be very good to have a friend like that. . . .

"It wasn't anything really, the abortion, like coming up from school for the dentist. Andrew's cousin George fixed it all up. It only took money. . . .

"It was only afterwards that I began to feel a bit low. I wondered if it might have been wrong. I thought of all the women who can't have children and I'd . . . Andrew said women often think like that afterwards. It isn't just something you can strike out of your mind, he said. Poor little baby, he said. I liked him for seeing it like that, that it was a person, not a thing. He can be nice, Agnes. Kind, in a strange way.

"But after that was all over I could see that he was beginning to be bored with me. He wanted to move on, but he wouldn't just drop me. Then one day, here, his cousin George looked at me, and I knew. . . . You see, George is older. He's a man. That seemed to make a difference. I thought, Goff passed me on, and now Andrew wants to pass me on, and that's how it's going to be. Once you start, there isn't any end. I didn't want it to be that way. The other night I felt so low I just . . ."

She raised her bandaged wrists and let them fall again.

"What about your mother?" Agnes asked again.

"She's been out of the country for weeks. This very important program on South Africa. She thinks I'm staying with Karin. I couldn't bear it if she found out. She's worked so hard and done so well since Daddy died. She despises the kind of woman who gets into a mess over men. She'd be so hurt if . . ."

"Not half so hurt as she'd be if you'd killed yourself," Agnes said grimly.

"Oh, I don't feel like that anymore, really. It was only that two nights ago I was here by myself and feeling so tired, and I thought it would be the best thing for everyone. Of course I botched it. Even while I was doing it, I knew it wasn't really what I wanted and that if I could get away I could try to make it different. Anyway, Andrew found me and got me out, and this girl George knows came and bandaged me up, and she says the wrists are healing nicely."

"Darling, you must let me take you home tomorrow," Agnes said. "Think no more about Andrew or this George creature. You have to—"

They both stiffened as they heard Karistides at the door. He smiled so confidently that Agnes felt a stab of her old dislike for him, and she found hateful the intimacy of the manner in which he yawned and loosened his tie.

She saw Deborah safely to bed, noting with relief that the apartment was large enough for her to have a room to herself. After she had kissed the girl goodnight, she allowed Karistides to call a cab and wearily returned in it to her own apartment, wishing she need never have been involved in any of it.

Next morning she conquered the reluctance she felt and returned to the penthouse. She found Deborah already up. The bandages were smaller today. Soon they would be no more than Bandaids. The outward scars, at least, would be minor ones.

"Get your things," Agnes ordered crisply. "We're leaving at once."

Karistides stood by the window. The light had gone out of him this morning. He looked squat, almost a peasant. When he spoke, his beautifully modulated voice was more than ever at odds with his appearance.

"Is there anything you want me to do?" he asked when Deborah had left them.

"I think you've done enough," Agnes said. She had a strong desire to conclude with him as soon as possible. "I'd like to pay for Deborah's abortion, Andrew, if you'll tell me how much it was."

"I couldn't let you do that," he protested. "It was nothing."

"Why should it come out of your pocket? Have you had anything from Goff?"

It was a question that cost her much, yet she had to ask it.

"Goff?" Karistides laughed abruptly. "*He* couldn't afford it."

"It's a pity he didn't think of that beforehand," Agnes said bitterly. "He comes out of all this very badly, you know."

Karistides shrugged.

"He never wanted her, Agnes," he said.

"But he had her!"

"He never intended that initially. He only wanted you." He raised his brown eyes to meet her gaze. "It was very abrupt, the way you threw him over."

Agnes was silent.

"He couldn't take it, when you phoned that time," Karistides continued inexorably. "I told him how it was, that he mustn't blame you. But you know Goff doesn't like to be turned down. You must have realized you couldn't do something like that and expect no re-percussions. I believe he rather hates you now."

"I'd prefer to have him hate me than hanker after what he can't have," Agnes said, though the words hit her like a blow.

"Hating hurts, too," Karistides said, surprisingly. "You were his first woman. He was dragged away from you almost before it began. He was raw, open. And this girl was available and willing. What would you have expected him to do?"

"Just what he did, of course," Agnes said wearily. "But afterwards, to be so callous . . ."

"Perhaps he was ashamed. I don't know. When I went back to school and told him, all he said was 'Oh shit!' He was throwing a ball around at the time. He said, 'Oh shit,' then he took a run and knocked the ball clean over the bar. 'Get her off my back, Andy,' he said. 'Bloody females!' What could I do?"

"Well, she was your girl by that time," Agnes said severely. "The idea of passing her on to your cousin, that was nasty, Andrew. Why couldn't you simply let her go?"

Irresistibly she was reminded of herself, years ago, rebuking the sulky, indifferent boy for some shortcoming in his grammar exercise.

"It wasn't like that," Karistides said defensively. "George likes her. Is that so bad? George treats his girls very well. Sex always has to be something bad to you, hasn't it? You're a typical English Puritan. Look at the trouble that's brought us."

There was no rancor in his tone, and Agnes couldn't resent what he said. Suddenly touched, she went across and put her hand on his arm.

"You've been very good," she said.

His brown eyes were unmoved.

"What do you want me to tell Goff?" he asked.

"You must do as you please." She dropped her hand. "I'm not happy with his part in this. I wish I could tell him so."

"Why don't you, then?" Karistides said mildly.

"No. Enough damage has already been done."

"Yes. We are all guilty!"

When Karistides laughed, he showed strong white teeth like those of a healthy young carnivore.

In the hall he said his good-byes to Deborah. Agnes was struck by how young they both looked. A normal couple of kids. It made her want to cry. Silently she held out her hand to Karistides, and then they left him.

In the three days that followed, she stayed at Marcia's flat. She tolerated the strains that imposed as if they were a penance. She looked after Deborah, entertained her, took her out, listened patiently to reminiscences of Goff, of which there were many. It was these last that she found the most painful penance of all.

Marcia was to return at the end of the week. Already Deborah seemed more cheerful, resigned to going back to school, to immersing herself in work. She was young, she had everything ahead of her still. Agnes saw that she would survive.

"Will you come and see me sometimes?" the girl asked on their last evening together. "You know I'd like it very much."

"Darling, so would I. But for a while I'll only be able to write. I'm going to America, for a year at least. It's all been arranged."

"Will you work there?"

"Yes. I've been taken on by a college in the Midwest. They've set up a course in writing for children. They think I have something to offer in that direction."

"You'll do awfully well, Agnes."

"I wonder. I'm not much of a teacher, and I never had any training myself in how to write, but that's the way they do things there. When I come back I'm going to buy a little place in the country. Then you must come and stay with me."

"I'd love that. But perhaps you won't come back. Maybe you'll meet some nice man in America and stay there and marry him and be happy."

"I doubt it, my dear." Agnes stifled a yawn. "For someone like me solutions are not so easily found. Anyway, I'm going to try, at least, to make a fresh start."

Within three weeks she was gone.

Part III

ᕯ NINE ᕽ

Agnes, traveling through Hampshire by train, marveled at the beauty of the English countryside in the hazy heat of a June morning. During the past two years she had forgotten the exact quality of its freshness that is like no other.

At Andham Station she was met by a car, which took her straight to St. Fenrins. Although a room had been booked for her at the Cock, she would not make use of it until evening.

The town was as she remembered it. It seemed odd that not far away lived Harold, to whom she was still attached by law, and that nearer still her sister-in-law and Jeffrey Miller and their two children were spilling out of what was termed a "town house" in one of the better suburbs. It was unlikely that she would have any contact with them during her brief stay. They had no part now in her life.

It was while she was in America that Agnes had created her most inspired character, a malevolent, cream-colored goat named Capricorna. If Agnes never produced another book in her life, she would be able to live comfortably for the next forty years on the cornucopia this animal provided. Capricorna was becoming a minor industry. From her had sprung foreign, paperback, and television rights, a syndicated column in newspapers, and an approach by the Disney studios, who were anxious to put the goat on film.

Agnes had been on vacation in the Caribbean the previous December when a letter had reached her from Tim Sergeant, asking if she would be guest of honor at an anniversary prize-giving at St. Fenrins. At first she had dismissed the idea, but it had intrigued her and, since she was now in a position to indulge certain whims, she had finally agreed to attend.

Sitting up as they approached the school gates, she noticed how far the suburbs had spread. Yet behind the high wall all the land belonged to the school, as it had for over a century. Once again they were back in the past, and Agnes was elated by the knowledge that such an escape was possible still.

When she saw the tall figure of Tim Sergeant waiting for her on the steps, she thought how little he had changed in the eight years since she had first met him. Entering the main hall with him, catching a glimpse of a fresh-faced boy in gray uniform, she was swept into a distillation of time past.

She had the same sense in the study, where she was greeted with a kind of reserved effusiveness by Susan Sergeant. The Headmaster's wife wore exactly the kind of faded cotton dress she had always worn. I have traveled so far, Agnes thought, conscious of the contrast with her own blue silk subtly shot through with suggestions of pink roses. And she has stayed here safe, knowing always exactly what her position is.

After she had accepted coffee and talked of old times, understanding that the Sergeants had a great deal to do on such a day, she asked if she might wander around for a while. With an impish smile, Tim sent for a Sixth-former to escort her.

"Such a pity," he said, "that there isn't a single boy from your time left here. However—"

He was interrupted by a tap at the door and flung it wide.

"Ah, there you are. Jolly good! I have something I want you to do for me. Come along in."

As he stepped aside, Agnes saw Goff standing there.

The sunny room spun. In a wild, whirling moment she thought, it's all right. The atonement must have been sufficient. They are letting us have a second chance. It was all very quick, the thoughts swirling around her brain in a matter of seconds.

". . . Mrs. Stratton, Fitz, whom you know better as Agnes Vale," Tim was saying genially. "This is the last of the Willoughbys we shall see for a while, Agnes, but a good one."

"How do you do, Mrs. Stratton?" the child said, extending his hand.

The room swung back into place as she grasped it.

"How like your brother you are!" she murmured faintly.

She heard Tim saying how everyone remarked upon it but that temperamentally there were differences. His eyes, she now saw, were of a darker brown and with a quite different expression. When he had been given his instructions, he led her from the study solemnly and a little self-consciously.

"We do like your books, Mrs. Stratton," he said, as they paused in the corridor. "Upper Sixth don't normally read children's books, but we all devour yours. I like Capricorna best. She's very wicked. Is she based on a goat you knew?"

"As a matter of fact, she is. One I met in America."

"You ought to put her in a book with Wolfram. What a combination! Where would you like to go first?"

"The garden perhaps." Agnes felt breathless, suddenly craved the open sky. "Might we take a look at Mr. Erskine Fawcett's bees? I was amazed when Mr. Sergeant told me he still lives in his tower. He seemed so old when I was here."

It was very bright outside. The mulberry trees shimmered, the grass dazzled, flowers rioted at their feet. Agnes felt safe here. Nothing was known. She felt a resurgence of ease. The place would protect her. When she put out her hand to it, the old stonework was warm.

"You know I was English mistress of Fifth when your brother was in it?" she said to the boy beside her.

"Yes. I remember hearing about you when I was little."

"It was a long time ago. How are your family, Fitz?"

"Pretty fair. My sister's been married ages, of course. And Goff's going to Oxford in the autumn."

"What's he going to read?"

"I think it's Modern History."

They had reached the apiary. The little tower peeped through the trees, but of its occupant there was no sign. A few bees were buzzing amiably among some pinks against the south wall. Agnes stared at them dazedly.

"My mother always said it was a pity I missed you," Fitz remarked. "I can never catch up with Goff, you know. He was gone before I got here. Would you like to see the pool?"

"Let's do that. It must be hard to follow your big brother. People always make comparisons."

"Yes. I'm not a patch on him at History."

"How about English?"

"So-so. Science is more in my line."

"When I taught here, there was a boy who was very good at both Science and English. His name was Blount."

"Ben? I know him. He stayed with us once in Ireland."

"How about sports? Are you another brilliant all-rounder?"

"No such luck." Fitz smiled. "Cricket's the only first team I've made. Here's the pool."

They stood together, staring into the bright blue water.

"It's magnificent," Agnes said. "When I was here boys swam in the river sometimes."

"It's becoming increasingly polluted, with the growth of the New Town," Fitz said seriously. "We still row on it, of course; I'm not bad at that."

Agnes said that she mustn't leave without a visit to the Chapel.

"Your brother had a fine voice," she said, as they approached it. "Do you sing, too?"

"I'm in the choir—but not as a soloist. I'm not like him, you know!"

Poor child, she thought, always to be set against his more illustrious brother! And yet he seems the more contented soul.

Inside the Chapel, amid the familiar mingled smells of must and furniture polish, someone was practicing in the organ loft, although Agnes knew that Justin Lord had departed long since. As she saw how the polished eagle of the lectern caught the light and how the names of St. Fenrins boys fallen in World Wars were thrown into sharp relief, Agnes was suddenly sweepingly joyful. She had a sense of peace here in the gloom, speaking in muted tones to this pleasant little boy while the organ softly played.

"There was a leak," he whispered, indicating a damp spot over the choir stalls. "The rain fell on me and nowhere else. The drips came at precisely thirty-three-second intervals. I counted during the Psalm." He grinned ruefully. "It was a jolly long one!"

The music stopped. Quick footsteps descended from the loft. Agnes glanced along the aisle.

For the second time that morning it seemed that her heart stopped. Fitz followed her petrified gaze.

"Oh, hello there, Goff," he said matter of factly. "I wasn't sure you'd show up."

"Didn't I say I would? Hello, Agnes." He made her a cool little bow. "Rather fun for you to come back here as a celebrity, yes?"

He paused within a few feet of her. She had taken a step back and had braced herself against a pew. The slight discomfort of the edge against her spine gave her a kind of reassurance.

"Hello, Goff," she said.

As he had advanced down the aisle, by a trick of the light he had seemed impossibly tall. She now saw that he had in fact grown about four inches. He was quite painfully good-looking, so much so that her heart gave a leap, but his expression was severe.

"I was showing Mrs. Stratton where the rain dripped on me during the storm last November," Fitz explained. "The drips fell at precisely thirty-three-sec—"

"Yes? Well, you'd better cut along now," Goff said dismissively. "Mrs. Stratton and I want to talk about . . . old times." His eyes, fixed on Agnes, widened with insolence and irony.

"She's due back at the study in approximately seven minutes," Fitz said. "Mr. Sergeant—"

"I'll see she arrives on time," Goff said, stooping slightly to address him. "You push off, Pussy Face."

Fitz hesitated.

"You heard. Toddle!" the elder brother said.

Fitz looked doubtfully at Agnes. Since she was unable to speak, he received no guidance. Reluctantly, he turned to go.

"Have you seen the old man?" Fitz asked his brother. "He's coming early, too, for the Governors' do."

"I know nothing of his plans," Goff said casually.

"Will you stay for lunch?"

"Not likely! I shall go to the pub. And I have things to do this afternoon. So long, Pussy Face."

When the Chapel door had closed, the building was dark and silent. Somewhere outside in the warm noon a hen was clucking. Agnes's eyes were fixed on Goff's face as she stood, still wedged against the pew. His eyes, on the other hand, flickered up and down, taking in the details of her whole person.

"I like your brother," she said at last, when the silence had become unbearable.

"He's a worthy chap," Goff agreed, putting his hands in his pockets. "And how are you?" His eyes swept her once more. "You're thinner."

He turned away and picked up a hymnal.

"It's all so predictable, this place," he said as he flicked the pages. "How could you bear to come back?"

"How could you?"

"I knew you were going to be here. I wanted to see you."

"That was an exercise in futility, surely?" Agnes said.

Although her tone was flat, she was inwardly tremulous. In the flesh he was infinitely more comely than her memory of him had been. Her heart ached.

"I wouldn't have thought you would want to see me again," she said.

He put out his hand toward the brass eagle and caressed the highly polished knob of its head.

"You never can tell. So when are we going to have a talk?"

"Is there anything to be said now?"

"Everything. When?"

The old pressure of his persistence turned in her like a knife.

"I must go back. They're expecting me in a couple of minutes."

"When?" he repeated.

He was so close that she could see the dark dots of his beard upon his shaven skin. She thought that if he touched her, so much as laid a hand upon the sleeve of her dress, she would collapse. His expression was cold, yet at the same time there was something of pleading in it.

"I don't know—" She put her hand weakly, impotently to her face.

"Where are you to stay?" he asked practically.

"I have a room at the Cock for tonight . . ."

"I shall come after nine-thirty. Do you know the number?"

"Room one-one-five, but I can't . . ." Her voice had a fretful note, like that of an invalid.

"We can talk then," he said soothingly, as if she were indeed ill and needed soothing. "We can talk, Agnes. Now I'll take you to the study. Come."

Dumbly she allowed him to make way for her. Once outside the Chapel, the atmosphere seemed lighter, but all the while she was aware of him like a dark shadow at her shoulder. They paused outside the study and heard the hum of voices and clink of glasses from within.

Goff made her a small, ironic bow and opened the door with a flourish. She passed inside it to be greeted and given gin and tonic. She was aware of herself smiling prettily, shaking lots of hands, hailing Hillary Willoughby with never a tremor. But it was another woman, of course, who was doing all this, or a preprogrammed robot, perhaps.

Later there was the noisy swirl of lunch, then she was in the midst of the summer cloud of the afternoon. And she acquitted herself well, so far as she could judge, looking charming in a big-brimmed straw hat with streamers and roses.

There was only one moment when she faltered. It was when she was making her speech to the assembled company on the west lawn. Raising her eyes, she saw Goff framed in the rose archway opposite, his body curved in negligent elegance, his shirt open at the throat. Momentarily he was more dazzling than Lucifer.

She paused in a moment when a pleasing little breeze came like a breath from nowhere and played tentatively with the streamers on her hat. As she recovered herself and continued to speak, she was aware of some powerful emotion moving in her that became diffused so that suddenly she felt a calm, matriarchal love for all those whom she addressed.

It was only after she had distributed the interminable awards and had sat down again to the cheers of the boys that she dared to direct her eyes to the rose archway. It was empty now.

At last the crowds rose, stretched, dispersed. Folding chairs were stacked, the caterers carried off the remains of the strawberry teas. Boys scurried excitedly toward parents to be taken home for half term. Soon only frail, forgetful Erskine Fawcett was left among the roses while his bees filled the air with humming. Agnes had a sudden longing to remain, too, to become no more than a shadow peaceably haunting the innocuous place.

Outside the gates the real world waited. She received the Headmaster's final effusions, was seen into a taxi together with a huge bouquet of roses, and was borne through the straggling suburbs of Andham New Town to the Cock in the old High Street.

When Agnes came into the room reserved for her she found it blessedly cooler than the evening outside. At once she bathed and changed into a flowery robe of chiffon.

Emerging from the bathroom she found that the roses, so full, so strongly scented as to seem almost unwholesome in their fecundity, had been placed in a bowl on the table.

Throughout the evening her spirits rose and fell by turns. She wondered whether Goff would come. She had to admit that she wanted him to find her desirable still, shallow though that was. She despised herself, yet still left a single lamp softly lighted so that he might find her in as becoming a setting as possible.

The clock of the parish church chimed the half-hour. She leaned out the window and smelled the honest wallflowers in a bed beneath. She had a sudden yearning to be down in the velvety half-dark rather than in her room where there was a hothouse artificiality about everything. But she was held there in a prison entirely of her own making. There was no way out for her.

It was about nine-forty when a soft knock came. She opened the door, and Goff entered without preliminaries.

"Not very late, I hope," he said, staring at her.

His face was bright with insolence and an elation that suggested he had been drinking. In a tight blue cotton shirt and tight jeans that flared below the knee, with his springing dark hair and fiery eyes, he had an almost hurtful glow that was totally male. It stabbed Agnes that she must do her best to douse the brightness of him.

"Would you like some wine?" she said. (Odd how even in extremity the rules of hospitality must be observed.) "The waiter left the ice bucket after dinner so it's probably cool still."

"Thanks, wine would be nice." (A ritual response of the same kind.) He lifted the bottle from the bucket. "Hock? Surely champagne would have been more appropriate after the triumphs of the day?"

"Champagne is for sharing. And as one gets older one finds less and less to celebrate." She handed him a glass. "I had such an odd sense there today of things the same and yet changed."

" 'Time present and time past both perhaps contained in time future?' " he misquoted.

His face glowed with pleasure like a small boy's at the expectation of approval.

"So you're into Eliot?" she found herself forced to respond.

(Really, she must not let herself become interested in this.)

"We did some for an exam," Goff said. "I must say I quite enjoyed the dryness after all the Victorian lushness—"

"—to which you were overexposed at puberty," Agnes said tartly.

"Oh, I don't knock the romantics," he said equably. "They had their contribution to make to my . . . my sentimental education."

"But you're done with it now, the sentimentality," she said.

"I rather think I may be." He moved away, glass in hand, to look out the window. "It's good you overlook the garden here. I'm surprised the Cock hasn't converted it to parking space."

Agnes sat down on a rather absurd little chaise longue covered in maroon velvet, and offered him a cigarette, which he declined.

"It's good that you don't," she said. "Still the great sportsman?"

"I suppose so. I'm bored with it. Only three weeks more and I'll be free."

"Modern History, Fitz said."

"At Oxford? Yes. My father's old college. I'd like to have done something different altogether, but I'm stuck in the groove. You've been in the States, haven't you?"

All this time he had been looking at the garden. Now he swung around and faced her.

"You left without saying goodbye," he accused her flatly.

Now we come to it, she thought, the muscles in her stomach knotting.

"I was in no mood to talk to you, Goff," she said. "If I had, I would have said some harsh things."

"And do you feel . . . mellowed now?" he asked mockingly.

"Time tempers one's initial response; life would be unbearable otherwise. The fact remains that you behaved badly. That hurts me still." She stubbed out her cigarette.

"Hurts you!" She knew by the dark flush that overspread his face that at last she was reaching him.

"After seeing what you did to Deborah—"

"Oh, Deborah," he said. "Is that what worries you?"

"Certainly it worries me, very much," she said stiffly.

He marched to the center of the room and stood there squarely, glowering at her.

"If it hadn't been me, it would have been someone else. That girl sits up and begs for it!"

"Perhaps. That's no reason why you should—"

"Isn't it?" he flashed. "I think it's a reason. Perhaps I'm expert at hurting people because I had a very good teacher, in my English mistress!"

The triumphant glow in his eyes told her she was meant to feel crushed. He hates me still, she thought, with a pang for the injustice of it. Karistides was right.

"I know how badly I acted," she said soberly. "I blame myself bitterly. Won't you sit down, Goff?"

She thought he would ignore her, but he flung himself awkwardly into a straight chair beside the table.

"What happened in those few days over Easter three years ago was madness," she said. "A spring panic in me. How could I have put you so at risk otherwise? No, don't interrupt. I escaped lightly, thanks to Karistides. I was able to end it then." She stared into the roses. "Do you think it didn't hurt, to cut myself off from you like that? No, don't answer. I must finish now, finish finally, and let you go. Your hating me for what I say must be part of my punishment.

"It didn't have to be like that with Deborah, Goff. What frightens me is that you may have used what was between us as a pretext for behaving badly. I know that you can be arrogant and stubborn—No Goff, don't pull the petals off the roses, it's destructive and quite futile. But I also know that you have great potential for good. With your brother today I had a sense of . . . of decency. That hurt, because I can recall how much like him you were at that age."

She stood up and moved away in her turn to stand by the window. "You're going to have influence in the world," she said. "I don't underestimate you. It pains me to think that I may have had a hand in making you less than you ought to be. Use your power to construct, not to destroy. I can't ask you to do it for me, of course not, but do it for your own sake . . ."

Her speech was a horrible parody of a teacher lecturing a recalcitrant pupil. Her voice had the odious reasonable note of the pedagogue. Goff's demeanor, as he sat slumped with bent head pulling petals from the roses, was exactly that of the lectured child, sullen and resentful.

"End of sermon?" he said when she had finished.

She nodded and going to the table lit another cigarette.

"You're right, of course," he said quietly. "I'm a bit of a bastard. Always have been. Karistides has decided to be a doctor, by the way. It must have been the looking after Deborah that clinched it. Maybe I did some good after all. It turns out he's to be the savior and I'm the destroyer. So much for you as a judge of character!"

He flung the shredded petals on the table in a shower and glowered up at her.

"You're about the most hypocritical person I ever met," he said. "And self-deluding! You never took me seriously ever, did you? I was never more than a kind of plaything. All the time, right from the start, you've pulled me to you and pushed me away by turns. You know I'll never be free of you. Yet still you blandly voice your platitudes! You call me cruel. You're crueler by far, because you refuse to recognize my feeling for you for what it is. God, how I've hated you, hated you, you bitch!"

Until the last words, he had spoken in a monotone. Now suddenly he flung himself head first toward the table with such force that the bowl of roses rattled. He covered his face with his arms.

"I *hate* you!" he gasped, thus muffled. "No. Of course I don't. Curse you! I love you! Damn you to hell! I've always loved you and I always will. And, oh God, it hurts!"

Agnes sprang to her feet, horrified, began to go to him, then stopped in the center of the room.

"Goff . . ."

"I thought it would get better," he said, his head still covered. "But it never does. I'll never be any use. I know that. Karistides has more caring in his little finger than I have in my whole body. But with Deborah it didn't happen the way you think. I didn't do it out of spite. I was lonely. The days were empty. She was my only link with you. When Karistides came and said she was pregnant, I admit I wanted nothing to do with it. My mouth felt so dry. The whole of me felt dry. It will always be like that. I'll never have any feeling again, and life goes on so long . . ." His shoulders shook.

Agnes took a swift step toward him and gathered him in her arms, seeking to stifle his sobs against her breast. A terrible, thundering, breath-stopping joy coursed through her.

"Hush," she said, holding him. "Don't cry, darling. Don't be so unhappy. There's no need. Baby, don't cry." She rocked him against her. "Of course I love you, always love you. You know that, don't you, Goff?"

She wrenched his head from her breast where she felt its heat through the chiffon and looked down at his flushed face, in which anguish now mingled with hope. His hair was damp and flattened against his forehead, and his cheeks were streaked with tears.

"Oh, Agnes," he said chokingly. "Don't send me away. Only let me stay with you and I'll be good. Give me the chance to show how good I can be." He pressed her fingers fervently to his lips. "Don't make me hurt any more," he pleaded, her fingers still to his mouth. "Sweet Agnes, don't make me have to be hard any more, when it hurts so much."

She took her hand away and stroked his damp hair.

"Agnes, I love you so," he said, his face as bright now as though the sun were shining from his eyes.

Gently, with a reassuring smile, she disengaged herself from his clinging fingers. She stepped toward the bed, her movements like those of some old dance, some pavane or saraband. Carefully she unfastened the many small buttons of the chiffon gown until finally it slithered from her shoulders, and she turned again to face him.

His eyes, staring at her from out of the lamplight, had a strange look. As he got up from the chair she thought he would fall on his knees, but he stood a little way from her.

"Agnes," he said, "I want to tell you that I love you forever, even without . . . this."

For a wild moment she thought she had been wrong from the start, that what he had wanted was for her to be what was no longer permitted, his lady, and he her gallant knight. Fleetingly she thought that she had owed it to him to be always his *princesse lointaine*. But the demands of modernity had forced them into other roles. That other, the medieval conception of courtly love, would impose too great a strain on her. Anyway, it was too late for that.

"Do you want it to be without . . . this?" she asked a little sadly, indicating her nakedness.

A look of anguish crossed his face as he shook his head.

"How could I?" He took a step toward her and took hold of her. "Oh God, Agnes, I need you! It's been so long. How it throbs! I think I'll choke with wanting you!"

Her image of a *princesse lointaine* and a perfect knight faded on the bed in the lamplight.

Hours later Agnes smoked and watched him sleep, marveling at the ease with which he had fallen into it, at the capacity men had for expending themselves that women could never quite match. Gently, taking him by the shoulder, she shook him awake.

Returning to consciousness, he stretched deliciously, as the cat Uncle would have done if prodded as he lay curled, sleeping in the sun.

"Darling, you must go soon," she said.

"What time is it?"

"A little after four. Better if you slip out before anyone's awake."

"Of course."

He yawned and sat up, pushing the hair from his eyes. The sheet falling below his waist revealed a young torso with the painful perfection of a Michelangelo sculpture.

"You're not sending me off for good, though, are you?" he asked, putting a hand on her shoulder. "Not now?"

"No."

He seized her hand and put it to his lips.

"I thought you would be too grand for me now you're a famous lady," he said.

"Too grand for you? Never that! Are you really allowed to be away from school this weekend?"

"Oh, yes." He yawned again. "Attendance is more or less a formality at this stage. I was supposed to be going home for the night."

"Then what will your parents—?"

"I don't answer to them for my movements these days," he said haughtily. "They know better than to pry."

"But you're going to be good. You promised," Agnes reminded him.

"Certainly, so long as no one stops me from having you."

"You'll try not to hurt them, Goff. I don't want your mother to be—"

"They needn't know for the moment, if you'd prefer not. But we have to make plans for the summer." He caressed her arm. "Would you like to go and stay with Karistides? He's been asking me to the island for months. It would be very quiet and we could—"

"What had you in mind, a foursome with his sister?" Agnes said, suddenly stiff. "No, thank you."

"It was just an idea," he said mildly. "What do you suggest, then?"

"We could go to Europe, I suppose," she said. "Simply take off and not stop until we feel like it. I need to do some work this summer but—"

"We'll do that," he said quickly. "We'll take my car. We must go soon." Things were easily solved for him. "How quickly can you get away?"

"There are things I'll have to do first, of course." She ran her fingers through her hair. "I suppose about a month."

"That fits. I'll be done with school forever by then. We won't come back till summer's over, maybe not even then . . ."

"We'll come back for you to be at Oxford in October," she said. "You have a commitment."

"This isn't going to be just another summer affair, Agnes," he said, gripping her wrist tightly and staring at her with an intensity that recalled his mother. "It's not something that's going to be over."

How young he is, she thought, how sure! Three months of me, day and night, and he'll feel differently.

"You'll be surprised how nice I can be," he said, "when you get to know me properly."

"Darling, I know how nice you are. But you must go. Telephone me tomorrow. I shall be back in my apartment by late afternoon. Look how light it is. It was never fully dark. A white night, not one to be wasted in sleeping. Will you get dressed now?"

"In a moment. I feel so remarkably randy! I have so much catching up to do. I want you a hundred times before I go." He took off her gown and nuzzled her breasts. "When I've had you a thousand times I shall only want you a thousand times more and go on wanting you until . . . until . . ."

This time when they were finished she did feel tired. After he had gone she smoothed the bed, stepped back into it and slept, beautifully, healingly, and alone, until well into the morning.

ᦠ TEN ᦡ

Out in the bay the blue of sun and sky was dizzying. The little boat rocked gently as the oars splashed and creaked, taking it farther away from the becalmed beach.

"It's blissful out here." Agnes let her hand drift in the water. "Your idea of renting a boat was inspired. It's the only way to avoid the crowds in weather like this."

She squinted over Goff's shoulder to where the buildings of the shore line were reduced to a romantic line of spires and towers. Even the few blocks of high-rise hotels and vacation apartments to the east of the town were glamorized by distance.

The decision to settle in this place had been a spontaneous one. As they had moved steadily through France at the end of July, Goff had intended to drive on through Spain and stay in some lonely, secret place in the south. But once over the border they had come to rest instead in Perez, an unpretentious resort a few dozen kilometers to the west.

Agnes had felt a strange affinity for the place from the first. It recalled to her the northern holiday towns of her youth, places designed for the pleasure of plain people. She felt her roots pulling at her here. It seemed delightful that what she felt was transmitted to Goff, and he had seemed satisfied to take an apartment on the top floor of a shabby old hotel on the promenade.

"If this weather holds," Agnes said now, shifting the cushion at her back, "the place will be packed by the weekend."

"The heat brings out the plebs like flies in August," Goff agreed, resting for a moment. "But it won't last, not on this coast. There'll be a storm sooner or later."

"A storm from over the mountains, rain from the high Pyrenees." Agnes looked beyond the beach toward where the hills lowered in green mystery. "How impressive they look! Think of all the lost little villages up there . . ."

"If you want to go up, you know we can," Goff said.

"I think I belong down here in vulgar, jostling Perez. I can work in mundane places, you know. Although without you, all of it would underscore my isolation."

She put out her hand, cool and damp from the water, and rested it on the heat of his forearm.

"I told you I'd be good for you," he said complacently, picking up the oars again. "I'm going to row around to the harbor. We can tie up there and go for a drink."

"It's three miles at least, darling, and you have to face coming back . . ."

"Nothing to it. Once I'm in the rhythm it becomes mechanical."

"Fitz likes rowing too, doesn't he?"

"He should. My father had us out on the lake at Marlwood before we could stand. And we row in Ireland every year."

"Do you miss Ireland, Goff? This must be the first summer of your life that you haven't been there."

"Childhood's end," he said with satisfaction. "My mother's family have gone there since time immemorial. My mother clings to it more desperately than ever now that Father has The Floozy."

"I feel so sorry for her. It must be horrible."

"She deserved to have Pa go off," Goff said implacably. "Oh, don't worry, there'll be no permanent split. In the end, if he doesn't drop The Floozy entirely, she'll become just another habit with him."

"You're very cynical."

"But Mother's so wet! She could have been someone in her own right. Like you."

"I didn't have three children, Goff."

"If you'd had five, you'd still have been an individual. She's been content always to paddle along in Pa's shadow."

"Most women do that. The other way, my way, is very hard. She must miss you, Goff. If you were my son, I'd want you in Ireland."

"She has Fitz. He's me with the bad bits left out. If I were there that's all they'd see, the bad bits. All the good in me belongs with you."

How fixed he is, Agnes thought. But it's only been a few weeks. In a year he'll see things quite differently. In ten years he'll be with someone else while I . . .

"Nearly there," Goff said, as the masts of the harbor came into view. "What's the betting we run into the Firmans or someone the moment we set foot on shore? Let's try and sneak up to the cafe before we're spotted."

Perez Harbor bore little relation to the resort of the same name. It was the remains of the original town, a picturesque cluster of houses scrambling down to a stone jetty that had been extended into a fashionable sailing marina.

When Agnes and Goff had first gone exploring there, they had struck up a conversation in a bar with an English stockbroker and his wife whose son turned out to have been in the same House at school as Goff, some years before. Agnes, not without a certain sinking of her spirits, had encouraged the acquaintance to develop into something more.

She did it for Goff. She had her work to absorb her during any time she did not spend with him, but he had nothing to do except loaf around until she was finished. He would have been furious if he had realized that this was why she encouraged the Firmans. She had to allow him to believe that she enjoyed their company and that of the other lively, wealthy sailing folk to whom she and Goff were subsequently introduced.

He managed to wedge the boat among the others that jostled near the quay. Even as he helped Agnes ashore, an English voice hailed them and they saw the peacock figure of Miranda Firman waving from the steps.

"Darlings!"

"What did I tell you, spotted first go!" Goff murmured.

Miranda, a handsome, florid blonde in her forties, was hastening down the narrow steps as fast as her high-heeled espadrilles would allow.

"You surely never came in that?" She indicated the row boat. "How eccentric!"

She embraced Agnes, engulfing her in the mingled scents of suntan oil and French perfume.

"I've been so bored. Monty went off with the Van Hechts. The young people are in San Sebastian . . ."

"We thought we'd have a drink at Pablo's before we go back," Agnes said.

"Lovely!" Miranda nodded agreeably.

She took Agnes by the arm, and Goff walked in their wake. He might have been with his mother and one of her friends. It was only when he and Agnes were alone together that they could be completely natural. It was a relief when half an hour later Anneliese and Serge, a much younger couple, joined them in the bar, cheerful from a shopping expedition.

"San Sebastian was lovely, but so hot!" Anneliese cried, the focus of all eyes from the moment she entered the cafe. "Did you tell me once, Agnes, that people went there to be cool?"

She was a small, sinuous girl with black hair cut as short as a boy's and a face that shone with vitality. She and her boyfriend, a very solid Teuton, had rented a houseboat in the harbor for the summer.

"The Spanish court went there every year," Agnes said. "Don't worry, though, this heat won't last."

"Goff brought Agnes over in a rowboat," Miranda remarked.

"Remarkable!" Anneliese opened her eyes very wide. "But you have the muscles for it, Goff. Sergey has them also. You are as big, Serge?" She reached over to prod each boy in turn on the upper arm. "I cannot tell. Agnes, what do you say? Squeeze them both!"

"There's very little in it, Anneliese."

"See how hard they have made themselves!" The German girl's eyes danced with mischief. "Yet I think perhaps Goff is the most powerful."

She gave an admiring giggle as she stared at him. From the start she had made no secret of the fact that she found him devastating. Yet now she tempered her interest by hooking her arms lightly about Serge's brawny neck.

"We must go," Goff said impressively. "We only took the boat out for a couple of hours, and we're way overdue."

"Perhaps you will find room in your boat for me, Goff?" Anneliese said, arms still round Serge. "I believe books I have ordered from the shop in Perez have come. You will take me with you?"

"There isn't room," he said flatly.

"But I am little." Anneliese pouted. "And if you wish I will row for you and Agnes so you can lie back and be a seraglio."

"There isn't room," he repeated, scowling, and Agnes had to promise that they would fetch the books from the shop and that Goff would bring them over to Anneliese next day.

They were not permitted to leave until Goff had agreed to make up a foursome with Monty Firman and two other men for tennis the next morning, and Agnes was persuaded to agree to their all having dinner together in the evening.

"Come on, Agnes," Goff called impatiently from the doorway.

"So much energy. How can you keep up with him?" Miranda murmured.

"Don't forget my books, Goff," Anneliese called. "And remember, one day you *will* take me in a boat!"

Goff, holding Agnes by the arm, did not reply. They heard Anneliese's laughter from inside the cafe as they walked away.

"You mustn't mind being teased, love," Agnes said. "You've never liked it, have you?"

"That female irritates me beyond belief."

"Which is exactly what she's trying to do. She's an attractive girl, though, don't you think so?"

"Not my type."

They had reached the steps, and he helped her into the boat.

"You react pretty strongly," she said. "I think you're attracted to her in spite of yourself."

"I tell you I find her totally trivial." Goff crashed the oars and pulled away from the quay.

"You can't expect to go through life and find every woman leaves you cold," Agnes persisted mildly.

"Every woman does not leave me cold . . . as you're very well aware," he flashed at her. "Females in a gaggle talk such rot, that's all."

"Then it will do you good to go out with Monty tomorrow. You know I'll be quite happy at the hotel."

"You're always happy, whether I'm there or not," he said coldly. "I wish I had your self-sufficiency."

"I'd hardly be in the position I am in if I were self-sufficient," she pointed out equably.

He grunted and rowed on in silence.

Agnes felt weary of it. She was not at her best this summer. America and her sudden celebrity had robbed her of her vitality. Years ago, when Goff loved her first, she supposed she had had a kind of exuberant prettiness, which was what he still saw in her, but she felt that she was long past her blossoming. She wanted to be safe and peaceful and to relax in preparation for the extensive work program that lay ahead of her in the autumn.

Once they were clear of the harbor, the blue of the water revived her, and she admired the bright colors in the west where the sun was poised above the sea in a streaky sky.

"It's fresher out here, Agnes," Goff said in a conciliatory tone.

"It's delicious." She smiled at him.

"You know we can go somewhere else if ever you want to."

His face had cleared, and he rowed easily. It was at times like this that she liked him best.

"I do feel restless sometimes," she admitted. "But if one can be generally content, as I am now, one oughtn't to hanker after the elusive something more."

"We have to have permanence, though," he said. "We have to think—"

"Let's talk about it later," she said quickly, turning her eyes as the town came into view to the Promenade dark with figures. "Will you go to the bookshop? I think I'll lie down before dinner."

Their little sitting room on the sixth floor of the hotel faced the sea, and it felt hot and stuffy. Agnes's manuscript lay on the table by the window. She gathered up some loose papers into a folder and glanced out over the sea, reddened now and with a few ripples on its surface far out.

Only a few feet away from the window was the belfry of a church. Up here the bell looked powerful, virile almost, very different from the way it seemed when viewed from below. Every morning at six its great rolling notes boomed into the room, seeming to shake the floor and furniture.

The bedroom was through a connecting door; it was cooler and overlooked the town square with colored lights in the trees and a bandstand at the far end. Beyond this plaza and the pressing buildings of the old quarter was a glimpse of the green lower slopes of the Pyrenees.

In the apartment it was never completely quiet; yet all the sounds, except that of the church bell, were experienced at one remove, muted by distance.

Agnes used the creaking shower, noticing as she did so how thin she had become, how her body and limbs had lost the roundness they had possessed in youth. Afterwards she lay down on the big mattress and covered herself with a sheet. She was lying thus when Goff came in, carrying the books he had collected for Anneliese.

"Do you want to sleep?" he asked, going over to the bed and staring down at her.

"I'm not really tired," she said. "It's good to lie flat, though. I have to go down at eight. There was a call, and they're ringing back then."

"Who will it be?" Goff asked. "Hardly anyone knows you're here."

"It might be Levy. He had to know, of course."

Goff sat down on the bed.

"He wouldn't ring in the evening, surely?" he said. He put out his hand and began to trace her nipples under the sheet. "I want you now," he suddenly said, without looking at her.

"Darling, at eight I must go down—"

"But it's only seven."

He started to scramble out of his clothes. His enthusiasm for sex was something Agnes was never able to match. As he pulled the sheet from her and she shifted her body to accommodate him, she found herself wondering if his desire had been quickened by the earlier conflict with Anneliese. But it was unfair to think it of him. It wasn't his fault that she was nearly twenty years his senior. It was nobody's fault.

When he slid out of her, he was aware that she was unsatisfied.

"It's too quick, always, always," he murmured discontentedly.

"Darling, I've told you it doesn't matter . . ."

She pressed her face into his neck, waiting for the thudding of his heart to stop.

"Anyway, it will be better tonight," he said, and his philosophical tone touched her. "It will go on much longer."

She showered again and put on a long skirt and an embroidered smock and wrapped her hair in a bandana to go down to the hotel lobby. Goff was still in bed when she returned, half an hour later, her face bright.

"It was Justin," she said excitedly. "Old Justin Lord! He's in Irun for the night, on his way to Grenada, but he'll come here tomorrow and stay over. It will be such fun to see him again."

"I don't know that fun is quite the word I'd use to describe it," Goff said. Her eyes were shining, and she looked younger suddenly. "I didn't know you'd told him you were coming here."

"I sent him a card, darling. He'd mentioned he'd be in Spain sometime, but I never thought we'd actually see him. Senor Ramos has managed to find him a room as a favor. He's a sweet man." Smiling, she powdered her nose. "I haven't seen Justin in more than two years."

"I can't see why you've stayed friendly with him," Goff said sourly, remembering the tea shop. "He's a dreadful old poof."

"Perhaps that's why. Friendships with men can be so complicated until a woman's too old for practically anything. I've known Justin so long. He's a kind of bridge between one life and another. You're not cross? You mustn't worry that he knows about us." She stroked Goff's forehead tenderly.

"I don't worry about *that*," he said. "His opinion is of no importance to me."

"Darling, don't be pompous!"

"I don't mean to be." He swung himself off the bed and stood in the center of the room. "If you want to see him so much, I'm glad he's coming."

"At least he'll dilute the harbor crowd," Agnes said. "He's so comfortingly unathletic! He can talk to me sedately while you're all off being frightfully sporty and energetic."

The next morning was fine, but the clouds over the mountains looked threatening. After Goff had gone off to play tennis, Agnes felt energetic despite the heat. For the first time in over a month she had plans that did not center around him exclusively. This morning she found it easy to work. She had the maid open all the doors and windows of the apartment so that a breeze stirred through it. The sounds of cars and people on the Promenade were pleasantly filtered by distance.

She wrote while she drank her coffee, and after the maid had gone it was very peaceful. A pigeon flew onto the sill and looked in on her boldly. It had come from the belfry where it lived in a colony of its own kind, and it took the crumbs of her breakfast roll that she put out on the sill.

When she sat down again, the bird didn't fly away. Instead it settled on the ledge with tucked-in claws and puffed-out breast. It reminded her of Uncle, long ago, fluffed to twice his normal size with folded paws, hour after long hour in the kitchen at Tringham Grange, while out in the garden Auntie and Gertrude in drowsy immobility mirrored his pose. To see the Spanish pigeon reminded Agnes of the way she had felt then, carefree and in charge of her destiny, creating Wolfram out of the whirling images of her mind.

At noon the bell tolled thunderously, and the pigeon flew away with a rustle and a whirr. She laid her work aside reluctantly and changed into a bright dress. As she applied makeup she wished she had more color in her face, wanting to look her best for her old friend.

She waited in the lobby until he arrived at twelve-thirty, brought from the nearest railway station in a taxi. As soon as he and his baggage had been deposited, Agnes flung herself on him and hugged him.

"Agnes at last! What bliss!" he cried. "Such a journey, my dear, the heat! Now let me see." He held her at arm's length. "*Très elegante!* No resemblance to the little mouse mistress! When first you came to Fins, I remember Angus Ross remarking there was nothing to be got out of you and making a mental note to prove him wrong. Now here you are, able to snap your fingers at the lot of us, a veritable *femme du monde!*"

"Justin, you talk nonsense!" Agnes laughed. "You must be exhausted. Long cool drinks at once. You can go to your room later."

As she led him to the bar, she noticed that there was a roll in his gait and the well-cut cream suit he was wearing did nothing to minimize his bulk. Yet he seemed altogether easier. He was one of those men better suited to middle age than to youth.

His manner was both more affected and more assured. He had long since given up prep school teaching, for which—like so many of those who practice it—he was ill-suited. He now worked with his brother in London as some kind of broker, but he was vague and airy about the exact nature of his business.

"But what on earth are you doing in this place?" he asked. "Such a crush as we came through the town! Not restful, not fashionable either."

"No, the harbor is the fashionable end. You'll see that later."

Sipping his drink he regarded her keenly.

"I take it you're not alone?"

"No. Goff Willoughby's with me."

Justin raised his eyebrows.

"Ah, Goff!" He set down his glass. "You always had a very special place for him. I suppose now he's rather devastating."

"Utterly. I love him, Justin."

"My dear, he always had his eyes on you. I can remember you dancing with him when he was about ten years old."

"Dancing? With Goff?"

"Yes. Around Christmastime. Well, there were precious few ways of keeping warm at Fins in those days. Willoughby barely came up to your shoulder. You had to show him how to put one hand on your shoulder and the other around your waist. It was a pretty sight, quite affecting. The other boys had to dance together. That was incongruous, but you and Willoughby were just right."

"I believe I do remember," Agnes said excitedly. "A Snowball!"

Justin raised his glass.

"I drink to you both, then and now," he said.

"It doesn't shock you?"

"Bless you no, not after Fins. The very air there used to ache with lust. It's gratifying to know that one liaison at least has been consummated."

In the dead hour of the siesta Justin went to his room and Agnes returned to the apartment. No wind blew. The Promenade was baking in the sun, the pigeons were statues stupefied with heat, the flag drooped on its pole, a dead thing.

Agnes flung herself on the bed and lay dozing, thinking of winter at St. Fenrins for fully two hours until Justin joined her.

"So this is the love nest!" he said, panting from the stairs and flopping into a chair. "You're happy here?"

"Very happy."

"It has simplicity. How long do you propose to stay here?"

"Until the beginning of October."

"And then?"

"I can't say, Justin. I mustn't think so far ahead. After Goff begins Oxford, I suppose it will be best if he goes his own way. None of this should have happened. It isn't really my style, you know."

"Of course it isn't. I've known you a long time. The boy, too, to a lesser extent. I wouldn't see either of you as living for kicks."

"But isn't that how it must seem? These people I'm taking you to meet . . . I see the curiosity in their eyes. To them it must—"

"It can't matter to you how it *seems*. I envy you your courage." He picked up a magazine and fanned himself. "I have less of that. For a long while, all the time I was at Fins for instance, I deprived myself of what I really wanted. And little good it did me! You know I'm on my way to Grenada to meet someone? He seems congenial. It might be what I'm looking for. I have a little place in Kensington. If we get on, he'll join me there. My other involvements have all ended unsatisfactorily. One has a sense of time running out." He sighed.

"Well, I hope it works out for you this time," Agnes said warmly. He sighed again.

"At this moment I don't care very much. Heavens, how exhausting it is, this searching for a mate. I've been through it all before . . ."

Agnes patted his hand sympathetically.

"Never mind," she said. "We'll take a holiday from our problems tonight. I feel like celebrating, and your coming gives me the excuse."

When the evening came they joined the others and drank iced champagne until they were dizzy, and afterwards ate in a dim little bodega noted for its seafood.

They were all as merry as if it were carnival. Anneliese wore a black dress with no back at all and great gold hoops in her ears that she shook as she flirted with all the men. Miranda was in chiffon in dizzying swirls of color. Agnes wore a muted silk dress high at the neck and was rather taken with the restrained, uncompetitive dowdiness of her own appearance.

She found Goff heartbreakingly handsome in a pale suit. His hair and the arrogant tilt of his head gave him a Spanish look. His amber eyes were pale now in his tanned face. Agnes noticed how often Anneliese's eyes turned toward him, but he stayed beside her, her tall cavalier, piloting her with his hand beneath her elbow and squeezing her arm meaningfully from time to time.

Agnes was happy. Over dinner she chatted more freely than usual, telling the party of the things of which Justin had reminded her.

"Were you a strict mistress to Goff, then?" Anneliese jingled her hoops wonderingly as she tossed aside the shells of her prawns. "Did you beat him?"

"No. I only taught him English. He never got into trouble anyway. He was good at everything."

"Not at English," Goff put in gruffly. "She had her pets, the ones who could write. I was never one of those."

"You were a dab hand at music," Justin remarked. "Did you keep that up?"

"I don't have much time. I'll take it up again one day, maybe." Goff kept his eyes on Agnes.

"What memories you all have!" Miranda marveled. "With my Danny it's the same. His schools—prep and public—have meant so much to him, a thing apart where a woman can't enter. Yet you managed it, Agnes."

"My influence was negligible . . ."

"No," said Goff earnestly. "If you talk to boys who were in Fifth, even now, they won't have forgotten you."

"To be fixed in the minds of boys when they are men," Anneliese said. "That is the immortality I would like!"

After the meal they went to the plaza, where the band was playing. Anneliese seized Monty Firman and whirled him into the crowd. Serge squired Agnes more decorously. Goff gave his arm to Miranda, and Justin looked on. When the first sequence ended he took off his jacket and hung it on a bench and led Agnes back onto the dance floor. Anneliese and Goff followed close behind. The German girl's dancing attracted attention and admiration from the locals as she whirled around Goff like a black snake.

"That little sexpot has a yen for young Willoughby," Justin murmured in Agnes's ear. "Wasting her time."

"She's attractive," Agnes said. "How can he fail to respond?"

"Very easily, since he's clearly besotted with you!"

"That will pass. It must."

"Don't be too sure. He was always a stubborn little cuss. He had you marked down right from the start. He'll not let you go."

"I worry about him. This infatuation is cheating him of what he ought to have."

"What a conventional outlook! I'd have believed you possessed more originality than that."

"Surely the greater part of our lives is convention? It's what enables us to survive."

"So Goff is going to be cheated of what he wants most?"

"Only a small part of what he wants. And just for a little time."

"I think you're being crueler to him than you know," Justin said seriously. "You're refusing to acknowledge his possible commitment to something deeper. You'll hurt him, Agnes."

"Me hurt him?" As the dance ended, Agnes parted from Justin and looked at him in amazement. "Oh, how little you know!"

While they sipped iced drinks at a sidewalk cafe, the moon went behind a cloud and the only lights were the colored ones in the trees and in the shops. Thunder rumbled in the Pyrenees. The band played softly.

"This music is for couples," Justin said, standing up. "I shall take myself off to the Caballeros!"

Anneliese and Serge followed Agnes and Goff onto the dance floor. The two pairs moved languorously. Agnes could feel the whole hard length of Goff against her. Miranda and Monty Firman were dancing easily, in the manner of people between whom there is no mystery. Justin, returning, stood watching, a fair, portly Englishman with a smile on his face.

To Agnes, dizzy with wine and music, the night took on a dream-like quality. Lost in the swirl of the dance, she felt it must go on forever. She flung back her head and looked into Goff's face. He smiled at her, puzzled by the excitement in her eyes, and tightened his grip on her possessively.

Later, at the cafe table, the faces swam a little. Goff, upright and austere, was so young that suddenly she felt a stab of joy at having him, at the knowledge that at the last they would climb the stairs to the apartment together. She felt sorry for the others at the tables around, banal in their conventionality and security. At least, she thought, I have lived as I wanted to live.

"'Drink life to the lees,'" she declaimed, draining her glass of the Sangria she was now drinking. "'Enjoy greatly, suffer greatly.' Isn't that better than living a drab half-life?"

"Every time, Agnes," Justin agreed hazily.

". . . to see some Flamenco," Monty was saying.

"Oh, too commercialized," Miranda dismissed the idea.

"But real Spanish gypsies." Anneliese shook her earrings like a gypsy herself. "Those I should like to see."

"'What makes you leave your new-wedded lord, to follow the raggle taggle gypsies O?'" sang Justin in his clear baritone.

He was very drunk. They were all very drunk. I left my husband, too, Agnes thought exultantly. And she remembered another song.

"'He is no gypsy my father she said but lord of free lands all over' . . ."

"That is pretty, it has a lilt to it," Anneliese said.

"Irish," Agnes explained. "Sing it for them, Goff."

Alarmed, he shook his head. He had a pleasing light tenor voice, and it was only now that she realized how seldom she heard it.

"It's one of my favorite songs," she told everyone solemnly. "The greenwoods in spring when all the world was young. Goff knows what I mean. Do you remember the song from the Auvergne, Goff? How sad it was! I was sad then. Now I'm happy. Sing the Gypsy Rover, Goff. Sing it for me."

All at once it was important to her that he should—that they should—forget the others, the cafe and the street. With her eyes she told him so.

After a moment's hesitation, he conquered his embarrassment, cleared his throat, and began. He sang the verses, and Justin and Agnes joined him in the sprightly chorus.

"'And he won the heart of a lady,'" everyone hummed at the last.

As they finished, people at the nearby tables applauded. Justin made them a bow, but Goff collapsed darkly into his chair.

"You're wild tonight," he said to Agnes quietly, as the rest stood up to dance again.

"Don't you like me wild?"

How young she was tonight! She grasped Justin by the arm to include him in her happiness.

"I like you anyway, as you know," Goff said.

Then they were dancing again under the darkness of the clouded sky, dancing forever toward morning, and the thunder in the mountains was no more than the muttering of sleeping giants.

✌ ELEVEN ⸏

The following day the revelers paid for their pleasure. When they awoke the light beyond the window was gray. The softly falling rain muted even the great bell to a funeral tolling. Their heads felt heavy, and their mouths were dry.

"I'm a hundred-year-old wreck," Agnes said ruefully, wrapping herself in the sheets. "I wonder, was it worth it?"

She had no inclination to write today. Downstairs after breakfast, Justin, gray-suited to match the morning, kissed her good-bye. As she clung to him, his soft cheek smelled of cologne.

"You'll leave the rain in the mountains with us," she promised. "As the train takes you south the sky will clear, and the landscape will be golden as you ride through it. I'll be thinking of you as you wake tomorrow in faraway Grenada."

She watched him drive away with a forlorn expression.

"He's a fearful old fag," Goff said, as she stood bareheaded in the rain, waving. "Next time we see him he'll probably have some gilded little twat in tow."

"What of that? I'd prefer it to his remaining alone and sad forever."

"Absolutely. But he won't be satisfied. Poofs never are. Even when they get what they think they want, it brings them precious little satisfaction."

"They're no different from the rest of us in that."

"Aren't they? I'll get what I want. I have so far, haven't I?"

His tone was positive. Agnes felt that they were not close today.

"Perhaps you have," she answered. "But how long will it be before you want something else?"

She turned and walked off, but he came after her and caught her arm and talked to her determinedly and brightly of trivial things.

When they ventured out at noon, they were passed by Serge's red Volkswagen being driven by Anneliese. In a raincoat of shiny scarlet vinyl, she was a vivid streak against the drab morning. Her face was alive with anticipation and zest. Her eyes were fixed on a small traffic jam ahead, and she didn't notice them.

They walked along the beach, with the wet wind battering their faces. A mongrel dog persuaded them with excited yaps to hurl pieces of driftwood into the murky water.

"Fetch, boy!" Goff called as the animal scattered pebbles and sand, attacking the sodden wood with spurious ferocity.

"He's a Spanish dog," Agnes said. "He doesn't speak English."

"Animals don't have language barriers."

"I remember once you brought a dog to Tringham. Do you miss her?"

"Miss Flock? Not really. I'm away too much for that."

As he spoke, Goff was aware of a letter from his mother, folded in the pocket of his parka. In Ireland, of course, it was raining. His father had gone back to London in a filthy temper. She was very depressed. It would help if Goff came, even for a few days . . .

"Fetch! Good boy!" he called to the capering dog.

"I wish my Kashtenka were here now," Agnes said, but softly so that he didn't catch the words. She wandered off along the strand, lost in melancholy thoughts of her own.

After lunch she stayed in the sitting room, and Goff went over to the harbor to work with Monty Firman on his boat. The mechanical marine tasks soothed him, and he returned to the hotel drenched but in a better frame of mind.

In the evening they stayed upstairs for dinner. Agnes changed into one of her long robes and brushed her hair severely behind her ears. Throughout the meal conversation was sporadic, though cordial enough. While Goff was pouring coffee, she went out to the bathroom.

He glanced through Monday's edition of an English paper Justin had left behind. It had been raining there, too, and a strike was threatened by maintenance men at Heathrow. On the arts page, there was mention of an important exhibition soon to open at the Willoughby Gallery. So his father had had a valid reason for going back to London early, Goff thought sourly. He threw down the paper and drank off his coffee like medicine.

It was very quiet in the apartment. He could hear the rain on the roof and on the windows. Agnes had been gone a long time. The water had stopped running. After a while he went to the bathroom door and, finding it ajar, knocked and pushed it open.

She was standing on the white-tiled floor holding a towel in front of her. There were splashes of scarlet on the tiles.

"Are you all right, Agnes?" Goff said, not understanding.

"I think so," she said with a note of hesitation.

He now saw that she was holding the towel pressed between her legs.

"Is it your period?" he asked, knowing little about such things.

"It must be. It's due, anyway." Again there was doubt in her voice.

"Do you always . . . bleed so much?"

"No. Goff, will you fetch the bath towel? I left it in the bedroom."

When he came back with it, she pulled the one she was holding away and replaced it quickly, but not before some of the bright blood had spurted from between her legs and splashed on the floor.

She threw the soaked towel into the bath. As it fanned out, the blood, diluted to a soft pink, swirled around in the water like the petals of some exotic flower.

Goff remembered Karistides's lovingly detailed description of Deborah's cut wrists. He'd shut him up. "You can spare me the gore Andy," he'd said. "I don't want to know."

Now he wasn't to be spared. Not this.

"I don't think it's going to stop by itself," Agnes said, in a matter-of-fact voice.

"I'll get them to send for the doctor." He still stood in the doorway.

"That would only waste time. I'd better go straight to a hospital. Will you find out where there is one?"

"Of course. I'll take you there at once."

Now that there was something to do, he could move fast. He had some idea that if he didn't hurry there would be no blood left in her.

Senor Ramos was sympathetic, gave directions, and arranged for the porter to bring the car to the side entrance at once.

"The hospital sign is posted on the hill to the west." His brown eyes were full of kindly concern. "I telephone that you come."

Once in the car with the long skirt hiding the towel pressed between her legs, Agnes looked quite normal. No one passing in the rain would have known.

"Does it hurt?" Goff asked fearfully, driving with care.

She shook her head.

"Has it ever happened before?"

"Something similar, but never on this scale."

"It shouldn't, should it? Why has it?"

"Something's not quite right," she said vaguely. "I've known for years about it."

"When did they first tell you that?"

"Oh, ages ago. When the first baby died. My guts were in a mess, even then. That's why I had a miscarriage when I was at the Grange . . . you wouldn't know about that. They decided not to do anything drastic at the time, just to keep the matter under observation."

"You never told me."

Thank God, the sign for the hospital! Not long now.

"Women's complaints are so dreary, love. I shall have to get it seen to soon, of course. I've been so busy . . ." She shifted slightly. "I never went out without panties before!" she said brightly. "My poor mother would turn in her grave! Will you wipe the blood off the floor, Goff?"

"Yes."

"I don't like to think of its being there all night. I'm sorry—"

"Don't be bloody stupid. Of course I'll mop it up."

They swung into the gates of the hospital. He carried her inside. It was run by nuns in long habits that swished. Goff hated the initial incomprehension in their eyes, but they soon found someone who understood and took Agnes away.

She had been light when he'd lifted her. He hadn't realized she was as light as that. She'd never told him about her insides. He thought of all the times he had made love to her, brutally, and all the time there had been something wrong . . . But it didn't hurt, she'd said that. And it had been with her husband that things had first gone wrong, at the time of the baby that died, years ago . . .

The sister at the desk smiled sweetly at him. They had nuns in Ireland, too, and priests to pray for dead souls . . .

At last they said he could see her. His heart thudded wildly as he was led along rubber-floored corridors smelling of antiseptic.

It was a little room, a bare cell with a cross on the wall. She lay on a high, white bed. They had taken her bright gown and replaced it with a white one.

She smiled at him and squeezed his hand.

"All right now. All plugged up," she said.

"But will you be—?"

"They want to keep me for the night, but I can go in the morning. Will you come for me?"

"Of course."

"I hate it," she pressed his hand, "for you to be involved in something so—"

"Silly!"

"Oh, my poor darling Goff!"

"You must try to sleep now. In the morning I'll come for you."

"Better telephone first, to be sure they're finished with me. And bring something for me to wear."

"I'll see to it all."

"You'd better go now. Sleep well, darling."

She leaned back on the pillows and closed her eyes.

He slipped out without speaking to anyone. It had stopped raining, but the bushes on either side of the road gleamed wetly as he drove.

At the hotel he reassured Senor Ramos, thanked him warmly, and went slowly up to the apartment.

The blood in the bathroom had dried to a dull rust color. Only as he swabbed at the tile did it momentarily come alive again.

The maid had turned down the bed and left Agnes's nightdress, smelling of her perfume, on her side. Goff slept fitfully and woke as the last notes of the morning bell died away.

The day beyond the window was cool and overcast. Immediately after breakfast, Senor Ramos telephoned the hospital for Goff. While the Spaniard chattered incomprehensibly, fear nagged at him.

A sleepy black-haired woman in slippers swept the lobby and emptied last night's ashtrays. The swinging doors had been flung back to let in the salty gray morning.

Senor Ramos replaced the receiver smilingly and turned to Goff. "Is all right. The Senora may come home. You will collect her noon, twelve o'clock."

At half past ten Serge called to invite them to dinner, learned what had happened, expressed stolid sympathy, and went away again. When Goff returned to the apartment the bloodstained articles were gone, fresh towels were set out on the rail, and the tile had been washed again. Everything was white once more.

In the bedroom he searched for clothes and thrust them into an overnight bag. Though it was only a quarter past eleven, he drove up to the hospital and parked on the hill overlooking the town. By daylight he could see the gloomy gray building with its arched gateway through which old-fashioned ambulances intermittently rattled.

At twelve he went in, handed over Agnes's clothes, and waited as starched sisters and white-coated doctors passed to and fro. An old man was wheeled by on a stretcher, eyes unseeing.

Goff had a healthy person's distaste for hospitals. It was inexplicable that Karistides should want to study medicine, yet somehow typical of the fellow, morbid always, fascinated by sickness, decay, and death.

At last he saw Agnes coming slowly down the long corridor, dressed in the clothes he had brought, carrying the bag in which they had come. His heart lurched as he went to her and took the bag from her unresisting hand.

She was very pale. Her face and hair and eyes were all one noncolor, and the dress he had brought, beige and sleeveless, further contributed to the bloodless effect.

They walked quickly away. The clouds seemed to be clearing a little. Agnes took the air in gulps.

"It's good to be out. It was so warm in my room. The nuns were very sweet. It was like being in retreat. There was nothing to look at except a Bible in Spanish. I was searching in it for the story of Rahab. The Old Testament books are really gutsy!"

"Are you all right? What did they say?" Goff asked when he had settled her in the passenger seat of the car.

"Nothing very specific. I have to get it fixed soon."

"It made me feel so helpless."

"Poor Goff, horrid for you! It's nice up here, isn't it? Can you drive slowly? I feel as if I've been incarcerated for ages. I understand how Lazarus must have felt."

"We'll go back to England at once. We'll leave tomorrow. You must see the very best people."

"My love, I have before, lots of them. I'm all right for the moment."

"It's happened once. It will again," he said grimly.

"Oh, I'll get it fixed before it does. We were supposed to be staying here for another three weeks at least. I don't want to go yet . . . Let us stay, please."

"We can stay if you're sure it will be all right," he said severely. "But you mustn't be careless with yourself."

"I'm supposed to take things easy for a couple of days, that's all. Sex is out for the moment, of course. Beastly!" She wound the window down. "The wind in my face feels so good!"

At the hotel Senor Ramos greeted them with rapturous concern, promising to send up a light lunch of halibut and fruit. They found on reaching the apartment that he had had a bowl of roses placed there.

"Beautiful!" Agnes pressed her white face into the riot of colors. "What a comfort, when one is ill in a strange place, to have people around one who are simple and warmhearted!"

I wasn't much comfort, Goff thought. He felt an irritation, guilty and irrational, stir in him.

He couldn't have borne to see Deborah when . . . Blood, always blood . . . From the fetus first, later from the wrists . . . People like Karistides apparently existed to take care of such things. He'd always been helpful if anyone was injured, even in matches at school . . . Karistides would sit with the dying in times to come, no doubt about it . . . If they had gone to the island, as Karistides had wished, how much simpler all this would have been for Goff . . .

He kept his back to Agnes, jingled pesetas in his pocket, and wished himself far away, playing in a match at school amid that exclusively masculine roar when a goal was scored; wished he were in Ireland, fishing with his father and uncle, something hard and cold and physical, no need to think, no need to have anything to do with flowers and pale women.

Anneliese came after lunch, cutting into the pallid quiet of their afternoon. She flung off her scarlet raincoat to reveal a very short scarlet skirt and a brief white top molded against her small, round breasts. She brought pale yellow carnations, and Agnes exclaimed over them, sniffing at the cloying artificiality of the petals.

Anneliese was offered a peach. She bit into it without removing the skin. When the golden juice ran down her chin, she caught it on her fingers and sucked it up.

Goff left them talking. The shops were closed for the siesta, and the beach was deserted. The rain fell intermittently, and the sky over the Pyrenees was black still. He walked aimlessly in the wind.

When he returned to the hotel, he asked that a call be put through to his mother and went into the lobby to wait. People passed in wet clothes, smelling of damp. It was raining again, lightly but steadily.

He told his mother, when the connection was made, that he could not come. She was unable to comprehend. What could an eighteen-year-old boy have to do, her tone implied, that could prevent him, apart from the purely selfish priority of his own pleasure?

"Things are difficult here." In the past couple of years her voice had developed a whining note. "Your father had to go back about the exhibition. The Reynoldses are here, and the Pages arrive on Friday. It would be such a help if you—"

"I'm sorry, it's out of the question," her son said, another man letting her down. He wanted to tell her he was with Agnes Stratton, but it wasn't something he could inflict on her even as a kind of revenge.

"Is Andrew there with you?" she said. "Will you be going on to Greece?"

For a moment he failed to understand, then recollected that he had once told her he and Karistides would drive through Spain together.

"I suppose I shall simply have to cope," she said, when she realized it was hopeless. "Fitz is very good. Have fun then, my dear. See you in October."

As he replaced the receiver, it came to him that she was not the only woman he would betray.

Back in the apartment the air was smoky. He became involved in a tedious argument about dinner with Anneliese and the Firmans. Serge, it seemed, had suddenly gone off to Madrid. Agnes insisted that Goff go out, pleading that she preferred to be on her own, and Anneliese finally departed with it settled that she would pick up Goff at six.

It was still raining when the red Volkswagen arrived in front of the hotel.

"I thought we might drive fast along the coast road," Anneliese said when he got in beside her. "I am so very bored, and we do not have to meet the Firmans until eight-thirty."

"Drive as fast as you like," Goff said. "What's Serge doing in Madrid?"

"There is business there that he promised he would do for his father if it was possible. It was the rain that decided him to go today." She gave him a mischievous glance. "And so now I have the chance to pretend there is no Serge. And no Agnes. Only you and me. It will be fun to see how you are when no one else is there."

The road curved high on a bend, and the drivers of lorries going in the opposite direction shouted and whistled at her. She laughed and waved back at them.

"Always you are so stiff, Goff," she said. "You must try to relax. Just one time, for me."

She was thoroughly spoiled and ought to be spanked, Goff decided. Yet, in spite of himself, he was conscious that it gave him a sense of lightness and freedom to be speeding away from Perez with her. By the time they drove back to the harbor, his mood was almost cheerful.

They strolled companionably, arm-in-arm, along the narrow main street, and paused before the window of an antique shop.

"What do you think of that paperweight?" he asked.

"It is a child's thing. When you shake it, a storm of snow covers the little house."

"Agnes might like it. I'll buy it for her."

"Does Agnes have a husband?" Anneliese asked when they emerged from the shop.

"She had, still has technically, I suppose." Goff frowned. "They haven't lived together for years."

"When first I met you both, to be honest I could not see how it was suitable for you to be with her. You are so active where she is not. But today when I talked with her alone I could see that she is a nice woman . . . and in a strange way interesting."

"She's always interested me," Goff said. "By comparison, I find other women rather a bore."

"You are so old! You have known so many!"

"Enough."

"You are very handsome." She pressed his arm. "You could have any girl you wanted, just by reaching out. Yet that is too easy, so you must reach out to a woman the age of your mother, yes?"

"Not quite. And I don't see Agnes nor myself as being any age in particular. I've known her too long."

"She must love you very much."

"No more than I love her," he said defensively.

"And how is poor Agnes?" Miranda asked when they joined the Firmans in the restaurant. "So unpleasant to be unwell in a foreign country. Tomorrow I'll look in on her. I thought it better today to let her rest. I was surprised you didn't go to Madrid with Serge, Anneliese."

"The interior would be too hot." The girl lit a cigarette unconcernedly. "Besides, I should miss what is happening here."

Goff enjoyed the evening more than he had expected. After the meal they moved on to a smoky basement disco, where Anneliese inveigled Monty onto the dance floor.

"Lord, what fools men make of themselves at his age," Miranda remarked, dispassionately watching her husband's capering. "That girl is a real firecracker." Her expression changed. "I'm sorry about Agnes," she said abruptly. "Is it serious?"

"I don't think so," he answered, not knowing himself.

"There are times when she looks very drawn."

"She works too hard, that's all," Goff said.

He was following Anneliese's provocative progress, aware of the admiration in the eyes of other men. He wanted to dance with her, too, but was not yet drunk enough to allow her to make a fool of him as she was doing with Monty. Deliberately he emptied his glass and called for more wine.

Later, when the music was slower, he did ask her to dance. He found that with her he was able to immerse himself totally in the present. In contrast with his relationship with Agnes, where everything was mysterious and insubstantial, rooted in a veiled past, he found the new, harder idiom of this place and this music and the immediacy of this girl exhilarating.

After Miranda and Monty had disappeared, they sat on at the smoky table. When he lighted her cigarette their hands brushed, and the electric current stung him. He felt heady with his own power.

Later they went to the car, and she drove fast to an empty inlet over the water. As soon as she stopped he grabbed her, kissing her savagely to undo the hard knot of his desire and only succeeding in tightening it.

When all you felt was physical, how easy, straightforward . . . Anneliese wouldn't make any trouble afterwards . . . Silly little Deborah, how could she have thought it meant anything . . .

But the girl Karistides had fixed him up with. That had been different. Very pretty, knew every trick. And yet afterwards there'd been nothing. No better than Deborah. Ashes . . . Right down . . .

In half an hour it was going to be the same thing exactly here, all over again. All at once he couldn't face it.

Scowling, he pulled away from Anneliese, murmuring about its being late, about having to get back. He knew he must look every kind of fool. It increased his resentment. He despised himself, her, everything.

But he had to admit that she accepted his withdrawal with surprising good humor.

"I will take you straight back to your Agnes," she said, and there was only a trace of mockery in her smile.

"Thanks," he said, when she drew up at the hotel. "For the lift and for a very nice evening."

"We might all have supper together tomorrow evening, when Serge gets back," she said, seeming quite unconcerned. "If Agnes feels up to it. Sleep well, Goff. 'Wiedersehn."

He stood on the sidewalk and watched the red car disappear. His mouth still stung from the roughness of their kisses, and he had not lost his erection. I feel horny, he thought, and Agnes is no good. He had been a fool to let Anneliese go . . .

The town was quiet now. He played with the idea of going off into the narrow streets, of seeking out some anonymous woman, but he really had no idea where to begin to look.

Shaking his heavy head, he entered the hotel. Only a single light burned in the lobby, and the porter was fast asleep in his little hutch.

As he let himself into the apartment Goff felt a shamefaced irritation, removing his shoes and tiptoeing into the bedroom with fleeting mental visions of a seaside postcard drunk. How utterly and totally sordid life was!

She'd fallen asleep with the lamp on. Goff sat down gingerly on the bed and stared at her. The book she had been reading lay, still open, on the bedspread. *Le Rouge et le Noir.* He was unfamiliar with it except for its title.

How pale Agnes was, how softly she slept, her breath scarcely stirring the sheet! Once her hair had been long, and if she had lain as she did now she would have looked like Millais's drowned Ophelia. So pale, so still. She might be dead already.

As he looked at her, a great fear came over Goff. In the country of sleep she was ineffably far away. He was entirely alone. He no longer really cared for his family, his friends, or his way of life. Perhaps he had never done so. Agnes was the only person he had never despised.

He suddenly saw, with total clarity, that she was the only being who stood between him and nullity. The knowledge made him afraid.

All his earlier sexual excitement drained out of him. The intensity of his emotion turned him cold. He took hold of Agnes's hand, and that was cold, too. She had left him. He experienced an indescribable terror. Nothing had ever seemed so far away as her sleeping face.

In his panic he squeezed her fingers hard.

The instant she opened her eyes, her face flickered back into life. She blinked, saw him, and smiled.

"Goff." She sat up. Her hair was flattened against her head. "What time is it?"

She was completely alive. The color returned to her face, her hand was warm. He was cut off no longer. He was saved.

"Were you dreaming?" he said, remembering how far away she had been. Puzzled, she shook her head. Relief was flooding through him, liquid and warm. "Once you had long hair," he said irrationally. "I wish you'd never had it cut."

"I can always let it grow again." She smiled and put out her hand to him. "Kiss me. Mmm. You taste of wine. It's good. I've slept so long I feel healed. What time is it? Four o'clock? Almost morning. Did you have a lovely dinner?"

"Nothing special," he said.

When he had undressed and lain down beside her, he took hold of her carefully. His heart was thudding and he felt shaky, as if he had passed through a great ordeal. She was warm against him, and soft.

"I was so tired," she murmured and sighed and fell asleep immediately.

It was mid-morning before Agnes woke again. Goff hadn't moved. His arm was stiff beneath her. She had not gone, would not go away from him, not now.

"Shall you go out today?" he asked her as they sipped coffee.

"Of course. I haven't been ill. Healthy people make up any blood they lose very quickly, don't they?"

"I think so. I'd have to ask Karistides." He remembered suddenly and fished the paperweight from his jacket pocket. "I got you this," he said.

"It's beautiful." Agnes shook it and stared at it intently. "I always

longed for one when I was a child. The glass is so clear it's like looking into a crystal and seeing the future—and the future being the
pretty little house. Such a quiet thing! I shall use it to hold down my
papers when I'm writing and shake it whenever I take a break."

She peered into it with the solemn fascination of a child.

The weather had cleared. At noon they drove away from the sea
into the hills, left the car and wandered in the sun. They saw no one,
only in the distance a whole herd of yellow-eyed Capricornas bleat-
ing softly as they grazed on scrub and thorn.

It's always best when we're completely by ourselves, Goff thought;
other people spoil everything. He could not stop himself from glancing continually at Agnes, nor rid himself of the fancy that she was
back from the dead.

"It's peaceful here," she said contentedly. "I'd like to lie forever
with the sun in my face."

"Agnes, what are we going to do after this?" Goff rolled over onto
his stomach and plucked at a blade of grass. "After Spain, I mean."

"I wish there was no 'after Spain,'" she said. "October seemed far
away when we came here. I didn't need to think of it. But the future
comes nearer all the time, inexorably closer, until we're dead."

"What will we do, Agnes?"

"You're going to Oxford. You'll like it there. I shall need to be in
London for a while. There's a television adaptation. And there's this
latest book to finish. I'm so tired of goats and sheep!"

"But what about us?"

"I don't know." She smiled at him sadly. "I don't know about us."

"You must decide." He rolled over to face her and sat up. "We
have to make plans."

When she still shrugged vaguely, he took her firmly by the wrist.

"Listen," he said, staring into her face. "I want something
definite. You're so indecisive always. Don't start any rot about what's
best for me. You know perfectly well what that is. And don't tell me
that I'm going to outgrow you. You've been saying it for years, and
it's bloody insulting. I deserve to be taken seriously."

"Yes, of course," she said. "I do take you seriously, Goff."

"Then what do you want to do?"

"Oh, all sorts of things." She sat up also, resting her hands on her
knees. "You know I was in the West Indies last winter? I'm thinking
of buying a place there. St. Kitts. It isn't that I want to avoid taxes

or anything, I simply like the idea of an island. I believe I could work there. Write something altogether different."

"I should like to come with you," he said at once.

"Darling, how can you know? You've never even been there. A small island is no place for a young man."

"We could go there together, couldn't we? We could go at Christmas. Why not?"

"Goff, I'd love to go there with you. But Christmas is for families. You've always—"

"I'm on my own now." He brushed grass from his shirt. "I shall go with you to your island, and we'll live there forever."

"Try to be practical. First you must get your degree. I insist on that. You have to have something."

"Very well. Three years. But I'll fly out every holiday. And you can easily fix it so that you come to London during term time. We need never be apart for more than a couple of months at a stretch."

"But you must work . . ."

"Oh, I'll work. You know I can do anything when I really want to. I'll bring my books in the summer so you can make sure I do it, since you're so keen on my education! Three years, that's no time at all."

"But afterwards, Goff . . ."

"I'd like to open a gallery," he said. Agnes looked at him in surprise. "Out there. Ethnic stuff. The Americans come, don't they?"

"Increasingly. But things are all rather makeshift, you know. It's hardly Bond Street-on-the-Sea."

"I know that. A place like my father's is the last thing I had in mind. No, I'd like to try my hand at new stuff. It would interest me."

"There'd be competition . . ."

"I hope so. I need to compete. I might travel around, make contacts, build something up from scratch. What do you think?"

"It sounds feasible," she conceded, not wanting to hurt him, wishing things could be that straightforward. But perhaps for him they would be.

"You could help a lot," he said. "You're sympathetic. People respond to you, young people especially. And you'd recognize talent if it was there."

"It's an interesting idea," she said. "It could do some good."

"I'd like to do something for somebody," Goff said. "I have to get away from what I am. I know that. If I follow my father I'm going to end up pretty objectionable." Frowning, he looked away up the hill toward the peaceful goats. "I do know myself. I'm not particularly nice, Agnes."

"That's not true. You have a great many good qualities."

"They count for nothing when the bad ones are stronger. I prefer your point of view to mine. I can only benefit from prolonged exposure to you." He laughed and caught her hand. "We'll live on our island and you shall be Circe, except that you'll make men of pigs!"

His face was bright, like that of a small boy. So young, she thought, to seek to shackle himself to me. How long . . .

"There's absolutely no problem about money," he was saying confidently. "At twenty-one I come into my share of Grandpa Holder's estate. It's in trust, so they can't stop me from having it. I've already enough to tide me over till then, courtesy of Lady Holder, my mad grandmother."

"Do you remember her?" Agnes asked, willing as ever to be sidetracked. "What was she like?"

"Sprightly. I was taken there as a kid. She insisted on behaving as if everyone were an animal, or a bird or reptile. I had to be a puppy dog, which wasn't too embarrassing."

"Did she make the animals appropriate to the people's characters, like in *Volpone?*"

"More or less. She called Lucinda a cat. I thought that was rather good. Momma was only a sheep. My grandmother never actually *did* anything, so she was never sent away, only confined to the house and grounds. Lucinda and I thought it was all a bit of a laugh. We couldn't see why the grownups were so edgy. She *liked* animals, you see. You'd have got on well. She'd have thoroughly approved of Wolfram and Capricorna . . . Anyway, I shall be financially independent when I'm twenty-one. Then we'll get married."

"Married!" Agnes was startled.

"Of course. You can't expect me to live in sin for the rest of my life," he said coolly.

"You're the eldest son. You have to have children. I can't, Goff. Even if I'm not yet too old, I'll never have children."

"I don't want any. Let Fitz do that. He can have Marlwood and the galleries and the suitable wife and the children. Fitz won't let anyone down. And I shall be free!"

"Goff, when you're forty you're going to see all this differently."

"There's no guarantee of that. I certainly don't intend to wait to find out. But there is another matter that has to be settled." He looked severe and practical. "It's high time you divorced Harold. There isn't any point in letting that drag on." He took hold of her wrist firmly. "Isn't it about time," he said quietly, "that you proved to me that you're sincere?"

Agnes was shocked by the vulnerability she saw in the depths of his clear eyes. Do I have any real idea of him? she wondered. His grandmother saw him as a puppy. Haven't I done that, too? Has he ever been more than a pretty thing to me, a surrogate Kashtenka, a substitute for the baby I never dandled on my knee?

She was shaken to realize that he had a fixity of purpose of which she was incapable. Did I let it happen, all of this, she thought, because I was sure it couldn't last? How would I cope with a future in which it did?

Disturbed, she got to her feet and walked across the humpy grass to stare out over the hill, hands in the pockets of her full skirt, the wind tugging at her hair. The knowledge of the implacability of his will, the fixed strength of his purpose, made her feel cornered.

He came up behind her and took her by the shoulders to face once more his uncompromising stare.

"You do love me?" he said searchingly.

She turned in his arms, knowing he would never let her rest.

"You will prove it?" he persisted. "You'll make yourself free?"

Dumbly, she nodded.

He lifted her hand and slid the wedding ring from her finger. It came off easily because she was so much thinner than she had been. He held it up, the small circle of gold, so that through it she could see part of the green hillside. Before she could stop him, he tossed it toward a scree. Their eyes followed the arc it made with the sun glancing off it until in falling it was hidden from them.

Poor Harold, Agnes thought, to be so easily dispensed with!

"That was quite a gesture, Goff," she said. "You realize it was the only wedding ring I had?"

"You'll have another one day," he said easily. "One that you'll keep forever."

᪥ TWELVE ᪥

". . . and the upshot of it is that he wants me in the hospital tomorrow," Agnes was saying.

"Tomorrow, isn't that rather quick?" Goff asked doubtfully.

"It will only be for a couple of days, tests and things. Exploratory surgery. He mutters about further treatment. It all depends on what they find, I suppose. Don't worry, love, anything major will have to wait until after Christmas. I'm not going to let anything interfere with our Caribbean plans."

She smiled at him warmly, but he looked beyond her abstractedly. He was thinking, not for the first time, that London distanced them from each other.

They were eating, at his insistence, at a restaurant. Agnes would have preferred to stay in, but Goff felt the need of some kind of public display of their relationship, even though he knew it made her uneasy. From time to time other diners gave her curious second glances, wondering if they recognized her.

In the context into which he had forced her, she became almost a stranger, a smartly dressed, essentially urban woman, too thin, and with a strained look about the eyes. Even her voice had an unfamiliar note of greater maturity in it.

"Don't look so stricken, darling," she said. "Women's diseases are a piece of cake to them nowadays."

"How much further have you got with the divorce?" he cut in, brutal because he had to dispel the sense of being apart from her.

Agnes looked pained as she sipped her wine.

"I've arranged to see Harold next week," she said evasively.

"Why *see*, for God's sake?" Goff said. "Surely it can all be done through letters?"

"Yes, of course it can, but it seems more civilized, more human, to meet as friends."

"Friends?" Goff glowered at the candle discreetly flickering on the table. "I don't see what friendship has to do with it."

"Harold never had very much of me, you know," Agnes said placatingly. "The least I can do is tell him about this myself."

"He had you first. He had you before I did. Isn't that enough?"

"Much good it did him," Agnes said a little sadly. "I'd like to see him settled. I wish he could meet a nice, domesticated girl who can give him children and—"

"Then let him have the chance to find one," Goff said at once. "He isn't going to let you go until he's sure you don't want him. You must tell him. You will do that, won't you?"

His tone was severe. She felt the weight of his will on her. It would always be there now, she supposed, until he grew tired of her. She gave him a wan smile and patted his hand.

They left the restaurant after the usual tedious squabble over the check and walked back to her apartment slowly, arm in arm. As always, as soon as they were out of sight of others, their relationship seemed at once more lighthearted and deeper, and the problems it brought them receded.

Agnes's apartment had a cold feeling, despite the central heating. As he walked about the living room while she was making instant coffee, it occurred to Goff that the place reminded him of some kind of waiting room. She needs a home, he thought; she really hasn't much idea of how to look after herself. He felt warmed, as always, by contemplation of this aspect of her personality.

"Why won't you talk about Oxford?" she said, returning and placing a mug of coffee in front of him. "You know how much I want to know all."

"It's all puerile, everyone's so young," he cut in. "I don't like being a student."

"You might at least try to give me a picture," she protested. "Tell me about your rooms, your tutor, the societies you've joined so far."

"It's a script you can write yourself. It's about as familiar as the Authorized Version," he said impatiently. "I don't know what it is about the place that compels everyone who sets foot in it to quack on ad nauseam, but at least I shall spare you."

"It's different when it's happening to you," she said. "I have a personal interest in it."

"Then you'll have to come and see for yourself. Arthur O'Higgins is up this term, by the way."

"Dear old O'Higgins!" Agnes's face lit up, as it always did at the mention of anyone who had been connected with St. Fenrins. "What's he like now, Goff?"

"Grown up a bit precious, has old Arthur. Rather sensitive. It's what comes of writing pretty pieces to please your English mistress! Seriously, why don't you come though, Agnes? You can stay at the Randolph. I'll give you tea and show you around."

"People will think I'm your maiden aunt!"

"No chance of that. You don't look in the least like a maiden aunt and never could."

Laughing, she shook her head and pushed her hair behind her ears. She was letting it grow again, and already it had an untidy look.

"Let's have some music," she said. "Something pastoral because the lovely summer's gone. How about some Delius? *Brigg Fair's* one of my favorites."

When she had put on the record, she listened with the absorbed air of a child.

"Everything you like evokes the past," Goff said with amused indulgence. "You always seem to be going back somewhere you never were."

"I'm an escapist," she said, her mind on the music. "Surely you realized that long ago?"

He turned her toward him and kissed her.

"I don't mind anything you are, really," he said, remembering his earlier irritation in the restaurant. "You know that."

He took both her hands and kissed them, noticing that they were cold still.

"I'm sorry we can't make love," she said. "Under the circumstances I don't think—"

"Doesn't matter." He shrugged. "I can always wait for that. Look, I'll come to the hospital tomorrow."

"It hardly seems worth it. I shall be home on Thursday."

"Then I shall come up on Thursday evening. You'll probably need cheering up. You will come to Oxford next weekend? I'll book a room for you."

"All right," she said, laughing.

It can't be very nice for her, he thought, holding her, what she has to face tomorrow. He caught a sudden faint sense of what it might be like for her and tightened his grip. Yet when he looked into her face it was unclouded.

"I'm not worried about it," she assured him, as if she understood his thoughts. "It's rather like going to the dentist. Not as bad actually. With a general anesthetic, one doesn't know a thing. You must go now, darling, or you'll miss your train. I think I'll listen to *Brigg Fair* just once more before I go to bed."

In her ears there was a dull throbbing. Somewhere to the left of her, blackness hovered as a cloud above her head. But that had nothing to do with the landscape through which she walked.

She was crossing a lawn, very wide and green. She knew that it must be summer because the trees were so thickly clumped against a sky of dark blue. The softest, sweetest of summer winds was stirring her long hair as she walked easily over the springy turf. She was quite extraordinarily happy.

She realized she was at Marlwood. Someone in the big house on the far side of the lawn was playing a piano, a Chopin prelude. She heard the notes clearly in spite of a throbbing in her ears. That will be Mrs. Willoughby, she thought; how exquisitely she plays. It will always be summer now. Nothing so beautiful can ever end. She felt the beauty singing inside her, and everything was sharp and clear.

A small, dark-haired boy was sitting on the lawn in the shade of a lime tree. At first she thought it was Goff, and then she thought it was Fitz, and then she realized it was too young to be either of them. The music was very loud, and the blackness over her head shifted a little.

The child turned and smiled at her. Her heart gave an enormous lurch as she recognized him. It was her own son. He didn't die after all, she thought. They were mistaken. He is alive. Everything is going to be different.

The music almost deafened her as she reached out her arms toward him. She stumbled, and the hovering darkness came down and blotted everything out.

In the hot white sterility of the operating room the anesthetist shook his head tiredly. The machines stopped. The surgeon turned away without speaking, his face concealed behind his mask.

Goff arrived at the house at seven in the evening and let himself into the building with his own key. Outside Agnes's door he found the flowers he had ordered to be sent, huge, curly-headed, golden chrysanthemums, still in a plastic wrapping with the florist's gift card attached.

The living room of the apartment had a swept and polished air. The desk had been tidied, pens stuck in an ornamental jar. A few tradesmen's bills were held down by the snowstorm paperweight.

They must have kept her in, Goff thought. Irritation mingled with his disappointment. After all, she had promised to let him know if there was any alteration in her plans.

He picked up the flowers and a couple of letters that had arrived for her by the noon post, and set off for the hospital.

It was a cold, clear night, and he walked fast. Arriving, he thought that the broad white building in its sea of traffic had more the look of a hotel than a hospital. The cars will keep her awake, he thought, unless she's in a room at the back.

Inside, the brisk receptionist gave him a professional smile as he inquired about Agnes.

"Mrs. Stratton. Women's Surgical."

The woman consulted her list, frowned, turned back to him. She was unsmiling now. She asked if he was a relative; he said he was a friend, and she told him she was sorry but Mrs. Stratton had died that morning on the operating table. Goff asked her to check the list, and she did so and assured him that there was no mistake.

He looked blankly at her and turned away in the direction of the stairs, still holding the flowers. The receptionist called after him, but he took no notice. With a sigh she turned to the switchboard to alert the sister on the floor.

Goff climbed the stairs quickly, automatically following the appropriate arrows. The room was on the first floor, and the corridor was a long one with women in all the rooms who were not Agnes and people sitting with them emitting hushed little murmurs of conversation.

A sister came out of an office, smiling sympathetically at Goff talking about his coming to see Mrs. Stratton, and telling him that Mr. Stratton had left less than a quarter of an hour before.

Goff held the flowers up high in front of him and nodded all the time she was speaking. The sister, who was herself young and pretty, thought what a good-looking boy he was. He thanked her very politely and turned away.

Down the corridor he stopped, unsure what to do next. His only thought was that he would have to cancel the hotel reservation he had made for the weekend. He had a sudden vision of people at lunch in a hotel dining room, of white table linen and heavy, old-fashioned cutlery and the food on the plates, roast lamb and roast potatoes and bright green peas, with the darker green of mint bespattering the lamb.

As he stood in the corridor, people suddenly began to stream toward him. Visiting hours were over. He heard their approaching footsteps as from a great distance. He allowed himself to be swept along with the tide and found himself in the lift. It seemed to him that they were looking at him strangely, and he realized it was because of the flowers; no one carries flowers *away* from a hospital.

Outside the building the traffic roar struck him like a blow. The street lights were painful to his eyes. He went into a subway where it was dim and quieter. A hippie youth was playing a guitar and singing with gusto the old Irish tune "Whisky in the Jar." For some reason Goff remembered the legend of Orpheus and Eurydice and took obscure comfort from it. He left the subway with the singing still in his head and found himself in a park, where he walked slowly under dark trees.

This time she's gone, he thought. She had looked dead once before, in Spain, so it wasn't really so much of a shock as it might have been. Yet it seemed strange that she had gone and left no message for him.

When someone dies there is much for the person closest to them to do—certificates to sign and burial arrangements to be made and lawyers and city officials and undertakers to be seen. Goff had nothing whatsoever to do except cancel a reservation for a hotel room.

It was very cold. He thought suddenly that he could go back to her apartment and let himself in and lie down on her bed in the dark. Maybe she would come to him there. She had not, after all, been gone long. He began to retrace his steps quickly, humming the jaunty "Whisky in the Jar" under his breath.

Of course, there was always the possibility that she wasn't dead at all, but sleeping. Mistakes of that nature occurred often in stories by Poe. In one particularly gruesome one the beloved came shuffling up out of the vault with all her teeth knocked out. Not dead at all.

Catalepsy. In Poe, people with catalepsy were always being buried alive. Karistides had loved those stories. "Horrible!" he'd gloated, with shining eyes. But all that had been years ago.

Goff climbed the stairs to her apartment heavily, feeling depleted. When he reached her door he saw a light beneath it and heard voices from inside, so he rang the doorbell instead of using his key.

The woman who answered looked like someone he had seen before somewhere.

"Yes?" she said, frowning at him.

"It's about Agnes," he said.

Over her shoulder he could see a bespectacled man standing in a listening attitude in the little hall. He recognized him with a faint sense of resentment.

"I went to the hospital, and they told me she was dead," Goff said, speaking over the woman's shoulder to Harold Stratton, who stared at him blankly.

"I know! You're the boy Agnes used to coach in Latin," the woman said. She sounded satisfied with the identification, as well she might, since the last time she had seen Goff he had been thirteen. "One of her old pupils, Harold," she said, still holding the door.

"Of course. I recognize you now. Would you like to come in for a minute?" Stratton held out his hand. "It was very kind of you to go and see Agnes. It's all been so sudden. We've been knocked side-ways—"

"I won't stay," Goff said, nevertheless stepping past the still reluctant Jennifer into the hall.

"At least we can offer you a cup of coffee," Stratton said, motioning him toward the living room. "My sister was just about to make me an omelet."

"He's had nothing to eat since lunchtime. We only got in from the hospital twenty minutes ago," Jennifer said, leaving them together.

Harold sat on the edge of the sofa, taking off his glasses and polishing them disconsolately. Without the horn-rims he looked plainer than Goff remembered him, and older.

"So unexpected," he said. "I hadn't seen her since early in the summer. She seemed all right then. She hadn't been back from Spain long. She telephoned me last week. We arranged to meet in a few days' time. She mentioned she was going to the hospital. For a checkup, just routine, she said. She always kept in touch with me."

"What did they tell you?" Goff cut in. "At the hospital, what did they say?"

"There was something." Harold did not appear to notice the sharpness of the interruption. "The surgeon said it was malignant. They didn't know until they opened her up. Nothing they couldn't handle, you understand? It wasn't that that killed her. No, it was just that while she was under the anesthetic—some kind of heart irregularity—one of these chance things. They did everything possible, they said. And yet . . . one has one's doubts . . . so much talk lately of negligence . . . always reading of these things. Should we press for a full inquiry?" He spread his hands helplessly. "I don't know," he answered himself. "We'd have to get advice. There's so much to think about all of a sudden."

"Even if we do make a fuss," Jennifer said, coming in with a tray, "nothing will ever be proved. The layman never wins in these cases. Now, you eat this."

She placed the tray in front of Harold after deftly taking two mugs from it. Goff stared fixedly at the one she held out to him. Agnes had served coffee in it two nights before.

"Sugar?" Jennifer indicated a bowl. He didn't answer.

"So many years since we were all at the Grange," Harold said wonderingly. "We all have happy memories of those days." He sighed. "Her sister's coming down tomorrow." He pushed the omelet about on the plate. "She had to make arrangements about her family first. Jennifer very kindly offered to come up with me. It was a considerable shock to me. She was no age . . ."

He mustn't cry for her, Goff thought fiercely. She had nothing to do with him for years. He isn't to cry. He dug his fingernails into his palms.

"Jeff's looking after our brood," Jennifer said. "I shall have to get back tomorrow."

All three of them started when the telephone rang. For a moment they did nothing, then Harold lifted the receiver. He stared at the paperweight as he listened, saying "Yes" once or twice in a slow voice. He covered the receiver with his hand.

"Levy, the agent," he whispered to Jennifer, who nodded.

"So much to be sorted out," she said to Goff with satisfaction. "Money all over the place. All these copyrights and things. Harold will just have to ask for a few months' leave from the laboratory, that's all."

"I'm sorry about that," her brother said, replacing the receiver. "I've arranged to see him after the funeral. There's going to be a lot of fuss over the estate. I don't want any of the money, of course. I've been thinking, Jen, they might set up some kind of fund to help young writers, something like that. I'm sure Agnes would have liked . . ."

He sniffed suddenly, shook his head, took a few furtive sips of his coffee.

"We'll talk about it after the funeral," Jennifer said. "There'll be time enough for all of that then."

"I'm wondering what would be best about that," Stratton said to Goff. "Where she'd like to be buried. I don't think she'd like a town. I thought perhaps that church next to the Grange . . . She did go to the services sometimes, you know, Sunday evenings. The Grange was the nearest thing to a home she had."

"It wouldn't be difficult to arrange," Jennifer said. "I'm sure the vicar would appreciate a contribution to the funds," she added with a little laugh.

"If you'll excuse me." Goff set down his cup.

"Of course, we mustn't keep you." Stratton got to his feet. "I'm only sorry we had to meet again in such tragic circumstances . . ."

Goff stood in the hall and stared at them both. He wanted to tell them, the tired, plain man and his overbearing sister, that they had no place here. He wanted to shout that it was he who belonged here, that Agnes had been his. But he spoke none of the words that tumbled and churned inside him. Instead he shook hands with both of them and went away, leaving the chrysanthemums, still in their wrapping, on the hall table.

On the way down to the street he realized that he had Agnes's letters in his pocket, so he toiled back up and pushed them under the door. Then he left the building and began to walk, steadily and aimlessly, through the October night.

Karistides had spent the night with his girlfriend of the moment. As usual, he was up before her. He shaved, dressed with his usual care, and set coffee to percolate. While he was waiting for it, he brought in the milk and the morning papers.

He was drinking his coffee when a story on the front page caught his eye. Immediately he went into the hall, found his dark gray overcoat with the velvet collar, and put it on. He was about to leave the apartment when the girl, smudgy-eyed amid a mass of tangled hair, stumbled out of the bedroom, yawning.

"I have to go," Karistides said, without preamble or explanation.

"You told me you'd be staying today," the girl said, looking aggrieved. "The last thing you said last night was that you wouldn't go to the hospital. You said there was one lecture you could cut and you'd take me—"

"I know, but something's come up," Karistides said. "Someone has died. I've just seen it in the paper. I have a feeling I'll be needed."

"Andy, I'm sorry. It's not a relative, is it?" He shook his head. "Would you like me to come with you?" the girl asked penitently.

"That won't be necessary. I'll phone you as soon as I can."

He kissed her lightly as he opened the front door.

"You won't forget?" She held onto him. "I'll wait in this evening."

"Don't worry, I'll be in touch. If Willoughby phones for me—you remember him—Goff? Tell him I'm at my place. That's important."

"Shall I tell him you . . ." she called after him, but he was already gone.

Closing the door with a discontented sigh, the girl shuffled back to the kitchen and poured herself a cup of coffee. She glanced at the front page of the paper. *Agnes Vale Dies.* The name was vaguely familiar. Could this be what Andy was talking about?

"Agnes Vale, award-winning children's writer, author of the Wolfram and Capricorna books," (that was it, she remembered reading *Capricorna* to her kid sister) "died suddenly in a hospital today. She was thirty-seven. Obituary and appreciation on page four. Other obituaries page six . . ."

Thirty-seven. Karistides's girl shivered. What kind of age was that to die? An old friend? What sort of friend? Where would Andy have met someone like that? There was so much she didn't know about him. But thirty-seven . . . Feeling chilled, she took a gulp of hot coffee and turned quickly to the woman's page.

Outside, Karistides walked with a spring in his step. The adrenalin raced pleasantly within him. It was only at moments of crisis that he realized how bored he was for the better part of the time.

Back at his own apartment, he settled himself to wait. Goff must come in the end, he was sure of it. After all, where else was there for him to go?

Goff did not finally arrive until six-thirty in the evening.

"Where the hell did you get to?" Karistides said. "I've been looking for you everywhere. I phoned around—Oxford, Marlwood, the Gallery, every damn place I could think of where you might be . . ."

The triumph that flooded through him spilled out of his eyes, making them dance.

"Sit down," he said, sounding calm, matter-of-fact. "You look all in. Will you have whisky? Shall I fix you something to eat?"

"Presently." Goff flung himself into a chair and shut his eyes. "For the moment I'll settle for the whisky. I've been walking. I walked all night, most of today. That dreary little Stratton has taken over . . ."

"I phoned there, too. They told me you'd called last night. He's still her husband by law, you know." Karistides proffered whisky. "I even looked in at old Lord's this afternoon. There was a young chap there with an apricot sweater and hair to match. Said Justin was playing the organ at the church around the corner. Fluttered his eyelashes at me. Lovely boy. Remember what I always said about old Lord? Only goes to show."

"There was nowhere at all I could go," Goff said. "It's cold on the streets at two o'clock in the morning. No one knows a thing. We were so bloody discreet always." He took the whisky at a gulp and held out the glass. "I can't seem to take it in properly . . ."

"You stay here," Karistides said, refilling the glass promptly. "I know how you feel. You can stay as long as you like. I'll get us something to eat in a moment."

They stayed up all night, drinking and talking, friends since childhood, so much to be said. Karistides was happy.

THIRTEEN

The trees in Tringham churchyard were dying slowly, stricken with Dutch elm disease. Yet so appropriate was their leafless state to the raw, November morning that the old crow winging over the open grave toward its nest was blissfully unaware that in the branches around it the sap had ceased to stir.

Karistides was chilled in spite of his heavy overcoat. He wished he might move and stamp his feet. The priest who intoned the prescribed formula about the sure and certain hope of resurrection looked pinched and chilled, too, in his thin white cassock.

The mourners, frozen into a dark tableau against the gray light, amounted to fewer than a dozen. At the memorial service to be held later in London, the church would be warmed by candles, music, and the tributes of the famous. For today's interment there were present, huddled around the priest, only Harold Stratton and Agnes's sister and sister-in-law, each flanked by her husband.

A little way from them a slight, bearded man in a cityish overcoat stood alone. Farther off still, in a cluster beneath the dying elms, seeming onlookers rather than participants in the scene, were Goff Willoughby, Andrew Karistides, and, more surprisingly, Ben Blount, who had found out somehow and driven all the way down from Yorkshire that morning. Justin Lord, who had hoped to be present, was at home in bed with bronchitis.

When the earth had thudded against the coffin, the priest cleared his throat and closed his prayer book with ill-concealed relief. The tableau around the grave unfroze as the separate members mingled and moved, speaking in muted voices.

Goff advanced with deliberate steps until he was staring into the grave. The flowers on the coffin, roses of course, seemed in this season waxen and artificial. Karistides eyed his friend, watchful for signs of cracks in the icy surface of his demeanor. He must break sooner or later, Karistides thought, regarding his stiff back with a professional eye. He'd had no sleep in the last three days, and any eating he'd done had been mechanical.

". . . I'll be going straight back," Blount was saying, looking faintly ill at ease. "No point in my hanging about here."

"You've a stiff drive," Karistides said, his eyes still on Goff beside the grave. "Any chance of a lift as far as Andham Station? We came by train and took a cab out here, but we haven't thought how we'll get back."

"I can drop you off wherever you like." Blount looked glad to have something to do. "Just shout when you're ready."

"Aren't you two of the boys Agnes taught at St. Fenrins School?" Harold Stratton said, approaching and shaking hands with them warmly. "My wife would be very touched . . . It was years ago she used to teach them," he said over his shoulder to the bearded stranger. "This is Mr. Levy, by the way. He was Agnes's literary agent—"

"—and close friend over a number of years," the man said, looking keenly at the boys. "I'm proud to say I can remember Agnes Vale when she . . ."

Harold Stratton left them and turned toward the grave, where Agnes's sister, Dorothy, bulky in a fur coat, stood alone a few feet from Goff.

"That's Goff Willoughby," he murmured to her. "You might possibly remember him, Dorothy, from the Grange days?"

"Yes, of course I do," the woman said at once. "How are you, Goff?" She had a pronounced northern accent. "You used to come over to the Grange every day when we were on holiday down here, years ago. Isn't your home near here?"

Goff nodded.

"I thought it was. I wonder if you remember my boy? Martin? Mad for sports! He really looked up to you. It was Goff this and Goff that long after we went home. That was a very happy holiday. I still think . . ." Her face clouded. "My sister thought a lot of you," she said. "You used to bring her the most beautiful flowers." She hesitated a moment and then asked rapidly, "Is there any little thing of hers you'd like to have?"

"Any little thing?" Goff repeated, staring at her with eyes that had a diamond glitter.

"Some small token, some memento, you know," Dorothy said earnestly. "I always think it's a nice idea . . . I'm sure Agnes would have liked all the people who meant something to her to have a little remembrance. She was too young to think of it, of course, much too young. It's old people who make provision for that kind of thing. Perhaps you think it's out of date these days."

"I really don't think . . ." Goff looked down at the bulky woman with an expression that could have been taken as supercilious. "But perhaps . . . There *was* something. A record she had. She was very fond of it. It was of some French folk songs, songs from the Auvergne . . ."

"Folk songs? Sounds like Agnes right enough!" Dorothy began to laugh. "Ever since she was little. Folk songs and folk tales and fairy stories . . ." All at once her broad face crumpled. "Poor little Agnes!" she said. "She was such a child always. She shouldn't have died so soon—"

Tears glistened on her eyelashes and she pressed her lips together hard. Her face, so little like her sister's, possessed, fleetingly, riven in its moment of uncontrollable sorrow, something of Agnes's strange vulnerability. In Goff's eyes there flared for an instant compassion and an answering pain.

"Yes," he said, very low. " 'More Songs of the Auvergne,' it was called. The one she liked best was about three princesses under a cherry tree . . ."

"You shall have it, Goff," Dorothy said, "if it can be found in Agnes's things. It would be at her apartment, I suppose. I'll look myself as soon as I go there, and when I find it I'll mail it to you right away. The house where you lived was called Marlwood, wasn't it? I haven't forgotten seeing it on an invitation Agnes had stuck up on the mantelpiece. A pretty name." She held out her hand. "Thank you for coming, and good luck to you."

She shook his hand and turned quickly away. Her place was immediately taken by Jeffrey Miller, who patted her shoulder sympathetically as she passed him.

"Godolphin Willoughby? Recognized you straight off," he said. "A good few years since I've seen you. You'll have left school now, I suppose. This is a tragic business. It's hit me harder than I can say. Agnes and I . . . we were close, you know." He cast a quick uneasy glance in the direction of his wife in conversation with Dorothy's husband. "I hadn't had much chance to see her lately, she was too busy. I always knew she had that special something. In a class of her own, Agnes. To come back here, after all this time . . ."

He shook his head and sniffed while Goff stared at him silently.

As the three boys were walking toward Blount's car, which he had left in the lane, Levy hurried after them asking if he could have a few words with them later. Rather to their own surprise, they found themselves agreeing to meet him at the Cock in Andham in half an hour. Since Goff and Karistides refused his offer of a lift there, he hastened on toward his two-month-old white Jaguar and drove off alone.

"Wonder what he can want?" Blount said.

As they drove past the front gates of the Grange, Karistides noticed a For Sale sign fallen on its side and the hedge completely overgrown. The property, long vacant, had reverted to its former state of desolation.

"Whatever it is will be to his advantage," Karistides said philosophically. "He must have had a bit of a blow, Agnes dying so unexpectedly. It cuts off a lucrative source of income."

"Oh, I don't suppose it spoils anything for an agent when it's someone like Agnes Vale," Blount said thoughtfully. "In a way it increases her worth. Levy will know how to exploit it. He must be pretty adroit. He handles some of the country's top authors."

"Been checking him out, Ben?" Goff asked listlessly.

He'd said so little all morning, had looked so cold, that Karistides was relieved by the normalcy of the question. Perhaps it was due to the presence of Blount, an easy fellow who seemed to have changed little in the years from eleven to eighteen.

"I make it my business to know a bit about this sort of thing," he was saying now. "I'm rather interested in the writing game myself." He paused for a moment. "All a bit of a coincidence, really," he continued at last. "On the same day her death was announced, I heard I'd had an article accepted by one of the papers. First sale I've made. Only a small thing. Seeing the obituary after reading the letter of acceptance kind of shook me, though. That's why I came today, as a matter of fact. I couldn't help remembering the interest she took in the rubbish I wrote as a kid . . ."

"Congratulations, Ben. Agnes would be proud of you," Goff said.

Karistides looked at him sharply but could detect no irony in his tone or expression.

"It was a sort of gesture, I suppose, coming here," Blount said thoughtfully, turning the car onto the main Andham road and settling back in the driver's seat. "I remember the last time I saw her. We were still at Fins. Goff and I cut games one afternoon. She was living in an apartment right on the top of a hill, rather weird, crammed with books and pictures all over the walls—"

"Pre-Raphaelites," Goff said.

"That's right. Pretty morbid. But then, she was like that, Miss Vale. She had a peculiar taste for melancholy things but always seemed cheerful in herself. She was completely outside the run of teachers I've met before or since. Are we nearly there, by the way? This Cock place, will I be able park in front of it?"

It won't be long now, Karistides was thinking as he followed Goff and Blount into the bar; this is the last hurdle. Perhaps, in some innermost part of himself, he would have liked a confrontation on a grand scale. Up to now it had all been rather too low-key for his own taste.

The bar, newly opened, had a chill about it. Levy, having ordered coffee and rum all round, lighted a cigar and began to speak rapidly, with few preliminaries.

Blount had been right. Agnes might be dead, but that was far from being the end of it. There was a television program in the works scheduled to air after Christmas. The director wanted to speak to people who had known her at various stages of her life.

Goff's nostrils twitched as he listened.

"It sounds like a sort of posthumous 'This Is Your Life,'" he cut in at last, disdainfully. "Poor Agnes!"

The agent looked at him sharply.

"Not at all," he said. "Nothing like that. This will be quality stuff. They've one of the best directors in the business penciled in. And the executive producer is to be Marcia Farrow, of whom you may have heard. She was a personal friend of Agnes. The Americans are very interested. Agnes's work was always taken seriously over there." He took the cigar from his mouth and looked at it fixedly. "We're dealing here with more than mere talent, a touch of genius maybe. This is only the beginning of what will be said and written about Agnes Vale, you know. I believe I owe it to her memory to see that it's a good beginning. What I want," he leaned forward with all the vitality of a small, feral animal in his narrow face, "is for them to include an interview with someone from way back, from her days as a prep school teacher, let's say. After all, it was at about that time she turned to children's writing and found her métier." He glanced from one to the other of the boys. "She taught all three of you, didn't she?" he asked meaningfully.

"You can count me out," Karistides said at once. In spite of his yearning for something histrionic, he knew he would try to get Goff out of the place as quickly as possible. "I was never a satisfactory pupil. Ben here is your man for that. He writes himself. He's sold some of his work already—"

"Oh, it's all very trivial." Blount colored. "I hadn't had any contact with Mrs. Stratton for years. Goff knew her much better."

"Yes. Her husband was telling me. You used to visit them when they were at the Grange," Levy said, his bright eyes swiveling to Goff. "They'll be going back there for the program. Might get something very interesting, you talking in the room where she—"

Goff set down his glass.

"I really wouldn't be interested," he said with a cutting finality. "I'm afraid it's not at all my line, this sort of thing." He looked at his watch. "If we're to catch the eleven-forty we should go now, Andrew." He pushed the table forward and got to his feet. "I wish you luck with your research, Mr. Levy," he said, his voice spiky with dislike. "Ben here will do all he can to help you, I'm sure."

"Writing yourself, did you say?" The agent's eyes swung back to Blount. "An eleven-year-old boy in her class . . . listening, learning . . . one talent nurturing another . . . You know, this is exactly the kind of thing they'll want to use. Look . . ."

He acknowledged the departure of Goff and Karistides with no more than a flip of his hand. As they left the bar he was leaning forward once more, jabbing his cigar in the air, talking excitedly to the bemused Blount.

"Looks as if old Ben's got himself an agent!" Karistides said when they were outside, but Goff only scowled at the agent's car as he passed it and strode off in the direction of the station without a word.

In the train he said nothing either. He slumped in a corner seat with his long legs in front of him, staring at the brown fields, rigid, unreachable.

Back at Karistides's flat, it was cold. A damp mist seemed to be seeping into everything. Goff, still in his overcoat, paced up and down the room. I'll take him home with me at Christmas, if he'll come, Karistides thought. The warmth will be good for him, it will unfreeze him.

"Bloody Blount!" Goff burst out at last. "Always was her pet! He could write the sort of junk she liked. *I* never could."

He flung himself into the farthest corner of the sofa where Karistides sat, his eyes dark with resentment.

"What a farce this whole thing is," he said. "That little runt of a Stratton playing the grieving husband. Who the hell does he think he is? He didn't mean a thing to her." He pounded the back of the sofa with his fist, raising a small cloud of dust. "The *timing*, Andy, that's what was wrong," he said. "If only she'd lived even a few months longer, it would all have been different. Everyone would have known about us. I'd have made sure of that. It's such *bloody* luck her dying now."

"She had cancer, Goff," Karistides reminded him gently.

"I know. I know she had cancer, but it was nothing they couldn't treat, they said that," Goff answered irritably.

"It's true enough she might have been cured," Karistides said judiciously. "But there's always a risk . . ." He pressed his palms together. "If she was going to die anyway—we don't know, of course— but if she was going to die, wasn't it better this way?"

"Better? What do you know about what's better?" Goff turned on him, his eyes suddenly blazing. "She was mine. You think she would have suffered? She might have suffered, yes." He nodded his head several times in rapid succession. "You don't have to tell me it might have been bad. Yes. But I'd have been with her. I could have taken it on me, don't you see? Anything. However bad. Even an agonized *inching* toward death. It wouldn't have been bad. It would have been glorious. Because I would have shared it. I'd have done everything for her, everything. And when the time came when it was too much, I'd have been the one who—" He closed up his hands into fists. "What kind of a way was this for her to go? Like slipping out of a room when no one was looking. No time to talk, nothing finished. A fool of a husband pawing through her belongings, a jackal of an agent prating about a program for the masses to gawp at. And all the time not a soul knowing she was mine! Christ, Andy, don't you see, she was *mine* . . ."

His voice cracked. He'll break now, Karistides thought, bracing himself. At last. Thank God.

"I loved her." The words were choked. "Always. I could never make anyone take that seriously, not even poor, silly Agnes! All I needed was time to prove it—to her, to everyone. Now it's too late. Now no one will ever know—"

He covered his eyes with his fists. It was very terrible, the hardness of his grief. Karistides felt it like a stone within himself. Tentatively, he edged closer.

"Too late," Goff said brokenly. "Too late, too late!"

All at once he was crying. Tears, wet tears, were streaming from his eyes. Suddenly his shoulders were shaking and his face was pressed hard against Karistides's chest, and the warm tears flowed.

Gently Karistides patted him. Compassion stirred and rippled inside him, smooth and soft. He was melted by love and sorrow. He felt as if his heart were being bathed in warm oil. He put his arms around Goff and hugged him as he would a child.

"Hush," he said. "There, Goff, it's all right. I know you loved her, I know. I know how this hurts. I know. Hush."

The sorrow and pity that he felt sang in him like a kind of joy. To be able to feel such sympathy, such empathy, with another human being purified and ennobled him. Poor Agnes, dead. Poor Goff, alive. There were tears in his own eyes as he waited for Goff, shaking against his chest, to expend this unexpendable grief.

After a while the paroxysms weakened. Goff drew away from him, sat at the other end of the sofa, choked into his handkerchief; then vigorously blew his nose, looking like nothing so much as a lost child.

"What do you want to do now, Goff?" Karistides ventured at last.

"Oh, go back to Oxford, I suppose," Goff said dully. "I'll take the five o'clock train. I might as well go back." He frowned. "It doesn't really matter where I go from now on. It's going to hurt, anyway."

Another spasm of grief passed over his features, but this time, biting his lip hard, he mastered it and went to the bathroom to wash his face.

When he came back there was little sign of his outburst save about his reddened eyes. The rest of his face was composed, collected.

"I'll tell you something, Andy," he said, almost philosophically.

"I'll not be good again. I said I would be, for her. But now she isn't here, it doesn't matter. I shan't bother."

It sounded no more than the empty threat of a petulant child, but it was spoken in the weary voice of disillusioned age.

As they stood side by side, the friends, Goff's amber eyes were already glazing over into a hardness. It was the smaller, darker eyes of Karistides that were warm with life. It was to Karistides that those needing help would always in the future most usefully turn. Goff Willoughby no longer had anything to give.

After the front door had slammed, the Greek boy sat on alone in the twilight. He had his own memories of Agnes Vale, who, in a more innocent time, under summer trees, had called him her Ulysses. He was aware, had always been aware, that she never cared much for him. He found that the saddest thing of all.

At last he shook himself as a dog will, switched on all the lights, and turned to the telephone. A few moments later he was talking to the girl from whom he would take solace in the long night ahead.